The Troubadour's Tale

MORE BY THIS AUTHOR

Historical Fiction

The Testament of Mariam
This Rough Ocean

The Chronicles of Christoval Alvarez

The Secret World of Christoval Alvarez
The Enterprise of England
The Portuguese Affair
Bartholomew Fair
Suffer the Little Children
Voyage to Muscovy
The Play's the Thing
That Time May Cease
The Lopez Affair

Oxford Medieval Mysteries

The Bookseller's Tale
The Novice's Tale
The Huntsman's Tale
The Merchant's Tale

The Fenland Series

Flood
Betrayal

Contemporary Fiction

The Anniversary
The Travellers
A Running Tide

The Troubadour's Tale

Ann Swinfen

Shakenoak Press

for

Michael & Sally
With much love

Chapter One

Oxford, Winter 1353

It was snowing again. Alysoun danced in from the garden through the kitchen door, the hood of her capuchon sprinkled over like some costly sugar cake, her cheeks rosy with the cold.

'Boots!' said Margaret. 'I do not scrub this floor only to have you bringing in half the snow in the garden to scatter across it.'

Alysoun stood poised on the threshold, her eyes sparkling with delight. Ah, to be a child again, when snow bound winters did not mean worry about a good supply of logs, and the prospect of the well freezing, but only delight in a world transformed into a magical realm, frosted white as some delicate confection on the king's table.

'Come and see!' she pleaded.

Rafe ran for his thick winter cloak and capuchon.

'Boots!' Margaret cried again, this time catching Rafe in time to put them on.

I smiled at her. 'Let them play,' I said. 'Best to send them outside while we can, for we may be held fast withindoors before long.'

I fetched my own cloak and hood from the hook in the passage beside the door to Margaret's stillroom.

As I followed Rafe out to the garden, Margaret raised her eyebrows at me.

'I am going to see that all is ready in the stable,' I

said.

Fortunately, before the first of the snowfall, the carpenter and his boy had started work building my small stable at the end of the narrow alleyway running down the side of the building which housed both my shop and our home. The roof had been completed the day before the snow began, and for the last two days they had been able to work inside, completing the stall and manger. As dusk was closing in yesterday evening, they had arrived at the door, stamping their feet and blowing on their fingers against the cold, to receive their purse of coin for the work, with a little extra in thanks, to buy a hot meal at Tackley's Inn before they went home.

It had been too dark last night to see the completed stable, so now I tramped my way out through nearly a foot of snow to admire it by daylight. Although small, it could hold two horses, should I ever become rich enough to maintain them, and it was sturdily built, with an oak frame and lath and plaster in-fill. Unlike the house, which was tiled, it had a roof of wooden shingles, but in the summer I would have it thatched, for greater warmth. I opened the door and breathed in the heady scent of new cut timber. I had insisted on oak within, as well as without. It was more costly than a softer wood, but stronger and longer lasting.

I felt a glow of pleasure as I looked around. I had not possessed a stable since leaving my father's farm at Leighton-under-Wychwood more than eleven years before, and I realised how much I had missed the sweet scent of hay and horse. I had both straw and hay stored ready in the shed where I kept tools for the garden, and I began to carry them to the stable now. Alysoun and Rafe helped with the first load, but soon grew tired of it, and resumed building a snow castle near the hen house. The hens, with more sense than the children, had chosen to stay inside and take their feed from an old tin dish instead of scratching about on the icy ground.

It took me four trips to move all the hay and straw, even using my new small handcart, but it was satisfying to see the straw stored to one side of the stable and the hay piled up on the low half loft. I strewed straw on the dirt floor of the stall – deeply, for the earth below was solid frozen – and I piled the manger with hay. When I filled a bucket from the well, I was relieved to find that there was no sign of it freezing yet.

'Come and see!' Rafe tugged at my arm as I emerged from the stable, my preparations complete. 'Our castle is finished.'

'It is very fine,' I said, solemnly admiring a round keep, correctly built on a raised mound of packed snow to represent the motte. 'Do you plan to build a curtain wall? Else the enemy may find it too easy to attack.'

'I was going to build a wall,' Alysoun conceded, 'but my hands are like to *freeze*!' She held them up, clad in sodden woollen mittens which Margaret had knitted only the previous week.

'I'll help you,' I said, 'then it will soon be done.'

I knelt in the snow and began packing together a ridge of snow around the keep, and the children joined me enthusiastically, forgetting their cold hands. Unfortunately, the spaniel puppy Rowan was eager to help, and must needs be kept away before she knocked everything down, castle, wall, motte, and all. She was a full nine months old now, but showed no signs of maturity yet.

'There,' I said, sitting back on my heels. 'Done.'

'Nay.' Alysoun shook her head. 'We must have a gatehouse, you know. Else how can the people in the castle come and go?'

'Very well,' I said, somewhat reluctantly, for I was growing very cold myself now. 'We will build a gatehouse. Then who wants to come with me to the Mitre?'

This proved to be the solution to building a very simple gatehouse, then we all rushed back into the kitchen, removing our boots before Margaret could chastise us.

While the children hunted for dry mittens and capuchons, and warmed their cold hands and feet near the kitchen fire, I went through to the shop, where Walter and

Roger were working. I had set a brazier burning here before they arrived early in the morning, for no scrivener can work with cold hands, and they had been obliged to light a candle each, for although the reflection off the snow threw light into the back of the house, despite the overcast sky, here facing the street the window was too overshadowed by the buildings of the High to benefit much from this mirrored snow light.

'No customers?' I said, opening my strong box, and counting out the money I needed.

Walter shook his head. He removed his spectacles, letting them dangle from his ears by the loops of ribbon, and rubbed the bridge of his nose. 'Never a soul. All the students gone home for Christmas, of course, and most of the townsfolk are keeping warm at home. I doubt we'll see anyone today.'

'All the better for getting on with our work,' Roger said, without looking up.

'Aye,' I said. 'I shall be glad to see nothing of Lady Amilia, for I've scarce made a start on finding the songs for her book. The snow may be thanked for keeping her at their country manor.'

The children appeared, warmly dressed again, carrying their boots, and each carrying one of mine. We put them on.

'We are off to the Mitre,' I said.

The two men grinned at each other, but said nothing. I knew they thought this was a piece of folly on my part, but I had worked out the figures three times over and reckoned I would be no worse off, and perhaps even a little better.

As the children and I stepped outside into the High Street, we were met by a biting wind in our faces. The snow was heavier now, and the wind tore down the street, unimpeded by walls, as it had been in the garden.

'Take my hands,' I said, 'so we may hold each other up. The cobbles will be slippery under the snow.'

'Rafe could not hold you up, Papa,' Alysoun said

scornfully.

'I could!' he protested. 'And I am getting stronger all the time. Someday,' he added, with satisfaction, 'I shall be much bigger and stronger than you!'

'Not for years!'

They continued to bicker mildly, but fortunately the walk to the Mitre was quite short, and we stumbled along, heads down against the slap of wind and snow in our faces. Once at the inn, we made our way round to the stableyard and sought the head ostler, who was crouched over the logs in the tack room fireplace, stirring spiced ale warming on a trivet.

'Ah, Maister Elyot,' he said, 'come for yer horse, have ye? He's ready and tacked up.' He rose from his stool, leaving the fire with some reluctance. I handed him the purse, and he counted out the coins carefully, then nodded.

'All fine,' he said. 'I'll hand it to the maister. He said as how I was to deal with all.' He gave a sharp bark of laughter. 'Has no wish to leave his fireside, not he!'

We followed him out into the snow of the yard, and then into the stable, where Rufus had his head over the half door of his stall, thoughtfully chewing on his bit. The saddle and bridle were somewhat old and worn from his use as a hired hack, but I had bought them along with the horse, seeing no need to invest in new, while these were still serviceable.

'I've given him a blanket under the saddle,' the ostler said, 'for the cold. 'Tis but an old one. Keep it.'

He slid back the bolt on the door and led the gelding out, his hoofs ringing on the cobbled floor of the stable, then softened to a muffled thud in the snow of the yard. He would not be reckoned a gentleman's horse, but I had found him strong and willing, able to go at a steady pace for hours without tiring, while a more costly animal would have looked handsome over a short gallop, but would flag and tire on any longer ride.

'What do you think of him?' I asked the children.

Alysoun glowed with pride, at the thought of

possessing our own horse.

'He's very handsome, Rufus. Do you think he will like his new stable?'

'I am sure he will.'

'I hope he may not miss his friends,' Rafe said anxiously, looking at the ostler.

The man smiled at him. 'No need to fear, my young maister. Ye can always bring him a-visiting, for ye live but a pace along the street.' He winked at me. 'And he will have ye as a new friend, surely?'

Rafe reached up and patted Rufus's shoulder. 'I'll give him an apple when we are home.'

'And who is going to ride him there?' the ostler asked.

'The children,' I said.

I lifted Alysoun up into the saddle, then set Rafe on the horse's withers in front of her.

'Put your arms around Rafe's waist, Alysoun, that he may not slip.'

I shortened the stirrups as far as they would go, and she was able to poke the toes of her boots through the leathers, then I gripped the reins close under the horse's chin and led him out into the street, raising my hand in farewell to the ostler as he turned and hurried to carry the purse into the warmth of the inn.

Walking back to the shop was not as trying as the outward journey, for the wind was now at our backs, although the snow was inclined to swirl about and insinuate itself under the edge of my hood and down my neck.

'All well, my pet?' I said, though I had to raise my voice, lest the wind carry it away.

'Aye,' Alysoun said. 'He is a very tall horse, isn't he?'

She could ride a little, although she had only ridden ponies by herself. She had once ridden Rufus with me, but had soon fallen asleep.

'And you, Rafe?'

He merely grinned. He had a firm grip of the mane,

6

and his short legs stuck out on either side of the horse's shoulders.

Back at the shop, I paused for a moment beside the door, so that Walter and Roger could admire the young riders, but we did not linger, because of the cold, then we made our way down the side alleyway. I wished that I had thought to clear it, for in places the wind had blown the snow into drifts which overtopped my boots and soaked my hose.

The new stable was a warm refuge after the snow and wind, even Rufus seemed to appreciate it. He cast a calm eye around the unfamiliar place, but by all appearances was happy to accept it, for in his work as a hired hack from the Mitre he had known many strange stables. Once I had helped the children down, I showed them how to remove the saddle and bridle and hang them high on pegs in the wall, out of reach of any rats who might take a fancy to chewing the leather. Although any rat of sense would be tucked away warmly in this weather.

'We will give Rufus a quick brush down,' I said, 'for he hasn't come far, but after a long journey you must make a better hand of it. Then we'll put his blanket on again, and another I have here, before we leave him to settle in his new home.'

The second blanket was an old one from my bed, which Margaret had reshaped and fitted with buckled straps. Rufus seemed glad of the extra warmth. I checked his hoofs for any hard lumps of snow and ice, then we left him in his new stall, after Rafe had run to fetch him an apple. My only worry was that, alone in my stable, Rufus would not have the heat of the other horses to mitigate the cold.

As we were obediently removing our boots at the door, I saw that Jordain had arrived and was making up the kitchen fire for Margaret. No one was left at Hart Hall over the Christmas season, save for Jordain and his cook, now that the students had gone home to their families. Mistrusting how well Jordain might be fed, and knowing

7

the poor fare the cook produced even in term time, Margaret had given him strict orders to take the midday dinner with us each day. Jordain had demurred at first, out of mere politeness, but it had not needed much to persuade him.

'So-ho!' he said. 'You are now a knight errant, Nicholas, possessed of a mighty steed! When shall you be off on some quest, like King Arthur's men of old?'

Alysoun took his hand and swung on it. 'Do not be foolish, Uncle Jordain,' she said severely. 'Papa has no armour.'

'Then he must find a great lady to make him her knight, and provide the armour.' Jordain gave me a knowing smile.

'That is enough foolishness,' I said with dignity, draping our wet cloaks and hoods over stools near the fire to dry. 'Rufus is a good working horse, and no more. It will suit me better to have my own mount, instead of constantly hiring from the Mitre, and never sure what they will provide for me. He's still quite a young fellow and should serve me well for some years.'

'I was against it, at first,' Margaret admitted, 'but Nicholas has shown me the figures. There was the cost of the stable, of course, but the horse's keep will come to less than his hire, now that more of our customers live beyond Oxford. Even if they visit the shop to place their orders, Nicholas often needs to ride some miles to deliver their books when they are ready, or even to discuss the finer points. Lady Amilia, for example, lives a good ten miles away when they are not at their house in Oxford, and she is one of his regular customers.'

'Building up an extensive library,' I said, lifting the heavy stew pot on to the table, where it rested on a couple of roof tiles, to spare the wood.

Jordain brought the bread and breadknife, and pulled up a stool.

'And how is her book of troubadour songs progressing? he asked.

I rolled my eyes. 'Not well. So far I have but three songs complete with words and music, one set of words with no music, and one possible tune with no words.'

'They will need to be writ very large, then, to fill a book.'

Jordain grinned. He knew that the book of troubadour songs had been a worry to me ever since Lady Amilia had commissioned it.

'Alysoun,' Margaret said, 'run and fetch Walter and Roger. Tell them dinner is on the table.'

Ever since the weather had turned really cold, Margaret had invited the two scriveners to share our midday meal, instead of tramping through the snow to Tackley's Inn, where they usually ate. Walter had said that they should give up some of their wages in return, but I had told him to keep his coin.

'We had a good crop of vegetables this year,' I said. 'And with a little bacon or dried mutton, Margaret can make a potage go a long way. Or with smoked or salted fish on meatless days. You will not be depriving us.'

Roger, I noticed, looked relieved. He had said nothing, but I thought he was saving what money he could. I suspected there might be a girl in the case.

Alysoun came running back from the shop, with news in her face.

She was followed by three men, not two.

'Peter Winchingham!' I exclaimed, jumping up from the table. 'You have returned from Bruges!'

'You come most aptly, Master Winchingham,' said Margaret calmly, 'for we are about to dine.'

I noticed that she did not order him to remove his snowy boots and smiled to myself, then helped him out of his cloak and capuchon, and put them with the others near the fire.

'Nay,' he said, 'I do not come greedily to your table, Mistress Makepeace, but – I beg your pardon – I thought we had agreed to dispense with formality?'

She gave a slight smile. 'Very well, *Peter*, but you

cannot come in out of the snow and turn up that nose of yours, rosy from the cold, at the sight and smell of my very good potage.'

He rubbed his nose thoughtfully. 'Aye, 'tis almost turned to ice. And I would never refuse any meal cooked by you, Margaret, but – see – you have already a full table.'

'One more cannot hurt,' she said briskly. 'Nicholas, fetch a chair from the parlour.'

I did as I was bid, and wasted no time about it, for we did not normally light a fire in the parlour in such cold weather, living instead entirely in the kitchen. The chair itself was cold to the touch.

We arranged ourselves around the table, some on stools and some on chairs, then I spoke a blessing over the meal and ladled out the thick potage into bowls, while Margaret sliced the bread. Once the first hunger pangs were satisfied, Peter sat back contentedly and nibbled a little of the bread.

'Excellent, as usual,' he said. 'You cannot buy bread of this quality in Bruges.' Then, picking up what I had said earlier, he continued.

'Aye, I am back now from Bruges, Nicholas. My elder son safely married and settled with his wife in my old house there. We reached Leighton-under-Wychwood a little over a week ago.'

'You have brought your other children with you?' Margaret asked.

'Aye, my daughter Birgit, who is sixteen, and my younger son, Hans. He is but fifteen, but he is a big lad, and looks older. We took ship to Norwich, and hired a carriage for the journey into Oxfordshire, with three carts for our household goods! I had thought to travel lightly, but my daughter could not bring herself to leave behind her favourite pieces of furniture or her lute or her gowns and books. As for my son, there was all his hunting gear to bring. I persuaded him to leave his horse behind, thinking it a cruel journey by sea for a horse at this time of year. He will send for him in the spring.'

He laughed. 'I must confess to three chests of books myself. We did not travel light.'

'My father owns a horse now,' Alysoun said, with assumed carelessness.

Jordain hid his smile behind his hand.

'Indeed?' Peter turned to me.

'No mount of fine bloodstock,' I said. ''Tis the gelding I was forever hiring from the Mitre. I resolved to save money by buying him outright.'

'And how do you find Leighton Manor,' Margaret asked, 'now that you are living there?'

'Sound and comfortable enough,' Peter said, 'but there is work to be done, of course. Birgit does not care for the flamboyance of the last owner's fripperies, which have come to us along with the house. She is all for changing everything, but the season will not permit. She must content herself with bundling away the worst until we may hire in new workmen in the spring.'

'I am sure you will find the manor servants and men from the village will be able to undertake most of what you may need,' I said. 'I think Gilbert Morden had all the structural work done before he moved there. In the de Veres' time it was a beautiful house.'

'Aye.' A dreamy look came over Margaret's face. 'I remember it when I was a young girl. I used to think then that it was the most perfect home.'

'I hope to make it that way again.' Peter smiled at her. 'I hope you will be able to help Birgit restore it to what it once was.'

'Well, whenever we are next in Leighton . . .'

'And that is one reason I have come to call. I had some business in Oxford, and your cousin Edmond asked me to bring you a message.'

Margaret and I both looked at him somewhat apprehensively. Our mother had been growing frail in recent months and uncertainty hung over her plan to come to Oxford for the Christmas season. In the autumn it had seemed possible, but the early heavy snow had raised doubts in my mind about her making the journey. I had intended to send word with Geoffrey Carter when next he was in Oxford, advising her against coming.

'Our mother?' I said.

He nodded. 'Your cousin thinks it impossible for her to travel through this weather, even if you fetched her in a covered cart, but she is most anxious to see you all. She fears that it may be the last time, though who knows how God will dispose? Instead, he begs you to bring your family to Leighton for the Christmas season. And,' he inclined his head to Jordain, 'extends the invitation to the friends who came for the harvest. I am hoping very much for myself that you will come, to help us celebrate our first Christmas at Leighton with a fine crowd of good friends.'

Once again, Margaret and I exchanged looks, and she gave me a slight nod. Alysoun was bouncing up and down on her stool, and Rafe was grinning broadly.

'Christmas at Leighton!' Alysoun cried. Then her face fell. 'But Juliana and Emma were to spend Christmas with us here in Oxford.'

The same thought had crossed my own mind.

'Some of our autumn party cannot come,' I said. 'Philip Olney, Beatrice, and Stephen have already gone to his father's manor for the festivities. Away from Oxford with its prying eyes, Beatrice may live without censure as his wife. They are not likely to return until the beginning of the Oxford term.'

Alysoun tugged at my sleeve. 'But Juliana and Emma?'

'I do not know, my pet. Mistress Farringdon may not wish to make such a cold winter journey. And Cousin Edmond has invited those who helped with the harvest.'

'But see!' she said cunningly. 'Without Master Olney's family, and Uncle Jordain's two students, we shall be five fewer. And Mistress Farringdon and Juliana and Emma and Maysant are but four!'

'Your reckoning is excellent,' I said dryly, 'but we cannot make plans for other folk.'

'If there is lack of room at your farm,' Peter said, 'the manor has an abundance of chambers. There will be no problem with lodgings, should Mistress Farringdon wish to come.'

'I am loath to spoil their Christmas,' I said, torn two ways. I could not gainsay my mother's wish to see the family, but we had also made promises to Mistress Farringdon and the girls.

'I shall speak to Maud Farringdon.' Margaret said briskly. 'She is a country woman herself. Likely she will be happy to celebrate a country Christmas. As for the cold journey, if I can endure it, I am sure so may she. Leave the matter in my hands.'

I nodded. I was relieved to do so. I had been anticipating a joyful Christmas here in Oxford, after fetching my mother from Leighton, but I had been as worried as Edmond when the weather had turned so cold as early as it had. Yet I did not want to lose Emma's company during one of the happiest times of the year. Margaret, I suspect, would make a better hand of rearranging our plans than I should do.

Dinner over and the scriveners returned to work, Peter Winchingham donned his cloak and capuchon again, saying that he must see to his business in the town before spending the night at the Mitre.

'I shall set off for home at first light tomorrow,' he said, as I saw him through the shop and into the High, where the winter light was already seeping from the sky. 'Do you think you will have word for me by then, how many will come to Leighton?'

Jordain had already happily accepted, for he always spent Christmas with us. He had lost all his family in the Great Pestilence, save for one sister who was married and living in Canterbury, too far to travel in winter. Before leaving to work on his lectures for the following term, he had bid Peter farewell until they should see each other in Leighton.

Margaret, coming up behind us, had heard Peter's

words.

'I am going now to St Mildred Street to speak to Maud,' she said. 'I shall have your answer before you leave, Peter.'

She set off up the High, clutching her hood close about her face against the wind.

'I remember me,' Peter said, as he too turned to go. 'I have another inducement for you to come to Leighton. I think I may have told you that Birgit is a great lover of music. Before we left Bruges, she heard a group of musicians play at a friend's house, three of them, brother and sister, and the sister's husband. We engaged them for several evenings ourselves. She has employed them to entertain us over the Christmas period. They had another engagement, so could not travel with us, but they should be here within a week or so. They follow the troubadour tradition. You may mine their repertoire for your book of troubadour songs.'

I grinned at him. 'That is inducement indeed, though I needed it not to persuade me to Leighton! If I can secure their help, it could save me a great deal of worry over a book I thought I might never be able to complete.'

He clapped me on the shoulder. 'I hope to see you in the morning, then. And it would be good to see Mistress Farringdon and her family again. I may hope that they agree to come.'

'And I,' I said, perhaps more fervently than I intended.

Margaret was an unconscionable time returning home. I spent the afternoon in the shop, first sorting through the student *peciae* which had fallen into disorder during the last weeks of term. Those that needed mending I set to one side. A few that were past saving, I gave to Roger so that he might make new copies whenever he was not engaged on more profitable work, preparing another copy of the book of tales he had assembled earlier in the year. It was proving popular, for as soon as he completed one copy, it found an eager purchaser. Once the *peciae* had been sorted, I sat down with Walter to go through the collection he had been making of the stories his mother used to tell when he was a child. He was still nervous and hesitant about handing them over to Emma, so that she could make of them a beautifully illustrated book.

'I do not know, Nicholas,' he said doubtfully, fingering the pages of his rough drafts, with all their crossings out and amendments. 'They are not the grand tales to be found in true books. These are no more than a simple goodwife's old stories told to her family by firelight. The language is too plain and simple, and even those with a moral do not have the high literary tone.' He peered at me anxiously over the wooden frame of his spectacles.

'You have spent too much of your time copying university texts, Walter,' I said. 'Those are meant for study and deep thought, for disputation and analysis. Stories by the fireside are what many people truly want. Especially in the dark years since the Great Pestilence. They crave a return to the simple days of their childhood, to the stories told to them by grandam or nurse.'

I paused, thinking about it myself properly for the first time.

'Ever since those black days, we have all been groping our way forward into a changed world. With half the people of England struck down with the Pestilence and gone, it is difficult to foresee our future. Before . . . well, I suppose we all thought life would continue as it had done in our fathers' time, and our fathers' fathers' time, and back through the ages. We are lost now on a sea of uncertainty, however much we try to live our everyday lives as if the times had not changed. Your mother's old stories are a link to a past we have lost but do not want to relinquish.'

His head was lowered, as he stared down at the blotted pages.

'Do you agree?' I said.

'Aye.' He nodded slowly. 'I suppose you have the right of it.'

He shook himself. 'I will try to put aside my misgivings. But do you go through them once more with me. I have made some changes since you read them last.'

I fetched more candles, for it was growing dark early, the heavy layer of cloud blotting out any lingering scrap of daylight. Some of Walter's new amendments were good, but many were mere tinkerings. I saw that in the end I should need to take away his manuscript by force, or he would never cease changing a word here, a sentence there.

'I think this is ready to pass over to the lady Emma now,' I said firmly, when we had read through every alteration. Roger was already tidying away his work for the day.

'I have thought of one more story to add,' Walter said eagerly.

I laughed. 'Just one more? Very well. Three more days. Then, will-ye or nill-ye, I shall take your manuscript to the lady Emma, that she may start work. She has been fretting about it.'

What Emma had said to me was that she could not bear to look at the new desk I had had made for her, with no work to be done on it.

'I am away then, Master Elyot,' Roger said, donning his patched cloak.

He could afford a new one, I was sure, had he not been hoarding his coin.

'Watch your feet,' I said. ''Twas slippery enough this morning, with the spare bit of sun on the street. With the dark fallen, 'twill be worse.'

'Aye, I'll mind how I go,' he said.

'Wait you a minute,' Walter said. 'We'll take a sup of hippocras at Tackley's before going home. It will warm us for the walk.'

'Three days!' I called, as they were closing the door. 'Mind, I mean it!'

Leaving one candle burning in the shop to light Margaret in when she came at last, I went through to the house. During the afternoon I had checked on the children

16

from time to time, but they had been playing contentedly with some figures Margaret had helped them make in hard baked dough – rough models of people and animals. I had given them some dribbles of old inks which had become too grainy to use, and they had spent a happy time painting them in unlikely colours. I saw, with some guilt, that there were smears on the table as well as on their hands and faces, and sent them to wash, while I put the playthings on the hearth to dry and fetched the solvent we use in cases of disaster with a manuscript. The table was free of paint – although suspiciously shiny in patches – when Margaret came in, shuddering with the cold.

'I thought you had taken a fancy to walk to Leighton,' I said mildly, 'without waiting for the rest of us.'

'I called in on Mary Coomber first,' she said, sitting in her cushioned chair by the fire and holding out her feet in their sodden hose to the fire, where they began to steam. Had I done that, she would have warned me about chilblains, but I kept my tongue behind my teeth.

'I wanted to be sure she could feed our hens, if we are to go to Leighton.'

I fetched an old bucket and poured in some bran and bruised oats, before adding hot water from the pot sitting by the fire.

'Spoiling that horse already, are you?' she said.

''Tis his first night away from the warmth of the other horses in the Mitre's stable,' I said. 'And a bitter night. I reckon it will do him good.'

Before I could ask how she had fared with Maud Farringdon, the children came clattering down the stairs, eager to show Margaret the painting of their models. Only when these had been duly admired, could I ask my casual question.

'And what says Maud to the suggestion that they should come with us to Leighton?' I asked. 'I mislike breaking our word that they should spend their Christmas with us here in Oxford.'

17

'She is not quite sure, Nicholas. Maysant has a winter rheum and a cough. She is not well enough to make a cold winter's journey.'

I felt a sharp stab of disappointment. Maysant, Maud's grandchild, was about the same age as Rafe, and had lost both her parents in the Pestilence, as I had lost Rafe's mother. Unlike Rafe, she was small and delicate. It would certainly not be safe for her to travel if she was ill.

'So they will not come?'

'I told her we should not leave for a week at least. Mayhap the child will have recovered by then. While I was there I stepped round to the apothecary's in Northgate Street, to fetch the herbs and roots for my chest rub and for the infusion for Maysant to inhale. We made them up together and physicked the child. She was looking better by the time I left.'

She drew back her feet from the fire, and spread out her wet skirts to the warmth.

'Then I stopped at the dairy again. Now that Maud has a few hens of her own, they will need to be fed as well. Mary was kind enough to say she would see to it, when she is taking her milk round the town. If the Farringdons decide to come with us.'

'Oh, I do hope Maysant will be better!' Alysoun said. 'Then we can all go to Leighton together.'

'Aye,' Margaret said dryly, 'and a fine company we should be. Have you thought on it, Nicholas? A gaggle of women and children? You and Jordain will be our only menfolk.'

'And me,' Rafe said indignantly.

Margaret was right. When we had travelled to Leighton in the autumn, as well as Jordain and me there had been Philip Olney and Jordain's two students, all mounted. A sizeable company, enough to deter casual footpads. This time I alone would be mounted, and Jordain would drive the cart, with Margaret's assistance. In these troubled times, the roads were not always safe. Would the bad weather deter any masterless men prowling on the lookout for travellers to rob? Or would their misery and hunger drive them all the more readily to attack?

'I am sure we will be safe,' I said, with more conviction than I felt. 'Besides, it will make little difference in that case, whether the Farringdons come or not.'

I gave a final stir to the warm bran and oats. It had cooled enough to take out to the horse.

In the stable, Rufus sniffed the bucket with interest, then plunged in as I held it steady. While he gobbled the mixture enthusiastically, I laid my other hand on his shoulder, feeling the ripple of muscles under the skin. I could hardly believe that I now possessed a horse of my own. As a boy I had a pony, but it really belonged to my father. Rufus was wholly and entirely mine. The day had been so crowded, I had barely had time to enjoy the thought.

When the bucket was emptied down to the last scrap, I checked the hay and water, then made sure that the two blankets were held securely in place. I was pleased to discover that there were no draughts finding their way through cracks in the walls or round the door. The carpenter had done good work. The stable was as snug as a cottage. Better, by far, than the dirty hovels up beyond St Peter-in-the-East, in Hammer Hall Lane.

I gave Rufus a final pat, picked up the bucket and my candle lantern, and went out into the night. The heavy clouds of the day had blown away on the wind and the sky was clear, moon and stars sparkling, a bitter cold silver against the black. There would be no snow tonight, but there would be a heavy frost. I could feel it already, on every in-drawn breath. I checked that the bolt was across the gate where the alleyway joined the High Street, then made my way thankfully into the warmth of the kitchen.

Whether the Farringdons were to come with us or not, there were preparations to be made for a winter journey. In the autumn we had been able to cover the distance in one long day's travel, but we could hardly hope to do the same in

19

December. The daylight hours would be much shorter, so that we would be obliged to start later and stop sooner. As well, with so much snow on the ground, the road might be blocked part of the way. The going would be slow and it might be necessary to dig a way through in places, even though most of our route would lie along roads which were regularly used. In a snow storm, anything might happen.

The next morning, straight after breaking my fast, I called at the Mitre, where I found Peter Winchingham packing his saddle bags for his ride back to Leighton, and explained that, for now, we could not be certain whether Mistress Farringdon and the three girls would come to Leighton or not.

'Do not concern yourself, Nicholas,' he said, fastening the last buckles. 'I will explain all to your cousin. If you have the chance to send word before you leave, well and good. If not, come, however many you are. As I have said, there is room a-plenty at the manor, if there be not enough at the farm. Birgit will enjoy playing hostess in her new domain. I am sorry to hear that the little maid is ill, but children often recover quickly.'

'How did you find the roads on your way to Oxford?' I asked, as I walked with him to the yard of the inn, where one of the young stable lads was holding his horse ready.

Peter flung the saddle bags over the horse's rump and fastened them to the saddle.

'Quite deep snow,' he said, 'but passable. There is a fair amount of coming and going along all the roads between Oxford and Burford. The lane up to Leighton is worse. I thought to speak to your cousin and some others about setting some of the day labourers to clear a way through.'

I nodded. 'They would be glad of a day or two's work. There is little enough for them in winter.'

'Aye, so I thought also.'

'And no sign of trouble on the road?'

'I had no trouble, but it may be different for you, with a slow cart. Some might think it full of valuables.'

I laughed. 'I shall be hiring one of the Mitre's carts. It will hardly look like some nobleman's entourage.'

'To a hungry man, living wild in the woods, even a cart itself might seem valuable plunder,' he said seriously.

'Aye, that's true enough.'

And to tell truth, I was worried about the journey, although I had been trying to hide it from Margaret and the children.

'You could hire an escort,' he suggested.

'I could. It would be costly, but worth it, if it meant a safer journey. But again, if we travel with an escort, it might seem that indeed we are carrying valuables with us.'

''Tis a dilemma, I agree.'

He swung himself up on to the horse's back.

'Well, I hope you fare safely. When do you look to come?'

'No sooner than a week,' I said, 'to give the child time to recover. If she is not well by then, I think we must come without the other family.'

He nodded. 'I look to see you then. God go with you, Nicholas.'

'And with you,' I said, as he clicked his tongue to the horse and rode out of the stableyard.

I turned back to the inn, to make enquiries about hiring a cart for our journey.

Since few people are foolish enough to undertake journeys in December, I had my pick of all the carts the Mitre had to offer. I chose the largest, in the hope that our numbers would be augmented by the Farringdons and Emma. This was a long vehicle, drawn by two horses, and had the advantage of a canvas cover stretched over hoops to provide a roof, for an open cart would have been deadly for the passengers in this winter weather.

I inspected the cart with care, for we could not risk it breaking down on the journey, leaving us to freeze to death beside the road.

I tapped the wheels doubtfully. They looked somewhat dried out to me, shrunken within their iron rims, as though the spokes might work loose.

'You must have a wheelwright check these before it will be safe to drive,' I said to the head ostler, 'and the axles will need greasing. I think this cart has not been used for some time.'

'Nay, to be sure, Maister Elyot, it has not.'

I had long had dealings with the man, and knew that he was to be trusted.

'And the canvas had best be checked over as well. Have you someone who can do that?'

He grimaced, and ran his hands through his hair, forgetting he was wearing a woollen cap, which flew off and landed in the snow. He grunted in annoyance and picked it up, slapping it against his thigh to rid it of the snow.

'Nay, now, who could see to the canvas? I mind 'twas bought like that, with the cover, and no one has done aught to it since.'

'Mayhap one of the sail-makers down at the dock on the Thames?' I said. 'It will not be their usual work, but they will know if it is sound. And I do not suppose they are much occupied at this time of year.'

'Aye!' His face lit up as though I had made some great discovery. 'I s'all see to it at once, maister. They can mebbe patch it, if 'tis needed.'

'Good,' I said.

I climbed up into the cart, to examine the inside. It was clean enough, though a mite dusty. All the planks were sound, and the sides were high, which would provide excellent protection from the weather. We could cover the bottom with a deep layer of straw, then lay blankets on top. With cushions and feather beds, the women and children should be comfortable enough. It would be cold for the driver. I resolved to persuade Jordain to borrow some of my clothes, instead of clinging to his threadbare academic gown, which would be poor protection for him, seated outside in the cold. Perhaps we could also contrive some other way to keep him warm.

We had never made a long journey in such cold weather as this, and I found myself wondering how habitual travellers managed to survive. A brazier inside the cart would provide a welcome warmth, but would be dangerous amongst the straw. Then I remembered how Emma had once travelled in the cart which was also home to a family of candle-makers. She might remember how they had contrived their home in a wheeled cart. I would consult Emma.

Chapter Two

St Mildred Street opens from the High between the Mitre Inn and All Saints Church, so that it would take me but a few steps from the inn to Mistress Farringdon's house. Emma should be there now. She had visited her grandfather Sir Anthony Thorgold at his manor near Long Wittenham, after the end of St Frideswide's Fair, but she had returned to Oxford two weeks ago. I had seen her a few times since then, but she had been much occupied helping her aunt to sew winter clothes for them all. Sir Anthony had decreed that Emma should have an allowance from him, despite her determination to earn her own living as a scrivener and illuminator, and she had immediately purchased a large quantity of the best woollen cloth for gowns, cloaks, and capuchons, as well as sturdy new winter boots from the cordwainer in Northgate Street. If the family were to be able to accompany us to Leighton, at least they would be warmly dressed.

As I emerged from the stableyard of the inn, I nearly collided with a small woman so bundled up in cloak and blanket that she was practically spherical. She carried a tray suspended from a leather strap about her neck, on which were laid out a tempting array of sweetmeats and comfits. At this time of year, many of the goodwives of Oxford earned a few pence by making and selling small treats for the festive season, and these looked as good as any I had seen. Margaret had already begun to make her own for Christmas, but I had not thought to bring any with me. I decided now that it would be a kindness to take some for the sick child.

I chose a selection of the softer kind – jellies and marchpane and rysshews of fruits – thinking that they would better suit a child with a sore throat, but I added salted nuts and dates stuffed with almonds and hard sweet pastes for the rest of the household.

'I thank 'ee, maister,' the woman said, bobbing me a curtsey as she handed me the sweetmeats in a cone of coarse paper.

I laid the pennies on her tray in exchange.

'Ah, but that be too much.'

'Never mind,' I said. 'Call it a gift in the Christ Child's name.'

I slipped the packet into the breast of my cotte, and began to plough my way up St Mildred Street. I was surprised that a path had not yet been cleared along to the church, but there had been heavy snow falls during several days lately. Perhaps the vergers and their lads had not had time for it.

My knock on the door of the cottage close to the church was answered by several voices calling 'Come!', so I let myself in, stamping the snow off my boots and surveying the scene within, which resembled a tailor's workshop, every surface draped with bolts of cloth, or cut pieces, hanks of thread, ribbons, scissors and threaded needles.

'Sit, Nicholas,' Maud Farringdon said, round a mouthful of pins.

I looked about for an unoccupied stool. Her daughter Juliana jumped up and removed a basket full of pieces of lace from the only one in sight.

'I am afraid you find us in a caddle,' Maud said, having removed the pins, but continuing to stitch. The needle, flashing in and out of the cloth, caught the light from the fire, so that it seemed almost alive.

'Do not let me hamper your work,' I said, seating myself gingerly, fearful of more pins. 'I have been at the

Mitre and thought I would call to ask after Maysant.'

'She is in bed with two hot bricks,' Juliana said, 'and her three poppets, and a cloth cat Emma made her out of some of the scraps.'

'I have brought her some sweetmeats,' I said, 'and some for the rest of you, to cheer you at your labours. Shall I take these up to Maysant, or will she be sleeping?'

'Not she,' said Juliana. 'She is growing very bored and tiresome, but we cannot have her here, sneezing all over this fine new cloth.'

I smiled across at Emma, who was diligently hemming a gown, though not as swiftly as her aunt.

'Aye,' she said, 'Maysant will be glad of a visitor. We are all too busy to entertain her.'

I found the child sitting up in bed, talking to her toys, and she croaked her thanks, diving into the packet of comfits at once.

'Keep some for later,' I warned.

She looked a little flushed, but otherwise not seriously ill.

Downstairs I asked Maud whether Maysant was recovering.

'She is better today than yesterday,' she said. 'Better than when Margaret called to see us. I think her fever is almost gone, but she still coughs a good deal in the night.'

'Do you think you might be able to make the journey to Leighton with us?'

She looked dubious. ''Tis too soon to tell. But if we cannot go, Emma may.'

Emma shook her head. 'I will not leave you alone with a sick child over Christmas. Either we all go, or none.'

'I have been at the Mitre,' I said, 'bespeaking a cart for the journey. I have been able to hire a very large one, with a good canvas for a roof.' I did not mention the possible need for patching. 'There is plenty of room for straw bedding, and blankets. We can carry a good supply of food with us.'

I turned to Emma, who was folding and laying aside

26

the gown she had finished hemming.

'I wanted to ask you about the candle-makers' cart you travelled in. Had they some means to keep themselves warm?'

Emma closed her eyes, as if to visualise the cart better.

'It was summer, of course, so there was no need for extra warmth. I remember that they cooked over an open fire outside, although there *was* a small brazier, which I think they must have used when it was raining too heavily to light a fire, but I never saw them cook over it. It was a very large cart, if you remember, and a portion of it divided off for the brazier.'

She opened her eyes again. 'It would be dangerous, would it not? Even kept separate? A fire inside, especially if we have a layer of straw in the bed of the cart.'

'That is what I fear.'

'You could take hot stones or bricks, well wrapped,' Juliana said.

'Aye, but they would soon cool.' Maud shook her head. 'I am afraid Maysant will not be well enough to travel, with the weather so cold.'

'Nevertheless,' I said, 'I shall make the arrangements to fit the four of you in, hoping that she will have recovered by then.'

'Who else goes?' Emma asked.

'Just Margaret, the children, and me. And Jordain. Philip and his family are invited, but have already left Oxford for Christmas.'

'You know that we will come if we can,' Maud said. 'How long do you take over the journey?'

'With this heavy snow and the short hours of daylight,' I said, 'we cannot make the journey in a day, as we did when we went for the harvest. I thought we might spend the first night at Eynsham Abbey, and the second at the Priory in Minster Lovell. That will break the journey into about three equal pieces.'

Maud looked thoughtful. 'That seems a little less

daunting. We shall see how Maysant fares over the next few days. Margaret said you would leave in about a week.'

'Aye,' I said, and with that must be content.

Emma walked with me to the door. 'I should like to see the place where you grew up,' she said, 'but I cannot leave my aunt and cousins at Christmas.'

I nodded. 'I understand,' I said, despite my disappointment. 'We must hope Maysant will soon be better. In the meantime, I shall make the cart as comfortable as I can. There are benches we can fit inside, and if everyone wraps up warmly, we can make it quite comfortable.'

'Jordain will drive, and you will ride?'

'Aye.' I grinned suddenly. 'I have bought Rufus!'

She laughed. 'I am hardly surprised, with that stable a-building.'

'Also, Walter's collection of tales is near ready for you. He has just remembered another, but I have told him, only three more days, then I shall take the manuscript away from him, even if I must tear it from his hands!'

'If I do not come with you to Leighton, I can work on Walter's book.'

'I suppose you might do some of the scribing in Leighton.'

'But not the drawing and painting.'

'Probably not.'

I paused before opening the door. There was no excuse for lingering, and she was much occupied.

'Peter Winchingham called on us yesterday,' I said. 'Did Margaret tell you? He is settled now at the manor, and his daughter has hired a troupe of troubadours to entertain us during the festivities.'

'Ah, so you are hoping to gather more material for Lady Amilia's book.'

'Indeed.'

'I should dearly like to hear them.' She looked wistful.

'Last Christmas,' I said curiously, 'how did you

spend it?'

'On my knees, for the most part. The services at the nunnery were very long, celebrating the birth of the Christ Child.'

'Sire Raymond, our village priest, will hold a midnight Mass on the Eve, and a full quiver of services on Christmas Day,' I said, 'but he has no objection to more ancient festivities. He has a great interest in such things.'

She smiled. 'I like everything I hear about your Sire Raymond, but you must understand why I cannot leave my aunt. Last Christmas both my uncle and my cousin William were alive. Aunt Maud was comfortably settled in her own home, not in a cottage loaned out of charity. There was my uncle's pension from the king, and a hired manager for the farm. Juliana had the prospect of a good marriage in a few years' time. They have suffered such misfortunes in the last year, despite all that you and your friends have done for them. I cannot leave her.'

I reached out and touched her arm gently.

'Of course you cannot. Never think it. We will all pray for Maysant's good health.'

I was much occupied over the next few days. There was work to be done in the shop before we closed for the season of festivities. I also spent some time checking over the wheels and canvas of the cart, after they had been repaired, and selected the two cart horses who looked most fit for the work, requesting that they be shod with winter shoes by the farrier, to give them a better grip on icy ground. Rufus had already been equipped.

Two days after my visit to St Mildred Street, I rode Rufus across Oxford and down Great Bailey to the castle, where I found the deputy sheriff, Cedric Walden, in the blacksmith's workshop, where he was supervising the tempering of a new sword. He came outside, wiping the sweat from his face, and immediately began to shiver from the contrast of the icy wind. It was not snowing at the moment, but the heavy clouds threatened more before long.

'Come into my office, Nicholas,' he said, 'before we both catch the lung sickness out here.'

There was a cheerful fire burning in his grate, and a servant brought us hippocras and seeded cake. I described the journey I should be taking in a few days' time, and the worry of caring for so many on the road in these lawless times.

'Jordain Brinkylsworth and I will be the only men, and although Jordain is a fine man and a gifted scholar, he has no skill at arms. Mine is little better. Perhaps I am needlessly concerned. What word have you, of any trouble on the roads north and west of Oxford?'

He sipped his wine thoughtfully. 'Since that trouble at St Frideswide's Fair in October, I have heard of nothing from the French, beyond some petty raids on the south coast. Though I confess I do not think our precarious truce with France will hold for long. As for our own home-grown villains . . . I do not suppose we shall ever be rid of them! There are some advantages to winter travel, to offset the cold and discomfort. The villains themselves are like to lie snug if they may, unless they are very reckless or very desperate. And with the leaves stripped from the trees, the woods you must pass through will not be as dense as in summer, giving little cover for an attack.'

'Yet you think there might be an attack?' I said.

'There was some trouble on the road near Witney, about a fortnight ago. A group of ne'er-do-wells attacked a pack train of woollen bales coming from Northleach. They managed to inflict some small injuries on the drovers, and carried off two bales, without being taken themselves. So, aye, there might be trouble along that stretch of the road. Though it may be they are more interested in merchants' goods than in mere travellers.'

'What I fear is that such men might suppose our cart did contain merchants' goods, and not a company of women and children.'

He nodded. 'That is a danger.' He thought for a minute. 'Do you want me to provide you with an escort?'

I smiled ruefully. 'I doubt I could afford to hire a party of soldiers.'

'But that might not be necessary. I am ordered to send a dozen men to Gloucester, to provide armed protection for some nobleman – who has not been named – travelling here to Woodstock Palace. They could accompany you past Witney, where that attack took place. You turn off near Burford, do you not?'

'Aye. The smaller road, no more than a country lane, turns north a short way before Burford.'

'I think that could be arranged. No need to make it official, and no need to inform Sheriff de Alveton. You will simply be travelling the same way on the same day, and the parties join by mere accident.'

I grinned. Sheriff de Alveton, high sheriff of both Oxfordshire and Berkshire, was notoriously slack in his duties, and had been fined for corruption in the past. Here in Oxford and the surrounding country, it was Cedric Walden who maintained the law.

'That sounds like an excellent solution to me,' I said. 'When do your men travel?'

'Five days from now.'

'We shall be ready,' I promised. It was too fortunate a chance to waste.

That evening I told Margaret of Cedric's offer, and could see that it relieved her of a worry she had tried to conceal.

'No one doubts your courage, Nicholas, but should we be attacked even by a few rogues, what could you do?'

'Indeed,' I admitted with a smile. 'I am no swordsman. I might manage a swipe or two, but hardly more. With a dozen soldiers accompanying us, no man living wild in the woods will risk an attack.'

I did not mention my other worry. On our return journey to Oxford, we should have no such guard, but time enough to face that worry later.

I sent Roger round to Mistress Farringdon, with a message explaining the arrangement I had made with the deputy sheriff, hoping that it might help to persuade her to make the journey. Then I firmly removed the manuscript of tales from Walter, and sat down to read it through one final time, before handing it over to Emma.

When he had first embarked on the task of writing down his mother's stories, Walter had been hampered by a belief that he must use a style of high rhetoric, with the result that the stories seemed dull and stilted. Only after I had persuaded him, with some difficulty, to write them down just as he was wont to tell them to our family around the fire, in his own simple words, did they come to life. The final version I now held in my hands had all the vigour and sincerity of the true storyteller. I knew this would make a fine book.

It had not been commissioned by any customer, and I knew I would keep the first copy for myself, once Emma had scribed and illustrated it. Then I would be able to show it to customers, who could order their own copies, with simple text or with the full glory of Emma's illuminations.

When I took her the manuscript the next morning, she was eager to make a start at once, now that the sewing of winter garments was all but finished.

'If I can be spared from the sewing, I shall read through the whole,' she said, 'then suggest how we might arrange the tales, for your approval, before I start on the work.'

I nodded my agreement. I was pleased to see that Maysant was out of her bed and sitting with Maud and Juliana as they stitched collars in place, and added a few trimmings to the gowns.

'So,' I said to Maud, 'shall you come to Leighton with us?'

She glanced across at her granddaughter. 'Aye, I think she is well enough. Although I do worry about the cold.'

And so also did I, but I assured her cheerfully that we would pile up the cart with blankets and feather quilts enough to keep everyone warm. When I left the house, I went to see that my instructions for the cart had indeed been carried out.

The canvas had needed one patch near the rear end, but otherwise the sail-maker had declared it sound. With the wheels repaired, and the axles and tow bar greased, the working parts of the cart were as sound as they could be made. Benches had been secured down both sides, for those who wished to sit, and the cart was so wide that there remained plenty of room between them, for those who wished to roll themselves up in blankets and sleep on the floor. When I arrived, one of the stable lads was forking in the last of the straw I had ordered, making a layer about a foot or more deep over the whole of the floor. I could think of nothing else I could provide, until we added our luggage and bedding, and as many hot stones as we could fit in. I had decided I would not attempt to copy the candle-makers' divided section for a brazier. I was sure they would only use one for cooking, when the cart was stationary. To have a burning brazier in a wooden cart, lined with straw, jolting over rough roads packed with snow and ice, was to invite disaster.

Probably Jordain and I would have the coldest journey. If he became too cold, sitting on the driver's seat, I would offer to change places with him, but I was not sure he would care to ride Rufus. Margaret had stitched together a kind of sack from two old blankets, which she hoped to persuade Jordain to pull up over his legs to his waist. She remembered Geoffrey, the Leighton carter, using such a thing in wintertime. I hoped she would prevail. I had had difficulty enough convincing him to lay aside his old academic gown until we reached Leighton, and to substitute a thick woollen shirt, cotte, and cloak of mine. In the end, he had even humbly accepted new woollen hose Margaret had knitted for him.

'They were to be a Twelfth Day gift,' she said, 'but you had best have them now, else you might not live till Twelfth Day, frozen into a man of ice on the driver's seat.'

I knew that she intended to take over the driving from

time to time, but she was well supplied with warm clothes.

It seemed our preparations were nearly complete.

It was the night before our departure. Walter and Roger had left for their own seasonal holidays, each with a Christmas bonus of coin and a basket of goodies baked by Margaret. Walter, who had lost his wife and child in the Pestilence, was to spend the time with the family of the fishmonger in whose house he lodged. Roger was leaving the next morning with a carter who would take him as far as Cutteslowe, then he would walk the rest of the way to his widowed mother's home in the Otmoor village of Beckley. Alysoun and Rafe were so excited that it needed a strict warning from Margaret before they would settle in their beds, and their mood had communicated itself to Rowan, who rushed about the house, barking at imaginary intruders.

In truth, I could not rest myself. My original plan had been to fetch my mother from Leighton to spend Christmas with us in Oxford, as she had intended. We could have ridden comfortably with Geoffrey Carter, whom no vagabond would have troubled, for he was known on the roads about this part of the county, and rarely carried goods worth stealing. Instead, I now found myself in charge of a whole company of travellers, obliged to make the journey through winter weather far worse than was usual at this time of year, most of my companions women and children, and one of whom was barely recovered from illness. I was heartily thankful for the protection of Cedric Walden's company of soldiers for most of the journey.

I had spoken confidently of spending the two nights on the road at Eynsham Abbey and the priory at Minster Lovell, but we were a considerable number now. I counted up in my head, as I lay on my bed looking at the rim of snow light around my window shutters. Mistress Farringdon's family: four. My family and Jordain: five. A dozen soldiers. One and twenty persons. And two dogs: Rowan, and Emma's dog Jocosa. Although the monastic houses were obliged by their Rule – both were Benedictine – to provide food and lodging for travellers, we might strain their resources. The blizzards having come on so unexpectedly, they might already be overrun with those benighted by the weather, who would probably wish to wait before continuing, in the hope of a thaw.

And would the passengers in the cart be able to withstand the cold? At least by our breaking the journey down into three parts, none of them overly long, they would not need to spend too many hours in the cart. I would hardly be warm myself, mounted on Rufus, but the very act of riding calls into use the muscles of arms, legs, and back, which helps to stir the blood and fend off some of the chill, although I knew that my feet, face, and hands would grow numb. Images of disaster invaded my mind, until at last sheer exhaustion sent me to sleep. It seemed almost the next moment that Margaret was shaking me by the shoulder.

The smell of baking bread brought me fully awake, and in the kitchen I found a row of loaves cooling on a shelf, waiting to be added to the baskets which were already packed with provisions for the journey. Margaret was leaving nothing to chance. The children were seated at the table spooning up porridge liberally laced with honey.

I set to and made another warm stir-up of oats and bran for Rufus before I would sit down to my own breakfast. On the way to the stable, my feet crunched on the layer of ice which had formed on the surface of the snow. There had been no new fall for two days, and clear tracks had been worn through the drifts to the stable and hen house. I shivered, for there was but the merest pre-dawn light in the sky, so that the whole world was a wash of greys and whites, with a sheen of silver where that first hint of light caught the surface of the frozen snow. The branches of the trees in our small orchard were frosted over and eerily still, as though the world held its breath, before the next blizzard struck.

Back in the kitchen, I shovelled down my own bowl

of porridge, barely allowing myself time to enjoy the luxury of honey, while Margaret chivvied the children into as many layers of clothes as she could contrive.

There was a knock on the street door, and Alysoun ducked away from her aunt, running to open it. Jordain stood there, his bundle at his feet, looking sheepish and oddly secular in my spare clothing.

'I thought to leave this here,' he said, pointing at his bundle, 'while I go along to the Mitre, to see whether the cart and horses are ready.'

'Aye,' I said. 'I am just going to saddle up Rufus, and Margaret is readying the children and the provisions. We are to meet the soldiers from the castle at Carfax.'

I added Jordain's bundle to the heap already lying just inside the shop door, wondering whether we would, after all, be able to find room for everything, despite the size of the cart. Still, the more crowded the occupants, the less chance they would feel the cold.

By the time I had saddled Rufus and brought him round to the street, together with his nosebag, a sack of oats, and a net of hay which he was trying to plunder, Jordain had arrived with the cart, drawn by the two heavy built cart horses, and with Juliana and Emma seated beside him on the driver's bench. All three jumped down and began the awkward business of turning the cart. The High is a broad thoroughfare, surprisingly broad for a small town like Oxford, but the cart was exceptionally long and wide, and the two horses, though well trained and experienced, had not yet grown accustomed to it or to working together. I was surprised to see how well the two girls managed, but both were country reared and entirely lacking in the refined daintiness of high bred ladies. It was difficult for me, sometimes, to remember that Emma was sole heir to the great estates of her grandfather.

Once the manoeuvre was successfully completed, and the horses stood still, blowing out clouds of steaming breath, Alysoun and Rafe climbed up the short ladder at the back of the cart to join Mistress Farringdon and Maysant inside, while the rest of us loaded up the luggage. There was a kind of kist built into the rear of the cart, with a lock, meant for costly items, and we stuffed into it as much as we could. Everything else must go into the cart itself. The girls helped Margaret carry out the piles of blankets and feather quilts, and the baskets of food, while Jordain minded the three horses and I fetched two shovels from the stable, before locking up both it and the shop. Margaret had already given her keys to Mary Coomber, so that she might feed the hens and keep a watch on our property.

As I laid the shovels just inside the back of the cart, Rafe said, 'Won't there be shovels on the farm, Papa?'

'Indeed there will,' I said. 'These we may need if the snow is deep on the road and the wheels of the cart become stuck.'

'Oh.' His eyes widened.

I could see that the thought was exciting, rather than fearful. I hoped it might remain that way.

Before Margaret climbed into the cart, she insisted on swathing Jordain in her blanket sack, despite his protestations. Usually he submitted to her ministrations, but this time he set his jaw rebelliously.

'Nay, Margaret,' he said. 'I shall feel a very fool.'

'Better a fool than a frozen corpse,' she said firmly. 'Pull this right up to your waist.'

I was too wise to intervene, for I knew who would win the argument. I untied Rufus from the hitching ring and mounted. By the time I had ridden into the middle of the street, Jordain was sitting glumly wrapped in the sack, with the reins in his hands, while Margaret was aboard and lacing shut the rear flaps of the canvas cover.

'Ready?' I called.

'Aye, ready.' It was both Margaret and Maud who answered, although Alysoun shouted as well, having pushed her head out from under the canvas beside Jordain, watching in glee as we started up the High Street toward Carfax. As we passed, I saw Edric Cromer's journeyman come out of his vintner's shop to lower the shutter. He stared at our cavalcade with an open mouth. I saluted him gravely with a raised hand. Word would soon be all about the town that the Elyot family were off on some ill-advised journey through the winter snows.

With all the time spent on our preparations, I had been afraid we might keep the soldiers waiting, but they were just riding up from the castle as we neared the central crossroads of the town, twelve troopers and an officer. The captain introduced himself as Thomas Beverley.

'You intend only travelling as far as Eynsham today, sir?' He sounded faintly patronising, as if so short a way was hardly worth his men's time and effort.

I nodded. 'In such cold weather, the women and children may take ill if they spend too long in an unheated cart, and one little maid is but newly out of her bed of sickness.'

He looked alarmed at the word 'sickness', just as we have all become in these late years, but I hastened to reassure him.

''Twas but a rheum and a cough. She is mostly recovered now, but she is a delicate child and we do not want to run any risks.'

'Ah, in that case–' He did not finish, but it was clear that he no longer scorned the shortness of the day's journey.

Indeed, once we had begun to trundle up Northgate Street, with half the soldiers deployed before us, and half behind, I began to realise that the ten miles or so to Eynsham would not prove so short a journey after all. Even Rufus found it difficult to maintain the slow pace of the cart, and as for the soldiers' horses, they pranced sideways, and curvetted, and tossed their heads impatiently at being held back, but there was little we could do. The two cart horses, harnessed one behind the other between the shafts, plodded along, heads down, the muscles of their shoulders bulging. The cart would have been heavy even when it was empty. Now, filled with passengers and loaded up with luggage and bedding, it was clearly almost all the animals could do to drag it through the snow. Here within the town walls the snow in the streets had been churned up by all the passing traffic of carts, horses, and people. It might prove either better or worse once we were away from Oxford.

When we reached the North Gate, a look of concern crossed Jordain's face, and with good reason. There would be scarce room for the wide cart to pass through on a clear summer's day, but now the drifted snow had been pushed into hard banks on either side of the arch through which the road passed. Undecided, Jordain halted the horses before trying to drive through.

One of the soldiers, seeing the problem, jumped from his horse and threw the reins to one of his fellows. I was about to call that I had shovels in the cart, but he began pounding on the gatekeeper's door.

'Out here, you lazy bastard!' the soldier shouted. ''Tis your duty to keep the passage clear for all who must pass through the gate. What do you mean by this?'

The gatekeeper came out, grumbling and wiping his mouth on the back of his hand, no doubt disturbed at his breakfast and little caring for the state of the passageway. When he saw the number of soldiers, with their horses pressing close in the narrow area before the gate, he backed into the shelter of his doorway again.

'Jesu!' he said truculently. 'May a man not break his fast before being called out into the cold?'

Captain Beverley rode over to him.

'There has been no fresh snow for two days. Those drifts should have been cleared well before this. See to it now, or you'll not keep your post for long.'

Threats achieved what persuasion would never do. I could see that had we arrived at the blocked gate without an escort, we should have had a long wait before we could pass through. As it was, the gatekeeper yelled for his two sons, and they had soon cleared away the packed snow. Even so, it was with some nervousness that Jordain drove through, no doubt expecting at any moment to scrape the sides of the cart against the stonework of the gate.

Once we were through and into the wide sweep of St Giles, the sun began at last to cast a dull golden glow over the world. I rode up close to the front of the cart and leaned over to speak to Jordain.

'Now the soldiers have already proved their worth,' I said, 'even if we never meet with so much as the shadow of a footpad.'

'Aye,' said Jordain, whose brow was sprinkled with sweat, despite the cold, 'but I hope we have no more passages like that. To speak of camels, and the eye of a needle.'

I laughed. 'You will soon get the measure of the team and of the cart. 'Twas not quite as narrow as you thought.'

Indeed, as we proceeded along this easier stretch of road, Jordain began to relax, but it was clear we could not increase our speed. There was almost no one else about, but the snow was deep here, hardly beaten down by any passing traffic, and the horses were forced to labour exceedingly hard to move the cart forward at all. It needed no great discernment to see how irritating our slow pace was proving for the soldiers, accustomed to cover the ground, even in winter, at a canter or gallop, with intervals of walking to ease their mounts. We lumbered on, taking the left hand branch along the road that led to Woodstock.

It was past midday by the time we reached the crossroads, where the westward road would take us most of our journey, past Witney and nearly to Burford, and which the soldiers could follow further on to Gloucester. After some initial chatter from the children, who poked their heads out beside Jordain to see where we were, there had been little sound from inside the cart, but now it was Margaret who climbed right out and sat down on the bench beside Jordain.

'Nicholas,' she called, 'it is time to make a stop and take some dinner. We are hungry, and surely the horses needed to be bated.'

'Aye.' I rode forward to Captain Beverley.

'Time to halt for a meal,' I said. 'Will you and your

40

men join us?'

He shook his head. 'We have our own provisions.' He jerked a thumb toward his own large saddlebags. 'But no more than half an hour, do you agree? Else we shall barely reach Eynsham before dark.'

'I agree.'

Jordain simply halted the cart in the road, for the snow was so deep that it was impossible to draw into the side. Maud tied back the flaps which closed the canvas cover front and back, and the women began to set out the food while Jordain and I gave our horses their nosebags. There would be no grazing here.

'How has it been for you?' I asked, as I climbed the steps into the rear of the cart. It was a tumble of bedding, and the passengers looked creased and tired.

'Not comfortable,' Margaret said, handing out pieces of a mutton and bacon pie, while Emma poured cups of small ale for everyone. 'But bearable. And warm enough, if we huddle together. The jolting jars your very bones.'

'It is the hard frozen ruts under the top layer of snow,' I said apologetically. 'Nothing to be done about it.' I turned to Maud. 'And the little maid, how does she fare?'

'Slept most of the way, far the best for her. She is not feverish.'

'I am quite well,' Maysant said with dignity. 'Have you brought more sweetmeats, Master Elyot?'

'I am afraid I have not,' I said, 'but there is good food here a-plenty. Eat your fill, so that you may prove to us that you are indeed quite recovered.'

We were well provided with cold food, but I think we would all have liked something hot. My own hands were stiff with the cold, despite the thick gloves I had been wearing, and I had not realised how numb my feet had grown until they began to return to life under the blanket I had wrapped around them.

When I reckoned our half hour was past, I unwrapped the blanket, and gestured to Jordain.

'You may continue to eat,' I said to Margaret, 'if you

41

can manage, but we must move on. I do not like the look of that sky. It is growing too dark too soon. I fear we may have snow before we reach Eynsham. Lace the cover closed before we set off again.'

Once Jordain and I had climbed down to the road, I offered to change places with him, but he shook his head.

'I am used to the horses now, and I think Rufus will go better for you than for me.'

'He's an easy horse to ride,' I said. 'He has had many riders.'

But Jordain would not be persuaded.

'Besides.' He grinned suddenly. 'Do not tell Margaret, but her ridiculous sack is surprisingly warm.'

'Very well!' I laughed. 'Stay with your team and your warm sack. Not very much further to Eynsham.'

Within a few minutes we were on our way again.

I had said truly to Jordain that it was not much further to Eynsham, but that was without reckoning on the weather. Even during the short time we had been inside the cart, the sky had grown even darker and the wind, which had been blowing without much force from the east, had swung round to the north, gaining in strength every second. We had gone no more than a hundred yards when the first flakes of snow began to fall. Within minutes we were engulfed in a whirling mass which cut off all sight of the road.

Captain Beverley shouted instructions to his men to close up together and around the cart, so that we might not lose touch with each other, all too easily done when we were nearly blind. The road had been barely discernible even before the snow had begun to fall. Now in the raging blizzard the faint hollow of the road between the banked drifts was hard to make out.

'Aelwyn!' Captain Beverley shouted, 'do you lead the way. Edwin beside him. The rest of you, pair off.'

He turned to me. 'Aelwyn is from these parts. If anyone can find the road, it is he.'

I could dimly make out one man riding to the front. At the same time the other soldiers arranged themselves in pairs, the man on the right reaching out to grip his fellow's sleeve with his left hand, so that they should not be separated.

'We ride so in fog,' the captain explained. 'One man can be easily lost, but not so easily two. Never had to pair off in snow before. This is the very devil. You and I should ride either side of the draught horses. If the cart should end up in a ditch, I cannot answer for the consequences.'

I did as he suggested, riding Rufus to the right of the shafts, while the captain took up his position on the left. Perhaps the present task of escorting our party no longer seemed so much beneath his dignity. In spite of a certain air of condescension, I could see he was a practical fellow, and was more than grateful for him and his men.

If we had been going slowly before, now a very snail might have overtaken us. The man Aelwyn was feeling his way carefully forward, fearful of leading us off the road to tumble into a ditch or wander across uncharted ground wherever the trees drew back, but the slow pace meant even greater tribulation from the blizzard. I rode with my head bowed, my chin on my chest, but even so the snow drove inside my hood and down my neck. Every few minutes I was forced to rub the settled flakes from my eyelashes, but since my gloves quickly became caked, I ended by covering my face with more snow. I could barely feel my fingers, and my toes not at all.

Aelwyn made frequent stops, as he cast around to be sure of the way. During the fourth or fifth of these, my eye was caught by a reflection of light on part of the cart's harness and twisted round to see the cause. A flickering glow was coming from within the cart, and then another. I felt a momentary panic, thinking the dry straw had caught fire, but then the two lights steadied, and I realised that the passengers had lit two candle lanterns.

Margaret cautiously put her head through the flaps behind Jordain, then an arm emerged, holding a lantern.

'Nicholas,' she called. 'Will it help our guide to have a lantern?'

'Captain?' I said.

'Aye.' I could just make out his nod. 'Let Aelwyn have it. It may serve.'

With some difficulty, I took the lantern from Margaret and rode to the front of our cavalcade. Aelwyn took the lantern with relief.

'Aye, thank 'ee, Maister Elyot,' he said. 'I can just abouts make out the lie of the road, but I'm a-feared of missing the turn down left to the abbey. I thought us would have reached 'un by now, but 'tis hard to judge in this b'yer lady storm, and getting dark and all.'

'Do not worry,' I said. 'Better to take your time and be sure of the way. Should we overshoot, I'd not like to think of turning that cart around in this.' I gestured at the snow, which was coming so thickly now that I could barely make out the ground beneath Rufus's hoofs. I could not imagine how Aelwyn could find the way, but with God's help, we must trust in him.

Rather than try to turn Rufus back to my place beside the cart, I waited until it had rolled slowly up to overtake me, then urged Rufus into his position beside the shafts.

'How are you, Jordain?' I called, finding my own voice caught and thrown back into my very throat. The snow felt almost as solid and muffling as a blanket against my face.

'Cold,' he said grimly. 'I cannot feel the reins, but the horses seem to know that they must follow the others. Poor fellows, I do not know how much longer they may be able to continue.'

The same thought had come to me. It was hard going for the ridden horses, but the draught horses had the much heavier task, and with every step through the snow it grew even worse. The shaggy hair about their fetlocks had become matted with clumps of ice and frozen snow. Icicles were forming a tinkling fringe along their manes, where their sweat had gathered and frozen. They put their feet

44

down warily. Despite their winter shoes, more ice would have formed painfully about the tender parts of their hoofs.

It was growing so dark that the snow showed grey now, rather than white, and I was fearful the passengers in the cart might come to serious harm. Jordain was blue with cold, his hands slack on the reins. I do not suppose I looked in much better case.

Then at last there was a shout from up ahead, and the whole company came to a halt. Aelwyn was riding back to Captain Beverley, holding the lantern high above his head.

'I have found the turn, sir, but we must go cautiously. It is a mite sharp, and the snow is piling up. I think we must clear a way before the cart will get through.'

'I have shovels in the cart,' I called across to them. 'I will fetch them.'

I slid down from Rufus, glad to be doing something active at last, instead of turning slowly to a block of ice on the horse's back, though my knees buckled as I landed on the ground.

'We have reached the turn,' I called into the dimly lit cart as I pulled out the shovels. I could make out little but a cluster of shapes huddled around the single lantern. 'We must clear the way, but we will soon be there.'

Several of the soldiers had dismounted, and the captain handed the shovels to two of the strongest looking.

'Might one of your men ride ahead to the abbey?' I asked. 'To give warning to the hospitaller to expect us? They will need beds for one and twenty. Nay, two and twenty. And we shall need hot food.'

'Aye, well thought on,' he said. 'Another task for you, Aelwyn.'

The soldier nodded, turned his horse, and set off along the lane, hardly to be seen here, but clearer ahead, where a tunnel of trees had held back some of the snow.

It did not take long for the two men to widen the gap enough to take the cart, then they led the horses round in a wide circle until the cart could be manoeuvred into the lane. I tossed the shovels back into the cart and remounted, riding ahead of it with half the soldiers.

The lane was dark under the trees, and I turned to the captain, who was riding beside me.

'I hope Aelwyn knows his way,' I said, 'and we are not heading into some unknown wilderness.'

'He was reared partly at the abbey, after he was orphaned,' Captain Beverley said, 'and worked as a kitchen boy, before he left to take to soldiering. He will not have led us astray.'

And he had the right of it. We came round a curve in the lane and through the unremitting dense cloud of flakes, thicker than ever, as it seemed to me, there shone the warm glow of windows lit by candle light, and flaming torches in sconces beside a gate. And faintly, like some deeply sonorous heavenly choir, the sound of voices chanting the evening office. Eynsham Abbey.

Chapter Three

After the bleak loneliness of the road and the fearful trial of the blizzard, Eynsham Abbey stood squarely before us, looming up out of the darkness and the snow like a veritable town. The tower of the church disappeared out of sight in the snow clouds, giddy above us, but the rest of the buildings were solid stone structures of no more than two storeys, laid out in seemly order. Eynsham was a substantial establishment, one of the largest in this part of the county, aside from those in Oxford itself. As we came through the gateway, I could see the monks processing from the church around the cloisters, toward a building I took to be the refectory, for the service must have been Vespers and they were making their way to their supper. Their black habits stood out starkly against the snow, which lay deep and untrodden in the cloister garth, and on every gable, sill, and carved gargoyle of the buildings.

One man was hurrying toward us in company with Aelwyn, whose horse stood steaming just inside the gate. He wore the Benedictine habit, but his round, cherubic face, with its nose reddened by the cold, might have belonged to any jovial innkeeper. This, I hoped, was the abbey hospitaller. As he soon proved to be. I slid from my horse with little grace.

'Brother Elias,' he cried at once, seizing both my hands and pumping them up and down, which did something to restore feeling to them. 'Welcome to Eynsham Abbey. You poor souls! Come within, come within.'

'We are a great many, I fear,' I said, 'and, apart from the soldiers, mostly women and children. They have had a cold journey and need warmth and hot food before all else, if we may beg it of your kindness.'

'No trouble,' he cried. 'No trouble at all. This good fellow . . .' he nodded toward Aelwyn and gripped him by the arm, 'has given us fair warning, and you come most apt, for this is a meat day for us. There is stew of mutton and barley in the pot, and fires alight in the guest hall. And . . .' here he shook Aelwyn's arm, 'who but Aelwyn himself come back to us, after five years, and grown into a fine young man!'

At this Aelwyn blushed as much as any man might who was half frozen. Although Brother Elias never paused for breath, he did not waste time. Lay servants were summoned with a gesture and sent to take the horses to the stables. More came hurrying to help the passengers from the cart. As I had feared, they were stiff with the cold, despite the blankets and feather quilts. Emma lifted Rafe down to me, and when I was sure he had the use of his legs, she passed me Maysant. The child seemed to be asleep, and I hoped that it was nothing worse than that. Alysoun scorned help, but scrambled down the steps by herself, though she held on to the side of the cart until she could stand unaided. Her teeth were chattering.

'Go you in to the guest hall, my pet,' I said.

She was looking about her, wide eyed. 'Is this the abbey?'

'It is. Now do not stand about in the snow. Take Rafe's hand and get you withindoors. See? There?' I gave a nod toward the open door, from which a flood of welcome golden light poured out, turning the snow into harmless glittering jewels of amber, instead of a deadly threat.

'Are you coming?' She tugged at my cloak.

'In a minute, as soon as everyone is out of the cart.'

'It was very cold in the cart. After we had eaten, and the snow started.'

'Alysoun,' I chided. 'Rafe. Guest house.'

The dogs Rowan and Jocosa tumbled down after the children, Jocosa almost vanishing into a drift. They raced about, delirious with freedom after the confines of the journey.

Alysoun took Rafe by the hand and they set off, stumbling across the court toward the open door. The snow reached above their knees.

'How is the child?' Jordain had joined me. He laid his hand on Maysant's sleeve.

'Asleep, I think. Have you any life left in your arms, or are you still numb?'

'From the stinging, I'd say they are come back to life.' Jordain shook his hands loosely from the wrists and kneaded them together.

'Then take the child in beside the fire.'

I handed him Maysant, and helped Juliana down the steps. She was followed by Emma and Maud, both staggering a little with stiffness. Margaret came last, carrying the lantern.

'We may have need of the blankets,' she said. 'You know these abbeys. They think that to mortify the flesh is godly, but my flesh has already been mortified enough for today.'

I laughed. 'Go you in. We are promised fires, beds, and a mutton and barley stew. I must see to Rufus, then I will join you.'

'The abbey servants will care for the horses,' she said.

'I had rather do it myself.'

I fetched the two horse blankets from where I had bundled them into the cart near to the shovels, and set out for the stables. Since I had entrusted the care of Maysant to Jordain, I had best make it my business to see to his cart horses as well. I thought Jordain looked even colder than I, though I too was feeling the agony of returning life to my numb arms and legs. I rubbed my nose, to make sure that it was still there. It felt more like a frozen stone than human

49

flesh.

In the stables I found Captain Beverley and his men. Like me they were grateful for the assistance of the abbey's lay servants, who could allocate us stalls for our horses and find us straw bedding and fodder, but a man should always care for his horse before himself, and these horses had endured a hard time for the last several hours.

Rufus was already settled in a stall, with a full manger of hay, but he had patches of sweat where the saddle had rested, and it was unhealthy to leave that to dry on his skin. I took a fistful of straw and rubbed him vigorously all over, before strapping on his blankets and checking his hoofs. As I was finishing, one of the servant brought him a small measure of oats. It was not a great deal, but Rufus took them gratefully.

I found the two cart horses together in one large box stall, their heads drooping with exhaustion, too tired even to eat. Someone had found them blankets, but they too were sweat stained, so I took the blankets off and rubbed them down before replacing the blankets. One benefit of all this vigorous exercise was that it warmed me up and brought my arms and hands back to full life. I persuaded the abbey servants to give the cart horses extra oats, and finally they stirred enough to eat.

It had been a hard journey for them, and we were but one third of the way to Leighton. If the blizzard continued tomorrow, I was not sure what was best to do. In many ways I wished we had never set out, but it had not seemed so perilous in Oxford, after the snow had stopped falling there. We could turn around and go back, but if we did, we should need to part from our escort. That would be a shorter way than going on, but it would mean all today's misery was but time wasted. I must talk to the others and sound them out. But not tonight. Matters might take on a better appearance in the morning.

The captain and I made our way across to the guest hall together, his men having already finished with their horses and gone ahead. I realised that he had waited for me.

'It was good of you,' he said, 'to see to the draught beasts. Should not your driver have done so?'

It was clear that he was inclined to view me with more favour, after my labours with the horses.

'My driver? Oh, you mean Master Brinkylsworth? He is a Regent Master of Arts and the Warden of Hart Hall, a senior member of the university, no driver!'

Of course, there was no reason the captain should know much about our party. The deputy sheriff must have told him who I was, but little else.

'My apologies,' he said, inclining his head.

'You were not to know.' I smiled at him. 'And although he is a scholar now, he was raised in the country, and would have seen to the horses, but I asked him to look after the child who has been sick. I thought the women were probably themselves very cold and weary, as he is, but he is best in by the fire, instead of the stable.'

'I think I heard mention of a mutton stew,' he said. 'I hope they have left some for us. My men have great appetites.'

With that thought in mind, we hastened our steps, and came gratefully into the warmth of the guest hall.

Fortunately, good helpings of the hot food had been kept back for us – I suspected Margaret's intervention on our behalf – and we were soon seated at a long trestle table, where the rest of the party had progressed to an apple pie and were passing around great jugs of thick cream. I felt the warmth of the food reaching into every corner of my being, and found myself growing quite cheerful, now we were quit of our recent ordeal. The monks of Eynsham, it seemed, did not observe the practice of fasting and abstinence during Advent.

It soon became clear that I had been right to suspect that the abbey might already be playing host to other travellers. Four merchants and their servants shared the table with us.

'And we are not alone,' one of them told me. He was sitting opposite, a burly man with a north country voice.

51

'There are three churchmen staying here as well, one heading west to Gloucester, and two on their way to Oxford, but like us they have decided not to venture further until the weather improves.'

I looked about, but there was none sitting at the table in clerical dress. He followed my gaze.

'Oh, they are eating in the refectory with the monks, and they have given up their beds here to your party. They will sleep in the dortoir tonight.'

'That was a kindness,' I said, scraping up the very last fragment of mutton from my bowl. It had been delicious.

'I do not expect they will bed down any worse than we do. These monks make themselves very comfortable.'

One of the other merchants, sitting beside him, frowned. 'Is that not uncharitable, friend? We are more than grateful for their hospitality. Otherwise, where should you and I be now?'

I helped myself to some of the well filled apple pie, fragrant with cinnamon and enclosed in a crisp light pastry, while the two men continued to discuss the rights and wrongs of monastic comfort. I had no strong feelings on the matter, unlike John Wycliffe, but if tonight's meal was anything to go by, the monks ate well at Eynsham.

As if summoned by their conversation, Brother Elias bustled in.

'Is everything satisfactory, ladies, gentlemen? Here, Eddi,' he beckoned to one of the servant boys, 'more wine is needed at this end of the table. Now, Aelwyn, not so very long ago that might have been you, fetching the wine, and here you sit down at ease amongst your fellows! How the world turns!'

Aelwyn looked somewhat uncomfortable at the mention of his former humble role, but he was a good natured fellow and let it pass. The soldiers all seemed well content with their meal, which almost certainly surpassed their regular fare in the castle barracks.

As soon as I had finished my apple pie, washed down

with a cup of excellent wine, I made my way to the other end of the long table, where Maud Farringdon was sitting with Maysant.

'And how are you feeling?' I asked the child.

'I am perfectly well, Master Elyot,' she said. 'I slept a lot in the cart because there was nothing else to do.' She could not suppress a fit of coughing, however.

'It was very boring,' Rafe agreed from the other side of the table.

I should have thought of that. The children needed something to occupy them, but it was too late now to fetch some toys or games from home. I had noticed that all the women had brought needlework or knitting with them, though the jolting of the cart must have made it difficult to work, even before the blizzard and the darkness.

'Tomorrow,' I said, 'we must find something for you to do.'

'Will we go on again tomorrow?' Alysoun asked.

Emma glanced at me with raised eyebrows, and I looked from her to Margaret.

'We will see whether the blizzard abates,' I said. 'The two cart horses are very tired.'

'Poor horses,' Alysoun said, and her lower lip trembled. 'It was very hard for them, in the snow, with the heavy cart to pull.' She brightened and smiled at me. 'I could ride with you on Rufus, then the cart would not be so heavy.'

'Nay, you could *not*,' I said. 'Your slight weight would make no difference to them, and you would soon turn into a block of ice on Rufus's back.'

'But you do not turn to a block of ice.'

'I am busy riding him, that keeps me warm.'

'But I would be riding him too,' she said cunningly.

'That is enough, Alysoun,' Margaret said. 'Your father has said no. He is in charge of our party. He cannot be doing with you on the horse with him. And now it is time that you and Rafe and Maysant were abed.'

Alysoun grumbled, but both Maysant and Rafe

seemed quite relieved at the prospect, until Rafe discovered that he was to sleep in the women's dormitory. He stamped his foot in outrage.

'I am a *man*,' he cried, tears springing into his eyes. 'I should not sleep with the women!'

He was overtired, and so was I, but I managed to keep my voice calm.

'Very well. Leave him to me, Margaret. He may share my pallet. I am ready enough for bed myself.'

The soldiers elected to stay by the fire a little longer, enjoying the abbey's good wine, and perhaps proving that they had withstood the journey better than feeble townsfolk like us, but Jordain and I followed the merchants to the men's dormitory. Jordain had fetched some of our bedding from the cart, while I carried Rafe. After his manly outburst, he was nearly asleep on his feet.

Brother Elias hurried along beside us, ensuring that we could find the lavatorium and the garderobe, then telling the servants to bring in extra palliasses to lay on top of the pallets.

'For they are very thin,' he said, 'and I fear you would feel the cold seeping up from the floor. These gentlemen are already provided.' He nodded toward the merchants and their servants, who occupied the far end of the room.

He was satisfied at last, and went off, still talking.

'Papa,' Rafe said, half waking, 'my night shift is in the cart.'

'Never mind,' I said. 'We will take off our boots and sleep in our clothes.'

Rafe gaped at this novel idea, then he giggled. 'Aunt Margaret will not like it.'

'Then we will not tell her. Besides, I think all the night shifts are still in the cart. Aunt Margaret's as well as ours.'

I for one was not going out through the snow to bring them withindoors.

Jordain had removed his boots and was arranging two

blankets and a feather quilt on top of the palliasse.

'Look at this, Rafe,' he said. 'We shall sleep as soft as kings tonight.'

We were speaking quietly, for the merchants had already extinguished their candles and settled for the night. I made up our bed, then the three of us knelt to say our evening prayers.

As we crawled under our blankets, Jordain said sleepily, 'I shall attend one of the services in the monks' church tomorrow, and pray for better weather during the rest of our journey.'

I yawned. Rafe was already asleep, taking up more than half the bed. I eased him over on to his side.

'You could always attend Matins and Lauds,' I said, 'come midnight.'

'Never fear.'

I blew out our candle.

It took me some time to find a comfortable position on the lumpy palliasse, and I was just sinking into sleep when I heard the soldiers come up to the men's dormitory. They tried to be quiet, but the clatter of all those boots tossed off on to the bare floor was enough to waken Rafe, who stirred and mumbled and rolled over to occupy most of the bed. It was a long while before I could sleep again.

It must have stopped snowing at some point during the night, for when I rose after a fitful sleep and opened the shutters to look out across the precinct, it was past dawn and the early sky was a hard clear blue, like the shadows on a snow drift, and the whole world glittered, as if carved from ice. Everything was very still. The trees in the abbey orchard flung out their frozen limbs, rigid in the hard frost. Directly in front of the guest hall, the hummocks of the dead plants in the kitchen garden looked like crouching animals, while beyond it the cloister garth was smooth and untouched.

Rafe was still asleep, but Jordain was stirring, and the soldiers had already quitted their beds. The merchants were talking quietly as they dressed. I could do little but brush down my creased clothes and pull on my boots, then I wrapped my cloak about me before heading for the garderobe and lavatorium. Everywhere it was so cold that I walked in a cloud of freezing breath.

By the time I returned, Jordain and Rafe were both up, and we made our way down to the hall where, blessedly, there was a fire, and we could hear the abbey bell ringing for Prime. Jordain followed the monks to the church, but I sought out Captain Beverley.

'What think you?' I said. 'Should we continue on our way today? The sky is clear. I do not suppose it will snow. And the wind has dropped altogether.'

He nodded. 'I think you have the right of it. For my part, we would certainly be on our way, but will the women want longer to rest?'

He glanced over at the table, where the abbey servants were laying out breakfast. All the women had done their best to neaten themselves, although they too must have slept in their clothes. I was sure every one of us would benefit from a rest, but I was impatient to carry on while the weather permitted. It was not far to Minster Lovell. If we could make a start as soon as we had eaten, we could reach the priory easily before dark, even going at our slow pace.

'I will see what the women say,' I told him, 'and I will look to the cart horses. Much depends on them.'

Not to my surprise, I found that the others were all eager to be on our way.

'We should take advantage of the good weather,' Maud said. 'Sooner away, sooner there.'

'I am not sure it is *good* weather,' Margaret said, 'for there is a very hard frost. I stepped outside to tidy the cart, and the snow is frozen solid as ice, but I agree that it is unlikely to snow today.'

'What say you, Emma?' I said.

'If the horses are recovered enough,' she said, 'then I should be glad to be on our way. Should we take too long about our journey, your cousins will begin to worry. And besides,' she glanced around and lowered her voice, 'I have had my fill of monastic surroundings, although the monks here have been most welcoming.'

I reflected that we had barely seen them, apart from Brother Elias, who would have been equally at home in the secular world.

'And what of you, Juliana?' I said. She was on the cusp between childhood and womanhood, so it seemed only right to ask her opinion.

She flushed a little at being included amongst the adults, and smiled. 'I think we should go on while we may. If, as Emma says, the horses are fit.'

'I am going to see to them now,' I said.

'Nay.' Margaret laid a hand on my arm. 'Take some breakfast first, Nicholas. It is very cold out there. And if you linger in the stables, the soldiers may eat it all!'

'Very well.' I smiled. Ever since we were children, my sister had been inclined to mother me.

I knew she spoke sense, for I would have a cold ride, even without more snow falling, and there was a pot of steaming frumenty tempting me to the table, but I ate hastily, anxious to see whether the horses were fit, and – if they were – to make an early start. Once outside, I found Margaret's warnings to be all too apt. The cold air hurt my lungs each time I drew it in. It had not been possible to shave, and I could feel the moisture of my breath forming minute icicles on the bristles of my beard before I was halfway to the stables.

Within, the stable was warmed by all the beasts inside, and to my surprise, I found that the two cart horses were well recovered, their heads up, their eyes bright, thoughtfully munching on fresh hay. They were hardy fellows, and had shaken off their fatigue with the night's rest. That made the decision easy. I met Jordain coming to find me as I crossed back to the guest hall.

'How are the horses?' he said.

'In good heart. I think we should start as soon as we

may.'

'Aye. Let us be on our way to Minster Lovell.'

As I neared the guest hall, I found Emma, with Alysoun and Rafe, probing amongst the hummocks of the kitchen garden, seemingly picking herbs.

'Whatever are you about?' I said.

Alysoun held out a handful of red hawthorn berries. 'We just need some sprigs of rosemary. Emma is making us a game.'

'They need something to occupy them,' she said. 'They cannot move about, and it is very dull for them. I am going to draw an alquerque board on the floor of the cart, and we shall play hawthorn against rosemary.'

'I want to be hawthorn,' Alysoun said. 'It's the prettiest.'

'I don't mind,' Rafe said. 'Rosemary is useful.'

Grinning, I left them to it. I hoped that Maysant would also be allowed a turn.

Now that a decision had been made, we all hastened to set off. With the assistance of the abbey servants and one of the soldiers, Jordain harnessed up the horses to the cart, while Margaret prevailed upon Brother Elias to provide hot bricks for warmth and a basket of food. The soldiers were accustomed to swift departures and were mounted and ready long before our own company was assembled. Once I had mounted Rufus, I leaned down to shake Brother Elias by the hand.

'I thank you for your kind care, brother. We were a cold and sorry company when we arrived last night.'

He beamed at me. 'It is my pleasure to serve the cold and hungry traveller, Master Elyot. May God be with you for the rest of your journey.'

'And God grant you His blessing,' I said.

We rode out along the lane, which seemed much shorter by daylight, and found that someone, probably the abbey servants, had already cleared the snow which had again drifted across the turn into the road to Witney, so we had no delay there, but turned left at once on to the wider thoroughfare.

Because the snow had frozen hard, it was somewhat easier for the draught horses, since the wheels of the cart rolled freely along the top of it, instead of needing to be dragged through it, although sometimes the cart would slither sideways, making driving it a nervous business. When we reached an easier stretch of road, where there was no slope to send the cart into a slide, I rode up level with Jordain.

'Harder work than yesterday?'

'Nay.' He shook his head. 'As long as we proceed slowly, with care, and this team knows no other way!' He grinned. 'And it is a joy to be able to see where we are going.'

'Did you attend Prime?' I said.

'I did. It is a fine church. You should have come.'

'Perhaps on the return journey. At the moment it seems your prayers for better weather have been answered.'

'Aye.' Captain Beverley had ridden up beside me. 'Better weather for travel, but better weather as well for the rogues who prey on travellers. If you plan to halt to take your midday meal, do it soon. I had rather you were moving again when we come near their hunting ground.'

'Is it far?'

'Perhaps another mile or two before we are near.'

Following his advice, we made our stop soon afterwards, although I did not tell the passengers in the cart why the captain wanted to make an early halt. All the while we were eating, I fidgeted, anxious to be on our way again and past Witney as soon as possible.

Once we were moving again, I was on edge, looking from side to side, watching for any movement in the surrounding woods.

'We are near the spot where the last attack took place,' Captain Beverley said quietly. 'You see that beech spinney ahead? That gave them cover.'

I looked where he pointed. The coppiced beech trees, as is their wont, had retained their leaves during winter, only to shed them when the new growth begins in spring. Therefore, unlike the rest of the woods, where the leaves were stripped from the trees, this spinney formed a dense wall along a stretch of the road. Had we not been forewarned, I would have thought nothing of it.

The soldiers closed in more tightly around us, and several had laid their bows across in front of their saddles, with full quivers of arrows strapped to their belts. The rest had loosened their swords from the scabbards, and rode one handed, swords across their knees. Surely we must look too formidable a convoy to be attacked?

I rode to the back of the cart and leaned down.

'Margaret,' I called, and she put her head out between the flaps of canvas, looking surprised.

'We are coming to the place where there was that attack Cedric Walden described to me. I do not think we are in danger, not with this escort of soldiers, but 'twould be wise if you were all to lie down, so that you are below the level of the sides of the cart. Best to be safe.'

A look of alarm passed over her face, then she nodded and ducked back inside. I rode forward again.

'I do not suppose you can urge those two fellows along any faster,' I said to Jordain.

He shook his head. 'We must just plod on and trust in God.'

The attack came, as the captain had expected, when we drew level with the beech spinney. In the clear uncompromising light, we were an easy target. The first flight of arrows caught one of the soldiers on the shoulder. He yelped in pain, and blood began to flow down over his sleeve. Another arrow ripped into the canvas cover of the cart, and there was a shriek from one of those within, but it had struck high and none should be hurt. The arrow remained, quivering, caught in the canvas with only the flight feathers protruding. A third struck one of the shafts of the cart, just missing the leading horse, at which it was clearly aimed. The rest of the arrows, perhaps half a dozen, failed to find their marks. The intention must be to cripple the horses drawing the cart, so that we would become stranded, then they might pick us off at leisure.

The captain gave a shout and turned his horse toward the spinney. Half his men galloped after him, including the injured man, who looked more angry than in pain. The other half of the soldiers closed around us. The cart horses had shied and halted, standing shivering and wild eyed. Although Jordain urged them on, fear pinned them to the spot. I rode forward and leaned over, catching hold of the reins of the horse nearest me, the one who had nearly been struck. I jerked his head forward, and as Rufus moved ahead, he took a stumbled step beside us. His companion was forced by the harness joining them to move with him.

For some reason I did not feel afraid, not then, despite my lack of armour or any experience of fighting, beyond the occasional student brawl. I felt a curious sense of excitement and knew only that I must get the company moving on as quickly as possible, while Captain Beverley and his men dealt with the lawless rogues who preyed thus upon travellers. When they had made their attack before, on the pack train, there had been no soldiers near at hand. They might find their arrogance and daring cost them dearly this time.

Jordain was striving his best to help me move the draught horses forward. He would never use a whip on a horse, but he had drawn out the one stowed beneath his seat, and cracked it over their heads. The snap sounded fearsome in the cold air, and the horses took its meaning. The strain on my arm eased a little as they placed one reluctant foot in front of the other, but their pace was so slow, slow as a nightmare when you try to escape some enemy and your legs will not carry you forward.

To the right, behind the spinney, I could hear shouting, and the clash of sword on sword, but more arrows rained down on us. There must be a sizeable body of the rogues, if some could continue to shoot, while others fought off Beverley and his men.

I twisted round in my saddle. Close beside me was

the young soldier, Aelwyn, amongst those who had been told to stay with us. Could I dare to countermand his officer's orders?

'Aelwyn,' I called, 'do you go to the aid of the others. There must be a considerable company of outlaws there. You will do us more good by engaging those who are shooting than by staying here to intercept their arrows. We will make our way on, as fast as we may.'

For a moment he hesitated, for he had received his orders, but another flight of arrows fell amongst us, one grazing the same draught horse just above his tail, so that he flinched, and took a quicker stumbling pace forward. Then Aelwyn nodded, turned his horse and called to his fellows. As they galloped off around the spinney, I felt a sharp pain, like the sting of a bee, in my right upper arm. One of the arrows had found its mark.

It was not deep, I was sure, but the arrow remained lodged there, dangling from my cloak. I might not be wearing armour, but I was thankful for my thick layers of clothing, The cart horses now seemed to have come to an understanding of the need to move on sharply, for they followed me willingly enough, but I retained my grip on their reins with my left hand, controlling Rufus with my right. He was alarmed, but apart from a great tossing of his head, he remained under control, which was as well, for my arm was beginning to throb.

The noise of the fight beyond the spinney grew louder as the other soldiers reached their fellows, and their intervention, as I had hoped, put a stop to the shooting. By the time Jordain and I were beyond the beech trees, I thought I could hear the sound of hoofs galloping away to the north, so I twisted in my saddle to look. Most of what was happening was hidden by the trees, but I could make out two, or perhaps three, of the outlaws breaking away from the fight in an attempt to escape, with several of the soldiers close behind in pursuit. After that, I concentrated on covering as much ground as possible. The soldiers would overtake us when they could.

Once we were well clear, I released the cart horses' tackle, and leaned over to speak to Jordain.

'Can you halt the cart for a moment? I want to be sure they are all right.' I nodded back toward the cart, from which there had come no sound after that first shriek.

When I lifted the canvas flaps and looked in, I was met by a cluster of white faces peering up from the straw in alarm.

'Danger over,' I said, as cheerfully as I could. 'Captain Beverley is dealing with those rogues. It is safe to sit up again. We will carry on and they will join us.'

'I was winning at alquerque,' Alysoun complained, 'and now our game is spoiled.'

I laughed. If that was the worst she had feared, they had not fared too badly.

'Nicholas!' Emma said, 'You are hurt!'

I glanced at my arm. 'Not seriously. The arrow was mostly stopped by my clothes. It can wait until we reach the priory. We will continue now.'

Despite her protests, I would not stop to have my injury salved. We were still far too close to that beech spinney, and I wanted to put as much distance between us as possible. From the diminishing sounds of the fighting, the soldiers were pursuing such of the outlaws as were trying to make off. They would be occupied yet a while. Indeed we had almost reached the turn north to Minster Lovell by the time the soldiers caught up with us. There were a few injuries amongst them, and one of the horses was bleeding from his off fore knee, but I counted, and all the men were present.

'How did you fare?' I asked the captain quietly as we rode forward together.

'They will not trouble this road again, I think,' he said with a grim smile. 'One fellow escaped, but the rest will lie there as food for the crows. We have even gained three good horses.' He nodded to the rear of his men, where I now saw three of the soldiers were each leading an extra mount.

Within another half hour we had reached the turn on our right to Minster Lovell. The short lane was well maintained by Lord Lovell, and we found ourselves at the priory gatehouse some while before dusk, despite the delay caused by the attack. To tell truth, I felt I should be glad to dismount and have my wound dressed, however slight it was, for it ached abominably in the cold, a cold which had grown even worse as the day grew older. And there were others with worse injuries than mine.

Minster Lovell Priory is an alien establishment, daughter house of a Benedictine monastery at Ivry in Normandy, unlike the English establishment at Eynsham. Yet there must have been an earlier monastic house here, for the designation 'minster' bespeaks a Saxon house. And with being alien, and French, it had suffered depredations by the English crown, especially in recent years, during our uneasy relations with France. I hoped it would not affect our welcome here, for I could think of nowhere else nearby where we might seek shelter for the night.

We were met with courtesy, but reserve, by a monk I took to be the hospitaller, although he did not introduce himself, leading us to the guest hall, which was considerably smaller than that at Eynsham. This was understandable enough, for the priory was a lesser house than the abbey. The quarters were austere, like the hospitaller, and there was no welcome fire burning, although a servant was summoned to lay and light one.

'We keep the period of Advent strictly here,' the hospitaller said, finally condescending to speak. 'I will send you food when we ourselves take our supper. You will, I know, give thanks to God that you have found lodging here.'

I bowed. 'Indeed.' I found myself catching his own spare manner of speech.

'However,' I said, 'as you can see, we met with trouble on the road, an attack by outlaws near Witney, and several of our party have been injured. We would take it as a great kindness if your infirmarian could attend to the injured.'

He inclined his head. 'I regret he will be unable to do so until after Vespers.'

With that he withdrew.

'He is an Englishman,' Jordain said in my ear, 'but I think he has lived in France. I detect a touch of their accent in his speech.'

'A very different establishment from Eynsham,' Margaret said, 'and I think we should make a start on caring for the injured ourselves.' She turned to the lay servant, a scrawny, nervous looking fellow. 'Is there water to be had? We need to bathe the hurts, and I have salves in the cart. Where are we to sleep?'

'I will show you the dormitories,' the man said, darting looks about him, as if he feared that he was overstepping the mark. 'And I will fetch you some buckets of water. Our well is not yet frozen, else we must fetch water from the river.'

As it was clear we must shift for ourselves, we set about tending the horses – having found our way to the stables – and I borrowed a pot of Margaret's salve to spread over the graze on the cart horse's rump. While we were occupied in the stable, the women unpacked the cart, for there was little bedding provided here. The pallets were no more than an inch thick, each provided with one thin blanket, so we were grateful that we had our blankets and feather quilts, else I think we might not have slept for the cold.

Once Margaret and Maud had heated water on the fire, they set up an infirmary of their own beside it, while Emma and Juliana ripped into bandages an old sheet the servant had reluctantly found for us. I waited until the soldiers' wounds were dressed, for they were more serious than mine, though not as bad as we might have feared, the worst being a deep sword slash in one man's left arm. Fortunately it had damaged only flesh and not muscle or bone.

When it was my turn, I removed my torn cotte and

peeled my shirt down over the arrow wound. It was painful, for the cloth had begun to cling to the drying blood.

''Tis naught but a surface cut,' I said, 'though it stings.'

'Best clean it well,' Emma said briskly, 'for the arrow may have been dirty. Stay you still.'

She bathed my arm with the warm water in which Margaret had infused a handful of her healing herbs, then smoothed a layer of salve over it.

'That hurts,' I complained.

She clicked her tongue chidingly. 'Do not be a child. See how bravely the soldiers have endured.'

'They are trained to it,' I replied, carefully lifted my shirt up over my shoulder. 'I am but–'

'I know.' She laughed. 'You are nothing but a humble Oxford shopkeeper. Listen! They have stopped singing Vespers. We may expect the infirmarian at last.'

When he came, the infirmarian was somewhat less aloof than the hospitaller. He examined and approved the women's dressing of the wounds, offering only a drink to ease the pain of the man with the deep sword slash, which he refused. The infirmarian having left us, two of the kitchen servants arrived with our supper. After the previous night's ample repast, this meal reminded us that we were indeed in the austere period of Advent. There was a thin watery broth with a few dried peas and beans floating in it, followed by a very small piece of fish each, and some hard rye bread.

Jordain spoke the blessing over the meal, and though his thanks to God that we had found shelter for the night were sincere enough, I thought I detected a slight note of irony in his voice when he spoke of the meal we were about to eat.

We were the only guests of the priory, and since we had not been provided with enough wood to keep the fire up for long, there was nothing to be done but to retire to bed. I found I was glad of Rafe's warmth, despite his squirming.

The following morning Jordain showed no inclination to join the brothers at their service of Prime. Once again we were served by the lay servants from the kitchen, who brought us jugs of small ale and more of the hard bread. No fire was lit, so that the hall of the guest house was little warmer than the bitter cold outside. None of us felt any desire to linger.

It was only after the cart was readied and we were mounted, on the point of departure, that the hospitaller showed himself again.

'I trust you have fared well with us,' he said, glancing from me to Captain Beverley. 'It is customary for our guests to leave an offering for the priory, in God's name, to help in our work with the poor.'

'I confess,' I said, 'that I had not heard of your work amongst the poor, and I am from these parts, or nearby. I think we will save our charity and dispense it where we see the need, amongst the poor themselves. That way we may be sure that it finds its way to those who deserve it most. I bid you farewell, brother.'

With that, I wheeled Rufus about and headed for the gate. Behind me, I heard a suppressed snort of laughter from one of the soldiers. Captain Beverley grinned at me as we rode together through the gateway arch.

It was as cold again as the day before, but clouds were once again gathering in the north, and I feared more snow.

'Not long now until we part company,' I said. 'How long before you reach Gloucester, do you suppose?'

'Tomorrow, perhaps,' he said. 'We will travel more swiftly, once . . .'

'Aye, once you are rid of us. Nevertheless, we have been mighty glad of you. Had those ruffians attacked us without your escort, we had all been dead by now.'

I knew that I spoke the truth, and shuddered.

'The world is well rid of rogues like that,' he said. 'And we were glad of the physicking by your womenfolk. My men would have fared poorly at the priory, without them.'

'Curious, was it not?' I said. 'Two establishments, both Benedictine, yet so different. I suppose much depends on the head of the house.'

'And I suppose we must forgive the priory for some of their austerity,' he said. 'Being a French house, they suffer for it, even though some of the monks are English. Myself, I do not believe we should make war on the religious, even when our nations are at war.'

'I agree, for is not Christendom a greater nation than France or England?' I looked at him thoughtfully. 'How long do you think this present truce will hold?'

He shrugged. 'Not long, I fear me. Not while our king believes he is the rightful king of France through blood, and the French plot to keep him out and their jumped up baron on the throne.'

I sighed. 'There have been troubles enough in our lifetime, God knows, with the Great Pestilence. I could wish that the great men of both nations would leave us little folk to live our lives in peace.'

'Amen to that. And I should not lose my profession, for there will always be rogues like those we encountered yesterday to keep me and my men in employment.'

We rode on for a while in silence. The cart continued at its slow pace and I feared that the snow clouds would reach us before we came to Leighton, but there was no hurrying the draught animals.

At last we reached the turn where the lane led northwards off the Burford road into Wychwood, which would take us on the final lap of our journey. Remembering how we had made the whole of it in a single day at harvest, it had seemed interminable this time, but we could look forward to a warm welcome from my family, and I was eager to see Peter Winchingham established as the new lord of Leighton Manor.

Captain Beverley took his farewells of the party in the cart, and of Jordain, then shook me by the hand.

'Perhaps we shall meet again in Oxford, Master

Elyot,' he said. 'I am afraid I am no man for books, but perhaps we might dine together some day.'

'I should be glad of that,' I said. 'May God go with you the rest of the way to Gloucester, and see you safely back with your charge to Woodstock Palace.'

The soldiers lined up, two and two, with the captain at their head, then with a final salute to us, they were off at a full gallop.

Jordain laughed, watching the clods of frozen snow flying up from the horses' hoofs. 'They have been longing for that these three days past,' he said.

'Small blame to them,' I said. 'We must have seemed very tedious company. Come, do you need help in turning the cart into the lane?'

'Nay.'

He clicked his tongue to the horses and they lumbered round to the north. I rode Rufus into the lead, where I could keep a watch for any drifts or fallen branches, for this was a very minor lane. At last we were on the final stretch of the road to Leighton.

Chapter four

Some attempt had been made to clear the lane of snow, by shovelling the worst of it on to the banked up drifts on either side, drifts which in places rose as high as Rufus's back. Peter Winchingham and my cousin Edmond, together with the other better-off men in the village, must have carried through their plan of employing day labourers to do the work, and we found as we travelled further from the Burford road and nearer to the village that the lane was all the better cleared. In one or two places fallen branches had also been tossed aside on to the drifts, so that the first part of our journey up the lane went reasonably well.

Then, as I had feared from the growing dark and the north wind, insidiously rising, it began to snow again. As we were now travelling north, Jordain and I were face into the wind. Soon I was forced to pull a fold of my cloak in front of my face to protect it, leaving nothing but my eyes uncovered as I peered through the seething mass of flakes. Fortunately I had known this lane all my life, so there was no danger of going astray, but there remained the danger of newly formed drifts blocking the way, or branches breaking under the weight of the snow and either forming a barrier across the lane, or – even worse – falling on top of us.

Jordain kept the cart close at Rufus's heels as we moved up the latter part of the lane with caution.

Then, what I had feared came about. Since it ran much of the way through part of Wychwood, the lane was surrounded by trees. In the past the de Veres, who had held

Leighton Manor for generations, had kept the law by maintaining a verge on either side of the lane clear for the width of a bow shot, a measure designed to deter all but the most skilled archers from attacks on travellers. But the last of the de Veres had perished early in the plague and no work had been done to hold back the woodland for some five years or more now, so that the trees had begun to encroach, not only on to the verges but reaching out over the lane itself.

The burden which had lain heavy on the branches for days was being augmented every minute by yet more snow, for the weather was whipping itself up to a fair blizzard now. I could hear an ominous creaking a short way ahead. Trying to see through the blinding snow, I could make out nothing by sight, but unmistakably I could hear the cracking which heralded a branch collapsing under the weight of snow.

'Stop!' I shouted to Jordain.

I doubted whether he could hear me through the howling of the wind. He had the hood of his cloak close drawn about his face, but he must have seen me signalling frantically to him as I pulled up Rufus, who stood blowing out great gouts of steaming breath. I turned back, so that I could bend down and shout close to Jordain's ear.

'There's a branch coming down ahead of us. It may not fall on the lane, but best to wait and see.'

He nodded, tightening the reins, so that the cart horses stopped, thankfully enough. I slid down from Rufus and made my way cautiously forward on foot, for I had no desire to be struck down myself by the branch. No more than four or five paces on, I stopped, as the creaking of the branch became a great tearing, like a scream of the very tree itself, and I felt the rush of the branch as it fell, the snow billowing out toward me, like a curtain caught by the wind.

I felt Jordain bump into me from behind.

'Is it over the road?'

'Aye, I think so.'

We felt our way forward together and soon stumbled into the outlying smaller branches fanning out from the larger one which had been ripped from the main trunk of the tree itself. Like the spinney where the outlaws had lain in wait, this was a beech tree. No cause for surprise in that. By retaining its leaves in winter, it caught and held a much greater weight of snow that those trees which stood stark and skeletal.

'Jesu!' Jordain said. 'We should be thankful you heard that. If it had fallen on the canvas cover of the cart, those inside would have taken great injury.'

I nodded. My mouth was too dry for me to speak. All those I loved most dearly might have been killed.

I cleared my throat. 'We must shift it out of the way, else we shall never get past. We are nearly at the village.'

Jordain did not ask how I knew, for we could hardly see more than a few yards ahead, yet I was sure of it, without knowing why.

We set to, but it was a great limb, and very heavy. After struggling for some minutes, we had barely moved it a yard.

'What's to-do?'

It was Emma, taking shape through the blizzard, and Juliana a shadow behind her.

'Fallen branch.' I could barely get the words out, gasping and short of breath.

'We can help.' Emma stepped forward and seized hold of some of the projecting smaller branches.

'This is no work for women and girls,' I said, without much conviction.

'Nonsense,' she said. 'We have no wish to freeze to our deaths, marooned in that cart in a blizzard. Here, Juliana, catch hold beside me.'

There was no help for it. Without Emma and Juliana we should never move the branch. Struggling and panting with effort, the four of us managed to drag the branch to the side of the lane.

'Do you think you will be able to drive past now?' I

asked Jordain.

'Aye, I think so. With care.'

'Get you back into the cart,' I said to the girls. 'And my thanks. We could not have prevailed without your aid.'

Emma smiled, with the very faintest touch of mockery in her eyes, and Juliana giggled. They shook off the snow which had clung to their skirts, then ran back to the cart as Jordain climbed up again to the driver's bench. Mounted on Rufus, I led the way slowly past the branch, watching all the while over my shoulder to make sure that Jordain was able to manoeuvre past it. Once clear, we resumed our slow and measured pace along the lane. Within no more than a quarter of an hour I caught sight of the first lighted windows of the village.

I was not sure whether Rufus recognised the village from his previous visit, but he instinctively quickened his pace as he reached it, and turned without guidance into the lane leading up to the family farm. As if they understood him, the cart horses followed, even improving from a slow walk to what was almost a fast one.

The lamp set burning outside the kitchen door of the farmhouse was the most welcome sight of this whole long, wretched journey, and before we came to a halt in the stableyard, Alysoun and Rafe were shouting, and my cousin's family came tumbling out into the snow, with lanterns, and even blankets to wrap around us.

Despite the vigorous effort in shifting the fallen branch, I had grown cold again, even colder than before, were that possible, and for once I allowed Edmond to persuade me that he and his two sons, James and Thomas, were capable of caring for the three horses.

'A warm bran mash,' I insisted. 'They have strived valiantly for three days.'

'They shall have it,' Edmond said, clapping me on the shoulder, 'and so shall you, unless you are prepared to wait a little. Susanna is going to roast a pair of ducks she has trussed, ready to welcome you.'

'Then I shall wait,' I said, 'if it be not too long.'

By the time the whole company was gathered around the long table, somehow everyone had been made known to each other, and all of us were full of good cheer, though I think Jordain, like me, was still feeling a deep cold. When we came in, my mother, sitting ensconced in a cushioned chair close to the kitchen fire, beamed upon us. And although she looked somewhat frail, she seemed in better health than I had feared. I knelt down beside her for her blessing, and she took my hands in hers.

'God's bones, son,' she said, 'your hands are frozen solid. I had no notion you must make such a perilous trip when Edmond sent to bid you here for the Christmas season.'

'I shall soon grow warm,' I said, rising to my feet and giving her my arm to the table. 'Just to be out of the wind and the snow is comfort enough.'

Edmond invited Jordain to say the blessing over the meal, in acknowledgement of the fact that he was in minor clerical orders, although dressed in my spare clothes he hardly seemed so.

As Susanna and her eldest daughter Hilda began to serve us with roast duck and carrots and frumenty mixed with fried onions and flavoured with garlic and thyme, I could see that Alysoun was bursting to say something. As soon as the talk eased a little, she was able to break in.

Turning importantly to James, who was almost a man, and therefore worth impressing, she said, 'We were attacked by *outlaws*!'

My mother's knife clattered to the table and I raised my finger to hush Alysoun, but there was no stopping her.

'There were hundreds of them, shooting arrows at us, and the soldiers fought them, with their swords, and killed lots of them, and seized some of their horses. And My Father was wounded in the battle!' She sat back and looked about her in satisfaction.

All eyes turned to me, and I found myself flushing with embarrassment.

'Alysoun has been a little carried away,' I said. 'I

74

took no part in the battle. And I received no more than a graze from an arrow. They were trying to cripple the horses, so that they could rob us while we were halted, but we had an armed escort, so we were quite safe.'

Edmond looked at me seriously. 'Outlaws? Where was this, Nicholas?'

'Miles away,' I reassured him. 'Near Witney. And only one of the rogues survived. They need not trouble you.'

'Nicholas showed great presence of mind,' Emma said quietly. 'He sent all the soldiers after the outlaws, instead of leaving half of them ineffectually guarding us, and then he led the cart out of danger.'

'Aye.' Jordain seconded her. 'I could not persuade the cart horses to move, they were so afeared, but Nicholas managed to drag them out of the ambush.'

'We were never in real danger,' I protested. 'We were at greater risk of dying of the cold at Minster Lovell Priory that night.

The others laughed, and I managed to turn the conversation to an account of our whole journey through the blizzards.

'And now, what of the preparations for the Christmas season, Edmond?' I said. 'What do you need us to do?'

'First,' he said with a smile, 'you needs must rest after your travails, but the day after tomorrow, Peter Winchingham has invited those of us who wish to join him, to hunt a deer or two in his hunting grounds, to provide venison for the Christmas feast. I had not thought a cloth merchant from Bruges would be much of a huntsman, but it seems he is English and grew up in the country.'

'Aye,' I said, 'by all he tells me, he is a countryman at heart, and now that he has gained his fortune abroad, he means to settle here, though he will keep a small flock of sheep himself, and employ his own spinsters and weavers. I believe he is one of those men who will never take his ease, but will be working even in old age.'

'He is hardly an old man,' Margaret objected, taking

my words amiss. 'Although he has a son grown and married, he himself was wed young.'

I raised my eyebrows at this, but said nothing. When had Margaret learned this about Peter Winchingham?

'I should be glad to join the hunt,' I said to Edmond, 'if the blizzards have died away by then. Let us hope it will not furnish us with a corpse, like our last hunt in Wychwood.'

'Well, there is no hated lord at the manor now, and no discontent in the village,' he said. 'Master Winchingham has already made himself popular by employing many of the villagers in his schemes, and has discreetly offered charity where it is most needed. As soon as he arrived here he was in conference with Sire Raymond about the village poor.'

'And what of Alan Wodville?' I asked. 'Does he keep his place as huntsman?'

'Aye, and his young nephew to be trained up in woodcraft beside him. He is a good man, this Peter Winchingham.'

'And what of his children?' Margaret asked. 'A son and a daughter?'

'I have met the son,' Edmond said. 'A foreign name. Hans. He came with his father, bringing the invitation to the hunt. I have not seen the daughter.'

'Peter's wife was Flemish,' I said.

'I thought we women might call upon the daughter, if the weather be not too severe,' Susanna said. 'It seems she keeps house for her father, now that her mother is gone. If you would care to come?'

Margaret and Maud agreed, and Emma nodded. I saw that Juliana was not sure whether she was included, but let the women settle that for themselves.

We were all tired after our journey, and Maysant was coughing again, so once Susanna had dosed her with a honey and raspberry syrup, we made our way thankfully to bed. My childhood room up under the eaves seemed an haven of comfort after the last two nights, despite the narrowness of the bed. I should not need to share with Rafe tonight. To his great delight, he was bedded in the chamber with the two older boys, instead of with Alysoun, which he took to be recognition of his manly status. Nevertheless, he still demanded that I should tuck in his bedclothes and kiss him goodnight. I was glad that he did not feel himself too old, after all.

When I flung open my shutters next morning, it was to reveal a world glittering like a jewelled reliquary. The sunlight flashed off the frozen snow, glinting in pure hues of gold and azure and ruby, like the colours of the great stained glass windows of one of the Oxford churches – St Mary the Virgin, or St Frideswide's. As I shifted my gaze, the colours seemed to flash and change from one hue to another. Why did that happen? It was one of the mysteries of God's exquisite creation. The orchard trees sparkled with hoar frost, so that they appeared not to be dormant winter wood, but some vast costly ornament, made for an emperor, of spun silver set with crystal gems.

When I went down to the kitchen to break my fast, I found Edmond peeling off his boots and followed by his two sons, having been seeing to the animals.

'All well?' I asked.

'Aye, your horses are well rested,' Edmond said. 'And by all I can see, I judge the blizzards have ceased for this while. There's a clear sky and a hard frost, but no sign of further snow. I think we shall have our day's hunting tomorrow.'

'Good.' I smiled. 'We shall do our best to add some venison to the feast.'

'We shall not starve even if we do not.' He laughed. 'Susanna is providing goose, and great hams, and I know not what else. She will have Margaret and the others baking pies and making comfits before they have recovered themselves from the journey.'

'And that will be no hardship.' Margaret came down the stairs, tying on an apron. 'We shall spend the morning baking, then visit young Mistress Birgit Winchingham in the afternoon. Susanna thinks we may take the farm cart, Edmond, if you can spare it. 'Twould save us a cold walk.'

'Nay, I have no need of it,' Edmond said. 'Come, my stomach is as empty as a hollow drum. Has that girl Elga finished the milking, James?'

'Aye, Father. I saw her come in before us.'

There was milk fresh from the cow for our breakfast, a little thin, as winter milk is apt to be, but welcome especially for the children after nothing but small ale on the journey. Susanna stirred a spoonful of honey into Maysant's cup, for the sake of her cough, so of course Alysoun and Rafe must have some as well, and Edmond's two small daughters, Megan and Lora.

'This shall not be for every day,' Margaret warned. 'Except for Maysant, until her cough is better.'

I felt lethargic after the journey, but the women all claimed that the long hours of idleness in the cart had left them impatient to be busy about the preparations for the twelve days of the festival. Even my mother drew up a stool to the table and set to work making marchpane shapes and rolling balls of honey paste in a sprinkling of cinnamon. I spent the morning with Edmond, looking over the affairs of the farm. Although this was my childhood home, it belonged to Edmond and Susanna now, but he always treated me as though I had still some stake in the land.

'Since the colder weather came on,' he said, 'we have persuaded your mother to make her home here with us, instead of staying on alone in her cottage. That way we can be on hand, should she need us.'

'She is looking in better heart than I expected.' I said.

He nodded. 'Once she realised that she need not make the winter journey, despite her determination to do so, and knew that you were all to come here, her health improved. I think the worry was trying her.'

'I am grateful for all you do for her,' I said. 'Margaret and I would gladly have her to live with us in Oxford, but she will not come.'

'Nay,' he said. 'I think she would not wish to leave the place which has always been her home.'

The visit to the young mistress at the manor was duly carried out that afternoon, and afterwards I contrived to speak to Emma alone, to learn what she had made of Birgit Winchingham, and of Leighton Manor under its new owner.

'We saw Peter Winchingham only briefly,' she said, 'and his son Hans, for they were busy about some improvements to the stable. And he is extending one of the barns to make a workplace for the weavers he means to employ. The spinsters, of course, will work at home, but he proposes to set up looms at the manor, since the cost of a loom would prove too much for most in the village. He will bring in an experienced weaver from Witney to train some of the men from the village in simple weaving.'

'Does he mean to make Leighton into a rival to Witney?' I laughed. 'That is ambitious indeed!'

'Nay, nothing so grand, as I understand. It will only be the coarser sort of cloth they will make, for blankets and such. He will still deal in the finer goods produced here in the Cotswolds or in London. I think it is an amusement for him, to see all through from the sheep in his meadow to the blanket on his bed, instead of dealing only in the buying and selling of finished cloth.'

'And,' I said, 'at the same time providing useful work for some in the village.'

'Aye. That too.'

'How were you received by his daughter, young Mistress Birgit? What age would she be?'

'About two years younger than I, I would suppose,' Emma said. 'Around Hilda's age. Mistress of her household, but shy, almost like a child playing at being the mistress. I do not think her mother has been long dead, and she is still finding her way. She received us most courteously, and once that anxious shyness wore off, she became quite talkative.'

'She speaks English, then, not simply Flemish.'

'As fluent English as you or I, with no accent, but I heard her address one of the maidservants in what I took to be Flemish. They brought a few servants with them from Bruges, though most preferred to stay at their homes in Flanders. Otherwise, I believe all the servants are those who worked at the manor before.'

'You liked her.'

'Aye.' She smiled. 'Very much. And she told us with great excitement about these troubadours she has hired for the Christmas season, although she is concerned that they have not arrived yet. They should be here by now.'

'How many, did she tell you? I think Peter said there were to be three.'

'Aye, three of them. A man and a woman – twins, it seems – and the woman's husband. They come from Provence – or Occitaine, as Birgit called it. Their mother tongue is Occitan. But ever since the troubles there, it seems life is hard for the troubadours, and they must make a living by travelling from country to country. They have been to Italy and Castile and Navarre, some of the German states, and of course Flanders, where Birgit heard them. Mostly, it seems, they avoid France. The French are much hated in Provence, ever since the massacres which were encouraged, or even initiated, by churchmen, in the name of a crusade.'

'The slaughter of the Cathars?' I shook my head. 'That was a vile business. From all one hears, the Cathars were good people, and the French armies were not too particular about who they killed, Cathars or devout children of the Church. I have always believed it was not so much a religious crusade as an excuse to destroy the powerful lords of Provence and seize their lands.'

'Aye, I think you have the right of it,' she said. 'It seems that once the great courts of the south were destroyed, the troubadours lost their patrons, although their musical tradition lingers on. Birgit says that the brother and sister descend from many generations of troubadours and strive to keep their heritage alive. She knows less of the husband, who is very reticent. She thinks him something of a mystery, but that may be no more than girlish fantasy.'

I hid my smile when Emma spoke thus about a girl hardly younger than herself, though I was not altogether sure whether she was teasing me.

'Well,' I said, 'I hope they will fall in with this plan of mine, to make a book of troubadour songs. They may wish to hug their knowledge to themselves, and not share it with me.'

The next morning shone again clear and bright. The frost was still thick on the ground and the fallen snow hard underfoot, even treacherous in places, where a solid icy crust had formed. After an early breakfast, Edmond, James, Thomas, and I mounted our horses, who frisked about the yard as if glad to be out of the confines of the stable. We left the others behind, busy in the kitchen. Jordain had chosen not to accompany us.

'I am no huntsman, Nicholas,' he said, 'and to tell truth, I am heartily sick of horses for the moment. I shall be a drawer of water and a carrier of wood for our multiplicity of cooks, and help with such menial tasks as may be assigned to me.'

I nodded. I had not expected him to come. He was indeed no horseman, viewing a horse as no more than a means of travelling about more quickly than on foot, and for your true huntsman the joy of the chase is more in the riding, fast and dangerous, than in the slaying of the deer. I have no great love of the killing myself, though I can take pride in a clean shot through difficult woodland, bringing down an elusive quarry. And a man and his family must eat. However, I have no patience with some of the excessive slaughter carried out in the royal hunts, beyond the needs even of that vast household.

We trotted briskly down to the village, Edmond's dogs loping beside us. We had taken care to shut Rowan and Jocosa away safely till we should be gone, for they could only come to grief, should they become mixed up in a hunt. The lane up to the manor had been meticulously cleared, and as we rode up it I was reminded vividly of the disturbing events which had taken place here only a few months before. But such thoughts were soon driven out of my head by our hearty welcome from Peter Winchingham and his son, an unmistakable younger version of his father and, as Peter had said, tall and strongly built for a lad of fifteen.

Nothing would do but we must come into the house to meet Peter's daughter and take a hot drink before we set out on our cold ride. Birgit Winchingham curtsied and blushed prettily at being introduced to us, and I caught her eying James thoughtfully, which he seemed not to notice. They were close in age, for James was eighteen now. Birgit resembled her father not at all, being flaxen fair, with a small heart shaped face, both features she had probably inherited from her mother. She had silver cups of steaming hippocras ready for us, and little spiral cakes flavoured with honey and cinnamon of a kind I had never seen before. She urged us to linger beside the roaring fire in the great hall, but the three boys were eager to set out.

As we left, I glanced back, remembering the hall as I had seen it in August, filled with a mostly hostile crowd and with the body of Gilbert Mordon lying on a trestle table. Now it was warmed by huge fires in two fireplaces, there were colourful Flemish tapestries on the walls, and there was a scattering of large, comfortable furniture, nothing of the grandeur of Mordon's possessions, but lovingly polished coffers on which stood jugs holding arrangements of winter greenery and berried holly, and wide oak chairs piled with embroidered cushions, almost certainly the work of Birgit and her mother, not bought from some professional needlewoman, as in Lady Edith's time, to make a show of luxury.

Under the urging of the lads, we were soon mounted, and followed the huntsman Alan Wodville and his nephew

Rob into the part of Wychwood which lay within the manor's demesne and where Peter held the hunting rights. The manor's kennel servants ran alongside, with the lymers and alaunts held back for the moment on their leads. Edmond's dogs had also been taken over by them, that they might not disturb the game too soon. Amongst the hunt servants I caught sight of Aelfric, with whom I had had dealing back in the autumn, and who gave me an awkward bow,

This was to be a very different affair from the ceremonious hunt under Gilbert Mordon. In the bitter weather of December, it was not the season for sitting at our ease in a clearing enjoying a hunt breakfast in the company of our womenfolk. This was a simple pursuit of game for the table. The venison would need to hang before it was ready for festive eating, so if we failed to bag a deer today, we would probably be too late. We followed purposefully up the main ride through the wood after Alan, who told us that some of the deer were likely to be off to the left of the ride, where there was easy access to the stream which, further down, ran past the glade where we had previously picnicked.

'There's a small clearing where they can scrape away the snow and ice to uncover the grass,' Alan said, 'and I have been leaving hay there for the past week, to encourage them to come back. I think we should get a sighting.'

He was proved right. As we turned cautiously off the ride, the lymers quickly picked up the scent and forged ahead, noses to the wind or to the ground, moving in that curiously silent way in which they have been trained to follow game. The alaunts strained to follow them, but were held back, not to be released until they were needed to bring a wounded animal down.

We followed the lymers. We were down wind of the deer, who would not pick up our scent, but their sensitive ears would soon hear us, even though at this time of year the horses' hoofs made little sound in the snow, unlike the cracking of twigs during an autumn hunt.

Then the deer were sighted, there ahead of us. Perhaps half a dozen does, with half grown fawns at heel, and three stags – one the dominant male and two younger ones. It was the stags we were hunting, not the breeding does.

As we saw the deer, so they saw us, and one of the young alaunts let out a yelp. Alan sounded his horn for the chase, and heedless of any noise, we put our horses to the gallop, for the deer had spun instantly round and leapt away, not all together but in several different directions. Alan raised his arm and pointed to where the two younger stags had crashed away through the trees.

I ducked down, keeping my head low on Rufus's neck, mindful of the low branches, which can kill a man hitting one at full gallop. Rufus was doing his best to keep up, but Peter and his son, and James, were pulling ahead, close behind Alan. Out of the corner of my eye, I saw the whisk of an upraised tail as the biggest stag leapt a bush and disappeared. We were still following the other two.

I had nearly caught up when I saw Hans drop his reins and, guiding his horse with his knees, raise his bow and loose a shot at one of the stags who had swerved to avoid a dense mass of undergrowth. It was a skilled display of horsemanship, but the arrow embedded itself in the stag's upper breast near the neck and remained quivering, wounding the beast, but not deeply. It was not a clean kill. Unless we could prevent, the animal would flee deeper into the forest to die slowly and in agony.

Alan turned to signal to the dog handlers to unleash the alaunts, who would pull down the stag and kill it, but it would be neither clean nor quick.

'Wait!' Peter shouted. He hauled his horse back, stood up in his stirrups, and sent a second arrow which took the stag in the heart. It threw up its head, sank to its knees, then fell sideways, laying a trail of blood, crimson on the unblemished snow.

It was a magnificent shot and had spared the stag a lingering death, yet I looked with sadness on the young stag where he lay. His eyes, filming over, were turned up to the trees that he was never to see come into leaf again. He would never join the rut to claim the place as leader of the herd.

Then I shook my head and warned myself not to be a sentimental fool. Stags could kill each other during the rut, or they could break one of those delicate legs and lead a diminishing life until starvation took them. This stag would provide meat for the Christmas feast, and even the poor of the village would benefit.

When all the business of dealing with the stag was done, we started back to rejoin the wide avenue through the wood. The customary offering had been left for Wychwood, the dogs had been given their shares of the umbles, and the carcase was slung over the back of a sturdy pony.

We were, I suppose, about halfway between the place where the stag had been taken and the ride, when I heard a confused noise in the distance.

'What is that?' I said to Peter, who was riding beside me. 'Were some of your people to come and meet us?'

'Nay.' He shook his head. 'I do not like the sound of that.'

'I think it may be fighting,' I said. 'That is the sound of swords, is it not? And was that a cry for help?'

We urged our horses on, as fast as we could go, but it was difficult making our way back through the pathless woods. The others had heard the noise now, and we rode ahead of the servants bringing up the dogs and the stag behind us. Alan, who knew these woods better than anyone, set himself at our head to find us the best way through the trees. It seemed to take us much longer than our earlier gallop after the fleeing stags, and before we reached the ride, all sound of fighting had ceased. It was eerily quiet.

'I do not like this,' Edmond said. 'Perhaps those outlaws you met with, Nicholas, are not the only ones to be roaming in these parts.'

'Outlaws?' Peter said, looking across at me.

'Near Witney,' I said. 'We were attacked on our way here, but for certain it cannot be the same men, for only one survived.'

'Mayhap there was more of the band,' Edmond said, 'lurking elsewhere. Nay, James, keep with us.' For James had begun to ride ahead. Like the other two boys he looked excited rather than alarmed.

'It may be a trap,' Peter pointed out, as James reluctantly reined in his horse. 'Let us take care to make sure what is afoot before we plunge in, heedless.'

As we neared the ride, we went more cautiously, although the snow still muffled the sound of the horses' hoofs.

'Wait you here,' Alan said softly, and slid from his horse.

He moved forward silently, slipping between bushes and behind a hazel coppice. In a few minutes he was back.

'Travellers,' he said. 'They must have followed the track from the north of the wood, though why they would come this way, I cannot say. A small cart. One horse, no more than a pony, wounded. No sign of any people.'

We looked at each other. This could well be a trap. If we went to investigate, the outlaws might fall upon us. They would be armed, and we were not, save for our hunting gear. Bows and hunting knives would stand little chance against the swords of desperate men.

On the other hand, this cart and its possible passengers might be the prey of the outlaws – or whoever had instigated the attack. There might be no one to be seen at the moment, but there could be people within the cart. Wounded or dead.

'We cannot leave the cart there,' I said. 'Even if there are no people, the injured horse must be seen to. Let us go forward carefully, our bows strung, and keeping a sharp watch on every side. If Peter can fell a deer with such a shot, he can surely bring down the first man to attack us.'

Peter smiled grimly as he restrung his bow. 'I shall do my best,' he said, but we all knew we would have little chance if a large band of outlaws was indeed lying in wait. They might settle for no more than our slain deer, or they might be after richer prey.

As I had been the one to urge the move, I rode forward beside Peter. When we broke from the trees, I held my breath, keeping Rufus paused at the edge of the ride and looking about in every direction.

All was silent.

The cart was neither shabby nor rich, merely of the middling sort. The pony stood with drooping head. Blood was pouring from a great gash in his shoulder, down his leg, and forming a puddle in the snow of the ride. It was impossible to judge from here how serious it was. If a major muscle was severed, the pony must have its throat cut. If it could be saved, it still looked in no fit state to draw the cart any further.

As we hesitated, midway between the trees and the cart, the first of the hunt servants began to catch up with us.

'Send the fittest of your men into trees round about,' Peter said to Alan. 'Let them flush out any who may be hiding there, but they should go carefully, with their bows strung and ready.'

Alan nodded, and rode over to speak to his men.

'Look there,' I said, pointing up the ride in the opposite direction from the manor. 'Movement.'

The others swung round to see where I was looking. Too far away to be sure, but we could see the hindquarters of retreating horses. Their riders were little more than a blur. There was a spray of snow thrown up, as by the hoofs of horses, and more snow slid from branches brushed by passing riders, settling soft on the lane.

'Shall we go after them, Father?' Thomas said eagerly to Edmond.

He exchanged a gleeful glance with Hans.

'Certainly not,' Edmond said. 'Do not be foolish. There might be twenty or thirty of them. What could you do, of any use?'

Thomas looked sulky, but held back his horse.

As I began to ride Rufus cautiously a little nearer to the cart, there came the unmistakable sound of a groan, cut off short, as if a hand had been clamped over the sufferer's mouth. I came a little nearer.

'Friends here!' I called. 'Your attackers have ridden away. Are any hurt within?'

There was a pause, a listening silence, then a young man put his head out of the back of the cart. He was perhaps a year or two younger than I, with curling hair worn rather long, of a reddish brown. There was a cut below his left ear, against which he was pressing a bloodied handkerchief. He was glaring at me.

'Who are you?' he asked abruptly, with a trace of an accent I could not at once place.

'My name is Nicholas Elyot,' I said calmly, riding no nearer, so as not to afright him. 'I have a bookshop in Oxford, but I am visiting my cousin, who has a farm beside the village of Leighton.'

'Leighton?' he said, his voice sharpening with interest.

'Aye. And this is Master Peter Winchingham, lord of the manor of Leighton.'

The man's face changed. The glare gave way to a look of relief.

'Winchingham—' he began, as Peter rode up beside me.

'But this is one of Birgit's musicians!' Peter cried. 'Falquet de Béziers, he is hight. Man, what are you doing here, in this state?'

'We missed our way to Witney,' the musician said, 'and turned too far north, I think. But a woman at a farm over there,' he waved his arm vaguely up the ride, 'she told us this way through the wood would bring us to Leighton Manor more easily than retracing our steps to Witney.'

'Why, so it would,' Peter said, 'and so it has, but you have met with misfortune in Wychwood, so it seems.'

'A wood of witches?' the man said. 'Little wonder, then.'

'No witch did that,' I said dryly, pointing at his cheek, 'nor injured your pony.'

'He is injured?'

'Aye, a bad cut to the near fore. He'll not be fit to draw your wagon any further. We must send for another.'

'But, Falquet,' Peter said, 'are you alone? Where are the others, your sister and her husband?'

Remembering the groan I had heard, I said, 'Is one of them injured worse than you?'

He hesitated, then must have realised, since Peter had recognised him and spoken to him by name, we must be who we said we were, and could be trusted.

'Aye. Gaston. Those rogues went for him. Singled him out. I only got this because I tried to intervene.'

'And the lady?' Peter asked. 'Mistress Azalais?'

'Not hurt. We hid her away when they set upon us.'

'We had better see to the injured man,' I said, dismounting. 'May we?'

I indicated the step up into the back of the cart. He hesitated only a moment longer, then he nodded and tied back the canvas. The cart was very similar to the one we had brought from Oxford, though a great deal smaller and better equipped. I suspect it had originally set out with all the travellers' belongings neatly stowed away in the cupboards under the fixed seats, which probably served them as beds, but now everything was thrown about in wild chaos, clothes ripped, wooden cups smashed as though they had been stamped on. A beautiful vielle lay disembowelled on the floor.

Also on the floor lay a man, older and bigger than Falquet, who I now saw was slightly built. This other – it must be the brother-in-law, Gaston – lay very still. He was unconscious, blood matting his thick, dark hair. A young woman knelt beside him, weeping, and trying to lift him in her arms. This must be Falquet's sister, for she had the same reddish brown hair, carelessly tied back with a scrap of ribbon, and the very fair skin common to those with russet hair. Her face was streaked with tears, but she

89

appeared to be unhurt.

'Careful,' I said. 'It may be best to let him lie.'

She looked up at me, startled and confused, and clearly afraid, then she caught sight of Peter, climbing into the cart behind me, and let out a soft cry.

'Master Winchingham! Oh, the Blessed Virgin be praised! How came you here?'

'You are on my lands, Mistress Azalais,' he said, patting her gently on the shoulder. 'You are safe now, whatever evil has befallen you. Master Elyot has the right of it. Best let Master Gaston lie until we can attend to him.'

'Have you a cushion to put under his head?' I said. 'That will make him more comfortable. One that will not be spoiled by the blood.'

'Devil take the blood!' she said fiercely, springing to her feet and looking about. 'They have torn us to pieces. Here.'

She dragged a cushion from under a heap of clothing, and, as I lifted the man's head and shoulders, slid it in place.

She dashed away the tears with the back of her hand and gave a tremulous smile.

'How far are we from your manor, Master Winchingham?'

'Not far, but your pony cannot draw the cart any further. Those fellows have wounded him.'

'The pony as well? Is it serious? What shall we do?'

'Not too serious, Azalais,' the young man said. 'He will mend. But these gentlemen are right, he cannot pull the cart.'

'Hans!' Peter leaned out of the cart and called. 'Ride quickly back to the manor and fetch one of the work horses to take the place of the troubadours' pony. The smallest one, for we have no time to adjust the harness for a larger beast.'

'I will come with you,' Thomas said, and the two boys set off at a gallop down the ride.

'Have you a blanket, mistress?' I said. ''Tis bitter

December weather for a man lying still and injured.'

She was bathing the wound, which was bleeding freely, staining her skirts, and looked about, despairingly.

'We keep them folded on the seats, but now . . .'

'Here.' I found an end protruding from under the broken vielle and drew it out carefully. 'I fear they have ruined your instrument.'

She took the blanket from me and spread it over the injured man.

'Happily that is not the better one. The other vielle, and the lute, and the rest of the instruments are safely stored away.'

I looked around. I could see nowhere a large instrument like a lute could be concealed, and she gave me a wan smile.

'We have a box for the instruments built under the floor. They did not find the opening to it. There, by your feet.'

I looked down, but could see nothing at first, then I realised that there was a recessed hollow in the floor boards, into which one could fit one's fingers to lift a portion, a kind of trapdoor, which must form the lid of the 'box' of which she spoke. They must travel about in this cart from patron to patron, somewhat like the candle-makers Emma had known.

The girl got to her feet and began to restore some order to the cart, so I rejoined the others in the ride.

'I have sent the servants back to the manor, with the dogs and the stag,' Peter said. 'Edmond and Alan are seeing how serious is the injury to the pony.'

Falquet had unhitched the pony from the traces and led him to the side of the ride, where Edmond was bathing the blood from the lower leg with a handful of snow, while Alan delved into his satchel.

'I have some horse salve here,' he said, drawing out an earthenware pot, sealed with a cork. 'This will give him some ease till we get him back to the stable and decide whether the wound needs to be stitched.'

I nodded. I knew that both Alan and our blacksmith Bertred Godsmith were experienced horse doctors. I should not care to attempt stitching a wound on a horse, but they knew their business.

Whether the salve eased the pain or not, the pony seemed cheered by the attention, and Alan told his nephew to start leading him slowly back to the manor, while we waited for one of the farm horses to take his place between the shafts.

I was unaware how long it had been since we first set out on the hunt, but it was growing very cold and dusk was setting in by the time Hans and Thomas returned with the smallest of Peter's working horses. By then Edmond with his sons, and Peter and Hans, together with Alan and me, were the only ones left apart from the musicians, and I had begun to worry that the outlaws – or whoever the attackers were – might return to finish their business.

However, we soon had the new horse hitched to the cart, and Falquet took up the reins. The girl Azalais had lit two candle lanterns, which she hung above the driver's bench, and another which she fixed inside to a hook in one of the hoops which held up the canvas roof. The cart was now neat and freshly cleaned, and apart from the injured man, still lying unconscious on the floor, might have been the room in any small cottage.

Moving slowly, so that the jolting of the cart should not be too grave for the troubadour Gaston, so eagerly awaited by Mistress Birgit Winchingham, we set off on our way back to the manor house.

Chapter five

By the time we reached the manor house, it was nearly dark. We had been obliged to go slowly, for none of us were sure how badly injured Gaston was, and feared that too rough a journey might prove fatal. Before we were halfway there, Peter sent Hans ahead to warn Birgit that rooms must be made ready, with warm fires lit in all of them, and abundant bedding, for it was growing colder all the time. Hans rode off, again accompanied by Thomas, for the two boys were much of an age, and seemed to see nothing in the events of the day but excitement and adventure.

'I told Birgit we have an injured man,' Hans said as they set off. 'While we were waiting for the stable lad to fetch the farm horse for the musicians' cart. I think she is worried whether she is able to care for him.'

'There is no physician or apothecary in the village,' I said quietly to Peter, 'though we might send to Burford. However, in the dark and snow, it would not be likely that any man could be here before the morrow.'

'Our womenfolk will cope,' Edmond said with confidence. 'The man is breathing normally. It is when the breathing turns to uneven snorting that one must worry. That is when the head is badly damaged.'

I nodded. I remembered a student who had been knocked down in a brawl when I was not long in Oxford as a boy. He had struck his head on the corner of a step, and his breathing had sounded as Edmond described. He had seemed to recover briefly, though dazed, but died two days later.

Falquet had been listening to our conversation from his seat at the front of the cart. 'There is no need to prepare rooms for us, Master Winchingham. We are used to sleeping in the cart in all weathers.'

'Do not talk foolishness,' Peter said. 'This weather would freeze the very blood in your veins. There are chambers aplenty at the manor. Do you think I would leave a wounded man to sleep in a cart? Colder than my horses in their stable? We even keep a fire burning in the tack room these nights, with one of the stable lads always there, and he leaves the door ajar, so that the heat reaches out to the stalls. And Gaston's wife will want to be with him. Or are you choosing to martyr yourself, alone and perishing in the cart? When we reach the house you will bring in whatever you may need for the night, while we carry your brother-in-law to his chamber. Everything else can await the morrow.'

'Very well,' Falquet said submissively, but even in the failing light I could see that he was relieved at the prospect of a warm bed.

The manor house was ablaze with light, so that we could see it from afar, and I had a fleeting thought of the Magi, following their star at this season so long ago, then put it aside as possibly blasphemous. It seemed that the Winchingham family did not stint on candles. As we halted close to the front door of the manor house, I noticed a small cart already parked there, though the horse had been taken away to the stable.

'Is that not your cart, Edmond?' I said.

'Aye, it is. Whatever can that be doing here?'

We had not long to wait before we discovered. The door was thrown open at the sound of our arrival, and Hans came out with two menservants bringing a pallet to carry the injured man into the house. Crowding out behind him were not only Thomas and Birgit, but, to our surprise, both Margaret and Emma.

When I returned to the house after seeing to Rufus in

the manor stable, I found some of the company gathered in the small parlour, but no sign of the troubadours, or of Emma and my sister.

Birgit explained, pausing by the door with a bowl of warm broth in her hand. 'When I knew that you were bringing in a badly injured man, I feared I had not the skills to care for him, so I sent one of the servants to Master Elyot's farm, to beg for help. I was sure that Mistress Makepeace, or Mistress Farringdon, or Mistress Elyot would be far better than I, having all reared families. Mistress Farringdon thought she must stay with the her little granddaughter, who is not quite well. Mistress Elyot had her little ones, and sent word that she would care for your two, Master Elyot, so that your sister might come to my aid. The lady Emma has come as well, of her kindness.'

She hurried away.

'The women have all joined Mistress Azalais at Master Gaston's bedside,' Hans said. 'I am sure that between them they will soon make the poor fellow well again.'

He was quite cheerful, with the confidence of youth that all hurts could be mended with the right care. It was somewhat surprising, since it was not many months since he had lost his mother, but I guessed that his nature was one of those which always takes the most optimistic view of life and its dangers. In this, I could see his likeness to Edmond's son Thomas.

'He is the leader of the group of musicians, is he?' I asked Peter. 'This Gaston? I do not know by what other name he is known.'

'Gaston de Sarlat,' Peter said, 'although I am not sure–'

Whatever he was about to say, whatever he was unsure of, was forestalled by the arrival of Falquet.

'And how does your sister's husband?' Edmond asked. 'Has he come back to himself?'

'For a few minutes,' Falquet said. 'The women have cleaned the wound and Mistress Makepeace believes that the skull is not damaged. There was a great deal of blood, but now that it is all wiped away, the injury seems less serious. She has salved it, and the lady Emma is even now swathing him in a bandage, so that he will look like a turbaned Saracen. They were going to cut away his hair around the wound, but he is vain of his thick locks, and woke long enough to beg them to spare him.'

He laughed indulgently. 'We musicians for hire must have a care for our looks. If we please the ladies, we are like to be employed again.'

Peter clapped him on the shoulder. 'I do not think it was for your ginger curls that my daughter hired you, Falquet, but for your music. Now, I have told the steward that we will take supper here in the small parlour, which is warmer at night than the great hall, and we shall eat as soon as the ladies join us.'

Edmond and I made no more than a mere pretence of protest, for we had realised that we had never taken any dinner. With all our labours in the bitter weather, we were ravenous. When the others joined us, they were closely followed by a procession of maid servants bearing dishes from which enticing smells rose that made my mouth water. The cellarer, Warin Hodgate, himself supervised the men carrying in flagons of the good French wine still stored in the cellars since the de Veres' time.

'So the patient is awake?' I said to Margaret, as we sat down to table.

'He woke briefly, when we were dressing his wound, and sipped a few spoonfuls of Birgit's broth, but he is asleep now. True sleep, not the effect of the blow to his head. I think he will mend in a few days. It was a hard blow, but he has a sturdy skull. He was also beaten and kicked. The bruises will give him some pain by tomorrow.'

I looked across the table at Falquet, who was tucking in heartily to the good food. Probably meals were scrappy when the minstrels were travelling in their cart.

'Have you any idea why these men attacked you?' I said.

I had suddenly realised that we had been so concerned with securing another horse for the cart and bringing the injured man to where he could be cared for, that we had not discussed the attack itself, nor asked whether there could be any reason for it.

Falquet raised to me a face of bland innocence and shook his head.

'I have no idea at all, Master Elyot,' he said. 'Do they not attack everyone they encounter, these rogues? They live by their wits, such men, and prey on any who come their way.'

I studied him closely, for there had been neither time nor leisure to do so before. He seemed an honest fellow, of age perhaps in his early twenties. Neatly, but not expensively, dressed. Close shaven. His English was perfect, but had a slight accent of the Provençal – or, as I had learned these people called it, Occitan.

'Yet,' I said, 'I think these particular rogues did not encounter you by chance, nor were they lying in ambush within Wychwood, hoping for passers-by. They followed you.'

At first I was not quite sure why I said this. I had no concrete proof, for I had not examined the ground where we had encountered the troubadours, only caught that briefest glimpse of the attackers riding away up the avenue in the direction away from the manor. Then I realised what I had noticed without being aware of it at the time. There were no hoof prints in the snow to show that men had been hidden at the side of the avenue. And just as surely, no hoof prints at all in the snow in front of the cart, in the direction of the manor, not even the prints of our own horses, for we had left the ride and entered the wood some yards further down from the place where we had emerged in response to the sound of fighting. Between, the snow lay smooth and unblemished.

The attackers, like the troubadours, had come *down* the ride. Why? It led only to the manor. In order to continue on to the village, one must pass through the manor precinct.

Outlaws living rough in the countryside would not have the means to attack the manor, nor would they dare to ride through the grounds, for they would have been stopped. The only reason for them to have come down the ride was because they were pursuing the troubadours.

'Followed us?' Falquet gave a nervous laugh. 'Why should they do so? Our modest cart, a few simple musicians? Nay, if you have the right of it, and they did follow us, they must have mistaken us for some other party. Why, despite their brutal attack on Gaston, they took nothing!'

His voice sounded firmer as he made this assertion, so that I was sure that, in this last at least, he was telling the truth.

'Strange,' I said dryly. 'For such men would surely seize your food and anything of value they could find. And from the state of disorder in your cart, which is now restored to perfect neatness, they seem to have turned everything upside down. As if they were searching for something.'

He flushed, then repeated himself. 'They must have mistaken us for some other party.'

Edmond and Margaret were looking at me disapprovingly, as if they considered me unkind to question one of the victims of the attack so closely, for Falquet himself bore that small injury below his ear. Emma eyed me thoughtfully. On Peter's face, however, I caught a glimpse of something, as though he thought my questions important, but he said nothing. I decided I should leave the matter alone for now.

'Aye, well,' I said, helping Birgit, who sat beside me, to more bread, and taking some myself, 'you probably have the right of it. They mistook you for a merchant coming to the manor with valuable goods, or a king's messenger, perhaps!'

I grinned at the musician, but he bowed his head over his plate and flushed even more. He made no response to my feeble jest.

After we had eaten, Margaret made a final visit to the patient, but declared that he could be left to sleep until the morning. His wife had stayed with him all the while, taking her supper from a tray in their chamber.

'I think we may safely go home,' Margaret said to Peter. 'Birgit and Mistress Azalais know what to do, should he wake. I will come again on the morrow.'

Peter took both her hands in his and kissed them. 'We are most grateful to you for your trouble, Margaret. It would have been a great worry to Birgit on her own.'

She smiled at him. 'No trouble at all. It was a pleasure to come to your daughter's aid. I can see that Leighton Manor will flourish in the hands of the Winchingham family.'

Peter turned to Emma, and I noticed that Falquet, after murmuring brief thanks to them both, had slipped away. A servant had been sent to instruct one of the stable lads to saddle our horses and fix pillions for Margaret and Emma to ride behind Edmond and me. The cart would be sent back to the farm in the morning.

As we walked to the door and began our leave taking, Peter drew me aside.

'Are you free tomorrow, Nicholas?' he said.

'Aye, unless Edmond needs me, but I think he can have nothing urgent to discuss.'

He glanced over his shoulder, but there was no one within earshot.

'I would have a brief conference with you,' he said.

I nodded, and I had guessed the subject of his concern. 'This attack on the troubadours – it seems as odd to you as it does to me?'

'Aye, something not quite right. Like you, I suspect they were followed. And not mistaken for someone else.'

'Aye,' I said. 'But Falquet does not wish us to think so.'

'He does not. And I find that worries me. I have always believed them to be honest people, but if so, what are they seeking to hide? I mislike it.'

'It is strange,' I said, 'but perhaps we are making too much of it. Mayhap the outlaws came upon them by chance and followed them, or did indeed mistake them for someone else. All will probably become clear tomorrow, or soon. But I shall indeed attend upon you in the morning.'

Margaret was already seated on the pillion saddle behind Edmond when I mounted Rufus. Before Peter could assist Emma to mount, she had placed her foot on mine in the stirrup and swung herself up behind me. Waving our farewells to the Winchinghams, we turned our horses down the lane, Edmond's two sons riding in front. With their lighter burdens they soon drew ahead of us.

Emma wrapped her arms about my waist, and leaned her head into the hollow of my back.

'I am reminded,' she said, somewhat muffled, 'of another occasion when we rode two to a horse. And that was on Rufus, this sturdy fellow.'

'Aye.' I grinned to myself. 'He is quite used to our combined weight. Though the weather was milder on that occasion, as I recall.'

'It was. But now we may ride at our ease. No stepfather with his dogs is pursuing us.'

'He has not tried to make any further claim on you or your inheritance?'

I could feel her shake her head.

'Nay,' she said. 'My grandfather and his lawyers have so hedged all about with the bounds of the law, that he cannot touch it. And the matter of Godstow Abbey has been settled with the gift of a fine property in the north of Oxfordshire, so all are content, save my stepfather.'

'Good.'

We were alone now, the boys having ridden out of sight, and the other horse, double burdened with a greater weight, lagging behind.

'What do you make of these troubadours, Emma?' I said. 'You have seen more of them than I have. This attack on them – what do you make of that?'

She paused before answering.

'I like the girl, Azalais. They are very much in love, I think, she and Gaston. She was distraught about his injury. She kept saying, "They need not have beaten him so cruelly!" It seems that the men had just time to hide her in the compartment where they store the instruments, before the outlaws caught up with them.'

'It must have been very cramped.'

'Aye, but she is slightly built. She was curled up there in the dark, terrified, hearing the fighting above her head, with only the thickness of the floor boards between them. Did you not say that you heard the clashing of swords?'

'I thought so.' I cast my mind back to the chaos in the cart when I had first seen it. 'Although now I cannot remember seeing any swords belonging to the troubadours.'

'From something Azalais said, I think they must have hidden them away before you reached them, although I do not understand why.'

'Another oddity. There is much I do not understand about these people. And what do you make of Falquet's claim that they were not followed, or else they were mistaken for someone else?'

'I believe he was lying,' she said. 'That look of innocence was too contrived. Troubadours are also players of a sort. That was pretended innocence.'

'But why?' I said. 'If indeed they have enemies, should they not seek help from such as Peter Winchingham, an honest man, already known to them?'

'That I cannot guess.' She thought for a moment. 'There was something else which was strange. We told you that Gaston awoke for a time. I expect the pain of having his wound dressed brought him out of his fit of unconsciousness.'

'You did.'

'He started to say something in English, but Azalais laid her finger on his lips and murmured something to him in . . . well, I suppose it was Occitan. It was then that he pleaded with us not to cut away the hair from around his injury, but I am sure that was not what he was going to say at first. His voice was very weak, but I thought I heard the words "where is?", then his wife hushed him.'

'He might simply have been asking about her brother, Falquet.'

I felt her shake her head. 'Falquet was still there.'

'Or about the injured pony?' I said. 'Or the cart? He had woken to find himself in a strange room, surrounded mostly by strangers. He must have been confused.'

'Perhaps. But I do not think so. It may be that Azalais was just bidding him to rest and be quiet. Yet I do not think so.'

'It is all a puzzle, and there is something behind it which they do not wish to be generally known. But we must remember, they had found themselves amongst strangers, soon after a violent attack. Peter has asked me to speak with him tomorrow. Perhaps by then they will have confided in him.'

'Aye, let us forget the affairs of the troubadours for now.'

There was laughter in her voice and she tightened her arms about my waist. I laid my hand over hers, and even through our gloves I could feel their warmth. Thus in a close embrace we rode the rest of the way to the farm.

The next morning I went over to the manor house alone. Peter had sent a servant early with Edmond's cart, bringing a message to say that the minstrel Gaston was making a good recovery and Margaret need not hasten to his bedside. He invited our whole household to midday dinner instead. However, as the women were still much occupied with the preparations of food for the celebrations, the invitation was politely declined, although Margaret said that she would drive over in the afternoon to see the patient.

I found Peter in the estate office with his steward and the manor reeve, going through the account books partially written up in Gilbert Mordon's brief time at the manor, then kept in rough form by the steward in the months since

Mordon's death and the flight of Lady Edith and her lover.

Peter did not seem as wearied by his accounts as I am, for they come close to sending me to sleep the moment I open my ledgers, but he declared cheerfully that they had done enough for one morning and sent the other two men off about their duties.

'I wondered whether you might have had speech with the troubadours this morning,' I said, 'now that the house is not filled with people of whom they know nothing. Have they revealed anything of this business, which we both regard as odd and requiring explanation?'

'Not a word,' he said, leading me over to the window embrasure, where cushions softened the stone seat. 'They are mystified as to why they should be attacked. It must have been a mistake, so they say. Gaston de Sarlat is awake and fully in his wits now. He tells the same story as Falquet. Almost in the same words.'

'Agreed between them, you think?' I said.

'Certainly that is how it seems. A little too . . . contrived.'

'Very strange. And it seems Gaston was worried last night about where something might be, but was hushed by his wife.'

I told him what Emma had heard.

'Of course, it might mean nothing,' I concluded.

'Hmm.' He drummed on the window embrasure with his finger tips. 'Yet, do you recall, when we first reached them, they let slip that the attackers seemed to be searching for something. Later, they turned that into a reason why they must have been mistaken for some other group of travellers. Now, I am not so sure.'

'Could they be carrying something these fellows were searching for? But what? And something so secret they wish to conceal it from you, whom they surely know and trust?'

'I suppose they do not know me so very well,' Peter said.

'At any rate,' I said thoughtfully, 'I do not think the

attackers found it. They had turned out every possession on to the floor, even smashed that vielle, as though they believed something might be hidden in it.'

'Why are you so convinced that they did not find . . . whatever it was? What they sought?'

'Because of what Emma told me. Azalais hushed her husband when he tried to ask where something was. She must have looked quite calm, for Emma said that she might simply have been bidding Gaston to rest. Yet I think if . . whatever it was . . . *had* been taken, Azalais would have been distressed, and Emma would have noticed. She is most observant.'

'Aye.' He nodded. 'A good point. I think you probably have the right of it. And I suppose, in any case, it is not our affair. Let them keep their secret.'

'I suppose that is true,' I said reluctantly. 'Yet if they carry some dangerous secret, and men are prepared to use violence to seize it, I hope your household may not be in danger. How long do they remain here?'

'Until past Twelfth Day. Afterwards, I believe they make for London, in the hope of finding other patrons. That is, if the weather and Gaston's injury permit them to travel.'

'Did they not come that way, through London, from Flanders?'

He shook his head. 'They sailed from Bruges to Norwich, as we did. Then made their way here with their horse and cart, though they had meant to come through Witney, but missed the way.'

'How does their horse fare? Will he be fit enough to draw their cart by the time they leave?'

'Difficult to say, as yet. As you know, Alan Wodville physicked it in Wychwood, and he has had Bertred Godsmith here this morning to give his opinion. The two of them with Falquet were pondering over the leg together.'

'Bertred has a good knowledge of horses,' I said, 'not only their hoofs and shoes! With both Bertred and Alan in attendance, I would say the beast has a good chance of recovery.'

'Did you not say that the men who attacked you near Witney also tried to disable your horses?'

'They did.'

'So it *could* have been more of the same group.'

I shook my head. 'I cannot think so. The soldiers who were with us killed all but one of the outlaws. I do not support the notion that more of the same group were in hiding elsewhere, and came after the troubadours. Why should they divide their numbers? I believe they waylaid us in their full force. This must have been a different group in Wychwood, although I suppose there is nothing unusual in the tactic of stranding your victims by disabling their horses.'

I paused, looking out over the snow bound garden to the distant line of trees where the Wychwood forest began.

'Nay,' I said. 'I am sure that these were a different sort of men altogether. Not outlaws. Not men living wild in the woods, surviving by their wits on what they can steal from helpless travellers.'

Peter gave me a penetrating look.

'You seem very certain, Nicholas.'

'I am certain.'

'But why?'

'Because they stole nothing. Not even a loaf of bread.'

Despite my doubts about the troubadours' story, I agreed with Peter that we should give every appearance of accepting it. Until they decided to confide in him, should they ever do so. However, the whole business exercised my mind a good deal, and I found it difficult to leave off thinking about it. If our conjectures had come close to the truth, Gaston and the others had been carrying something of value which they must keep secret. It had been discovered that they were doing so, and someone wanted it, whatever it was, and was prepared to go to some lengths to get it.

Why had those attackers ridden off, abandoning the

attempt? If they were prepared to beat Gaston, why did they not carry him off with them? Perhaps it was not some *object* the minstrels carried. Perhaps Gaston had a message to deliver. A message he had memorised. Nay, that would not do, or he would not have asked 'where is?'.

Of course, there was always the chance that the attackers had heard us approaching through the woods, and rode off before they could be caught. We had made no attempt to move silently until the last stretch of the way, after we had heard the affray. We had been talking loudly, the whole company of the hunt. We were no longer stalking the deer in silence. Sound carries a long way in frosty air. They must have realised that we were a large party.

So, I reasoned, as I rode back to the farm for the midday dinner, if the attackers believed the troubadours had something which they wanted but had been unable to find, did that mean they would make another attempt while the musicians were at Leighton Manor? Before I left, I had cautioned Peter once more against this possible danger, but he was not alarmed. I had learned before that his experience as a merchant travelling all over Europe, along perilous roads and over stormy seas, had given him a quiet but clear eyed courage.

'I shall make provision, Nicholas,' he said. 'Fear not! I have been the prey of reckless and dangerous men before this, and I will not risk my family. I brought my own small band of armed men with me on our journey from Bruges, and I have already ordered them to keep watch. I think we shall be in no peril, though I cannot say what may happen to Master de Sarlat and the others when they leave here.'

There was again that slightly odd intonation – ironic – when he said 'de Sarlat', and I recalled that he had been about to make some comment on the name before, when we were interrupted by the arrival of Falquet.

'You do not seem to like the designation "de Sarlat",' I said.

He shrugged. 'I suppose these troubadours may call themselves what they will, although usually they take the place of their birth, or perhaps the manor of their most important patron. I am quite sure that Gaston was not born in Sarlat. Nor, I think, has he ever had a patron from Sarlat, for I have traded there. I do not know of any patron of musicians in or near the town.'

'Why are you so sure that he was not born there? A man may be born somewhere obscure, but leave to seek his fortune elsewhere.'

He smiled. 'You forget, Nicholas, that my business in many countries has made me very familiar with a multitude of languages, dialects, and accents. Gaston speaks Occitan like the brother and sister, and he speaks English and French as well. No doubt other languages, as it suits him. However, he has not quite rid himself of an accent which betrays that he was never born at Sarlat in Aquitaine.'

'You are tantalising me!' I grinned at him. 'What is this elusive and mysterious accent?'

'Castilian,' he said. 'I will take my oath that Gaston *not* "de Sarlat" was born in Castile.'

I pondered this revelation of Peter's as I rode through the village, nodding to my many friends there, and giving them good-day. Did Peter have the right of it? Was Gaston a Castilian? I was inclined to believe him. He was not a man given to baseless imaginings, and I knew very well that he had an excellent ear for languages.

Castilian? It was possible. Even in my brief encounter with Gaston, I had noticed that he had a much darker complexion than the other two musicians, though I suppose that, unconsciously, I had put it down to their reddish hair and pale skins. But Gaston did have a look of a Spaniard. Not that a Castilian would thank me for calling him a Spaniard, for it was a proud independent nation, like the other lands in Iberia and the Pyrenees, such as Aragon and Navarre. A cluster of little lands, always in alliance or enmity with each other.

A few years ago – it must have been the summer of 1348 – King Edward had despatched his young daughter Joan to be married to the heir to the kingdom of Castile,

Prince Pedro, a boy of similar age, who was now the king. The girl was only fourteen at the time, the same age at which Margaret had been married to that brute Elias Makepeace. It was a sad tale, and all England grieved at it.

None of us had realised, heedless in that summer, that a dark cloud was passing over the world. Divine vengeance, so some clerics would come to say, for the sins of mankind. Had our king realised the terror which was about to engulf us, he would surely have kept his daughter by his side, and never let her venture into the black plague making its way insidiously across France.

She landed with a considerable company at our main English port on the west coast of France, Bordeaux, and although the people of the town warned her of the plague stalking their streets, she took up residence in the royal castle there, only to perish, along with many of her party, one of the first English victims of the Great Pestilence, which was to rob me of my wife.

Although the marriage alliance had perished along with the Princess Joan, England and Castile had remained allies, in particular in defending Castile against its neighbour, Aragon. I knew little else about Castile, for we who live outside the circles of royal and noble power are little versed in these affairs, unless some great victory is won by our army, or some great defeat suffered.

However, in the time since Lady Amilia had commissioned the book of troubadour songs from me earlier in the year, I had been striving to learn what I could about them. The peak of the troubadours' fame had been reached some hundred years ago, only to be blighted by the vicious destruction wrought in the south of France during the *soi disant* 'crusade' against the Cathars. The musical tradition had spread out from Occitaine – Provence and Aquitaine – to northern Italy, to some of the German states, and, aye, to Castile.

Now that the troubadours, or the heirs to the tradition, were so dispersed and must earn their livelihood by travelling from place to place instead of dwelling comfortably in the shelter of some great noble's court, it was not surprising that a Castilian musician should have left his homeland, nor that he should have married a girl of the same heritage, albeit that of Provence. Why, then, should he pretend to be from Sarlat? Was it merely for professional reasons? It seemed to me hardly necessary, though there might have been some good reason for it which I did not understand.

And then there was the name, Gaston. That, surely, was not a Castilian name?

I had reached the farm. I shook my head, as though an annoying insect were buzzing about it. Irresistible curiosity had led me into trouble before. Into danger, even. This matter was certainly no concern of mine. I should let it go.

Margaret visited the manor that afternoon and returned to report that the musician Gaston de Sarlat was making a good recovery. He was sitting up, although still confined to bed, and had eaten a light meal at midday.

'And once again we are bidden to join the Winchinghams for dinner tomorrow. I did not feel I could refuse twice.'

'Nay,' Susanna said, 'that you could not. 'Tis no matter. Most of our preparations are complete, save for what must be done at the last minute in any case. We can finish the sweetmeats this evening and tomorrow morning, then go to the manor with a clear conscience, that we have done all that is needful. Are the children to come as well?'

'Aye, young Birgit invited them in particular,' Margaret said. 'What of Maysant, Maud? Is she well enough to go visiting?'

'Well enough, I think,' Maud said. 'She is wild to see the manor. She has been asking Emma if 'tis as fine as her grandfather's home.'

'Not as grand,' I said. 'Sir Anthony Thorgold's manor is part castle, part house. Leighton Manor is a fine gentleman's residence, but all the old fortifications have long been torn down and the stone used to extend the house and build new stables. I hope Maysant may not be disappointed!'

'I do not think she truly remembers Sir Anthony's home.'

'Peter Winchingham and his daughter have some new plans in mind, which they wish to discuss with us,' Margaret said.

'And what are those?' Edmond, coming in from the yard in a cloud of icy air, caught the end of the discussion.

'They will wait to tell us tomorrow,' Margaret said. 'Now, Susanna, set me to work. What have we that still needs to be done?'

'You might make me another batch of marchpane,' my mother said. 'Strangely, I had made a whole tray of Christmas stars yesterday, and today not one is to be found. They have quite disappeared.'

Her face wore a pretended look of complete mystification, but we exchanged a look of understanding. Both Alysoun and Rafe had a great weakness for marchpane, and I suspected that their cousins and allies, Lora and Megan, would know exactly where the Christmas sweetmeats had been stored for safety. However, I would not give them away.

The following day, our large party made its way to the manor in time for dinner just before midday. I had Alysoun before me on Rufus, while Jordain took Rafe, riding one of the cart horses, with a borrowed saddle. For the rest, we were a mixed party, some on horseback and some in Edmond's cart. My mother had confessed to some fatigue after all the busyness of seasonal cooking, and decided to remain quietly at the farm.

There had been another fall of snow in the night, which lay over the bed of frozen snow beneath, on the whole giving a better footing for the horses than the slippery surface packed down in the village street. As we passed the forge, I saw that Bertred Godsmith was fitting two more horses with winter shoes, which are slightly spiked to give the animals a grip on icy roads.

'Still hiring that same beast, Maister Nicholas?' he called.

'He is ours now!' Alysoun shouted. 'Not hired.'

I smiled. The novelty and the sheer grandeur of owning our own horse had not worn off.

'Do you think,' she confided, when we had gone a little further and turned into the lane to the manor, 'that some day I might own a horse?'

'You might,' I said cautiously, not wanting to commit myself to something I might be held to later. 'It would depend on whether you should have need of one. In Oxford, you may walk anywhere.'

'But I might not want to walk. I might want to ride, like a fine lady.'

'Emma walks everywhere in Oxford,' I pointed out, pleased with the astuteness of my argument. 'And she is a fine lady.'

Alysoun continued to ponder this as we rode up to the manor, clearly seeking an answer to counter my argument, but fortunately we were overtaken by the bustle of our arrival and Alysoun was carried off by Birgit along with the rest of the children.

In the stable, once I had removed Rufus's saddle and bridle, and buckled on a blanket, I paused to look into the tack room, from which I had been hearing voices. This tack room was more than a simple store for saddles and bridles, with a few stools for the stable lads. It was at least three times the size of any other tack room I had ever seen, with a substantial fireplace – the fireplace Peter had mentioned – in which a good fire of logs from the manor's woods was burning. The stools and benches for the men had cushions to make them comfortable, simple cushions of rough hessian, to be sure, but cushions nonetheless. I doubted whether even the stable lads in the king's palaces had better. One end of the room was fitted out as a workshop, with a bench and tools for mending harness, and a scattering of other half mended objects – a bucket with a broken handle, part of a manger, and, leaning against the wall, the door to a stall awaiting new hinges.

To my surprise, it was Falquet's voice I had heard, speaking to Aelfric the dog handler and one of the grooms whose name I did not know. He must be one of those who had come from Bruges with the Winchinghams, for he was not one of the villagers. Falquet had cleared a space on the work bench and laid out the pieces of the broken vielle. The three men were examining them.

'Is there any chance it could be mended?' I asked. ''Tis a great pity it has been smashed.'

Falquet glanced up at me.

''Tis not quite as bad as I feared at first. The body has come apart at the joins, but they may be glued together again. It is the neck which is broken into three pieces. I shall need a new piece to shape for that, but Aelfric here thinks he may find me something suitable. His brother is a carpenter.'

'Aye,' I said. 'So he is. What of the bow? And the strings?'

'No difficulty there. We always carry spare strings, and I have another bow. But I shall need to make new pegs for the strings.'

He laid a hand on the scattered pieces, caressing them sadly.

'It had a good tone, the little thing, but I may not be able to restore that.'

He shrugged. 'Still, it was as well it was not Gaston's great lute. That could never have been mended.'

'It was stored away beneath the floor, your sister told me.'

'Aye, there is no room for the instruments amongst all our other possessions. This would not have been in the cart, save that I was trying out a new melody while Gaston took his turn at driving.'

I wondered whether he might share his melody with me for my book, but decided that now was not the time to ask. Best to wait until the troubadours knew me better.

'And the lady Emma tells me that you were able to hide Mistress Azalais in the compartment beneath the floor when you were attacked.'

He looked for a moment alarmed, as though he thought I should not know this. I saw the calculation in his eyes, and the exact moment when he decided it did not matter, and relaxed.

'Aye,' he said. 'We feared what she might suffer at the hands of such men. Better to keep her safe.'

'Yet it seems they cared only to set upon Gaston,' I commented mildly, not looking at him, but fingering the broken pieces of the vielle. 'You told us you were only hurt when you tried to intervene.'

I risked a quick glance at him.

He looked at me nervously, and shrugged. 'Aye, well, it is clear to anyone that Gaston is our leader. No doubt they would have turned on me as well, in time, had they not heard your party coming up.'

'They heard us, did they?'

'One of them said, "There's people in the woods, coming this way." That was when they gave up their search, threw Gaston down, shoved me aside, and mounted their horses. We probably owe our lives to you.'

'And they gave up their search . . . for whatever it was,' I said.

He turned away. 'As I said before, they must have taken us for someone else.'

I thought it wisest not to pursue the matter, for Falquet already seemed suspicious of my repeated probing.

'You are very skilled,' I said, 'if you can really mend this delicate musical instrument.'

He shrugged. 'In our profession we must learn all trades. I can make you a melody, write you a lyric, sing you a *canso* or a *sirventes*, repair an instrument, physic a horse.'

He grinned at me aslant. 'I can even poach a rabbit and cook it for you, but I would never seek to shoot a deer.'

'I should hope not,' I said dryly, 'for there would be

little enough room in your cart to hang a deer carcase to cure. Besides, the penalties are somewhat severe, to pay for a little meat.'

At this he laughed merrily, his good humour restored.

'Ah,' he said, 'but I am looking forward to some grand feasts of venison over the Christmas festivities!'

We walked together across the stable yard to the manor house.

'You told us that you are a bookseller,' Falquet said.

'I am. I have a shop in the High Street of Oxford.'

'Yet your cousin is a yeoman farmer.'

'And so was my father, and my elder brother, before the plague took them. Since my brother was to inherit the farm, it left me free to become a student at Oxford.'

'Like Master Brinkylsworth?'

'Aye,' I said. 'We met as students and have remained friends every since, though our paths diverged. He became a scholar, I a shopkeeper.'

I paused. There was no reason he should not know my history, if I hoped to gain his confidence enough to learn some of his songs.

'My father wanted me to continue as a scholar, and then become a lawyer, perhaps in the royal service. My mother hoped for the priesthood, but Fate took me another way. I fell in love, and married, and so must abandon the life of a scholar.'

'Scholars may not marry?'

'They may not. My wife's father was a bookseller, so I went to work for him, and it was from him that I inherited the shop.'

With his hand on the door, Falquet said hesitantly, 'I think you no longer have a wife.'

'The plague took her,' I said.

For years after Elizabeth's death, I could not speak of it. Even now it cost me dear.

'I too lost a girl in the plague,' he said quietly. 'We were to be married, but we never achieved that happiness.'

'You must have been very young.'

'And you.'

'At least,' I said, 'Elizabeth left me the blessing of two children. And in that I am more fortunate than you.'

For the first time he looked me in the eye with no veil of deception between us.

'In that,' he said, 'you are indeed fortunate.'

Chapter Six

The dinner served at Leighton Manor was excellent, but not ostentatious. It was clear to me that Peter Winchingham was purposefully establishing his own manner of life as soon as he settled here, a manner which would be neither that of the de Veres in the past, a traditional but relaxed custom and hierarchy, nor that of the short lived Gilbert Mordon, all grotesque parade and ill bred hauteur. The table, dishes, and food were immaculate. The servants skilful but not obsequious. And (which I thought significant) both the troubadours and the children sat at table with us.

It was obvious to me, at least, that Peter wished to show the minstrels that he did not rank them amongst the servants. I could not be sure what they made of this, for their faces gave nothing away. From what I had managed to learn while planning my book of songs, in the past many of the troubadours themselves were of high rank, some even noblemen, while those who were of lesser birth had earned, through their talents, a high place in the households of their noble patrons. Amongst the great houses of Provence a hundred years ago, they would have been counted as courtiers.

All that had changed now, with the slaughter meted out by the French on those great houses, whether or not they were Catholic or Cathar. The troubadours, having lost their high positions, had themselves been driven into a wandering life, like this small group, and one could be sure that they were often treated no better than vagabonds or mountebanks, despite their musical and poetic skills, and their remarkable heritage. It was a tragic decline. In the past also, there had been a distinction between the troubadours, who wrote the songs, and the jongleurs, who performed them, the jongleurs often looked down upon by the troubadours. In our present day, groups of musicians like Gaston's might be no more than jongleurs, but others were both troubadours and jongleurs, writing their songs and performing them. From what I had already observed, these three were themselves composers of songs, perhaps even Azalais, for there were indeed trobairiz, women troubadours, the first women ever to write secular music.

We must hope that Peter's matter-of-fact kindness would earn the trust of Gaston, so that if he needed help, he would confide in us. There was little sign of that yet, but the last part of my conversation with Falquet as we walked over from the stable gave me some hope that he was relaxing his mistrust of me.

Gaston himself had left his bed and dined with us, having exchanged his large bandage for a much smaller one, although he still moved stiffly, due to the bruises Margaret had mentioned. Apart from this, he seemed much recovered, although there were dark shadows under his eyes, as though he had slept badly. No surprise in this, for he must have been in considerable pain. Margaret had offered him some of her precious poppy syrup, but he had refused it. Was this a determined stoicism? Or did he wish to remain alert, for reasons of his own?

I was delighted to find that our village priest, Sire Raymond, was also to be of the party, for I had not yet had the chance to visit my old teacher, although Margaret had seen him. I knelt for his blessing, and when I stood, he embraced me warmly.

'Ah, it is good to see you again, Nicholas!' he said. 'I had feared that you would spend the Christmas season in Oxford.'

'We thought it better that my mother should not

travel this winter,' I said.

'Indeed. But you have had adventures on your way, so I hear, as well as blizzards and bitter cold.'

'The attack near Witney?' I said. 'I was glad we were able to travel with a company of soldiers from Oxford castle. We were never in real danger.'

'Hmm,' he said. 'By what I hear, it came close. And what of these poor troubadours? That is a bad business.'

'It is,' I said soberly. 'And in Wychwood itself, so close to the manor house.'

'Sad times,' he said. 'Sad times.'

After we had eaten, Birgit carried off all the children to her own chamber.

'I have brought with me,' she said, 'all my childhood toys and games, for I could not bear to leave them behind with my brother in Bruges, but I have had no chance to unpack them yet. There are two whole barrels full! Would you like to come and help me? We can see what we shall find.'

The invitation was greeted with delight by all the children, who ran off with her.

'I will come with you,' Hilda said, clearly having no wish to sit long over sleepy after dinner talk.

'And I too,' Juliana agreed.

Peter smiled at their retreating forms.

'Birgit knows already what I want to discuss with you,' he said, 'and she is fond of children, not much past childhood herself. Let us adjourn to the small parlour, where I have sent for wine and nuts.'

The three boys also asked to be excused. They were eager to exercise their horses while the winter daylight remained, and ran off to the stables.

'If you have no need of us, Master Winchingham,' Gaston said, bowing, 'we would like to tune our instruments and practice a little. We must think what to prepare for your entertainment at Christmastide.'

'Aye,' Peter said, 'if that is what you wish. Will you

stay here in the hall?'

'Not at present. The chamber you have given to me and Azalais will serve very well.'

They left us, going first out to the barn where their cart had been stored, to fetch their instruments – all but the broken vielle, I supposed. As we crossed the passage to the small parlour we heard them climbing the stairs, talking softly in Occitan.

Once we were settled, with cups of wine and dishes of nuts, Peter beamed round at us all.

'I have invited you here not merely for the pleasure of your company over dinner, but because I have a scheme in mind which I shall not take forward without your advice and encouragement. We have here my old friends Margaret, Nicholas, and Jordain, together with Maud Farringdon and Lady Emma from Oxford, Master and Mistress Elyot from here in Leighton, and Sire Raymond to speak for the church.'

'This sounds most solemn,' Edmond said, 'but I pray you, do not stand upon ceremony. We are Edmond and Susanna in this company, if it please you.'

'I shall be most happy.' Peter bowed in acknowledgement.

'Now,' he said, with the air of coming to the matter at hand. I could envisage him thus, sitting down to do business with a party of fellow merchants, and smiled to myself.

'I have heard something of the history of this manor,' Peter said. 'It was held for generations by a family both honoured and loved hereabouts, the de Veres, who are remembered still with great affection in the village.'

'That is very true,' Sire Raymond said.

'The world is so changed, these last days,' Peter went on, 'yet it cannot be more than a few years since the death of the de Veres.'

'The last child, one of the girls, died four and a half years ago,' Sire Raymond said, 'near the end of the Great Pestilence. She was a lovely child, bright and happy, until all her family perished around her.'

I knew that Sire Raymond had sat with each member of the family in their dying agonies, but did not speak of it.

Peter nodded soberly. 'And then the manor passed to the king?'

'Not directly,' Edmond said. 'There was a kinsman in Leicestershire, but in those troubled times he did not want the responsibility of a manor so far from his own seat. Then I think he sold it to the king. At any rate, it passed into the hands of the king.'

'And he gave it to this fellow Mordon?'

The others looked at me, for I had found myself entangled in Mordon's affairs.

'We do not know the whole of it,' I said, 'but Mordon had made several large loans of money to the king for his French wars, and was given the manor to clear some of the debt. There was considerable deception in the matter, for the manor was worth much more than Mordon's lawyer claimed. The king found that he had been cheated. After Mordon was killed, the king took possession again.'

'That is more or less my understanding of the matter,' Peter said. 'And both the king's lawyers and my own have carefully assessed the property and agreed a value which is acceptable both to His Majesty and myself.' He smiled. 'The king still has need of considerable sums of money for the wars, since no one expects the current truce to last. All now seems to be arranged satisfactorily, and I am in full possession of the manor and its rights.'

I wondered whether Peter had brought us here simply to make this clear, but that did not seem like him. As he moved about, refilling our wine cups, a distant sound of singing drifted down to us. A sweet, pure woman's voice soared above a man's deep bass, then a tenor joined, his melody following after the treble, weaving about it, like figures in a dance. I found myself gaping at Peter.

He smiled. 'I told you they were gifted.'

'More than gifted,' I answered. I nearly said 'the voices of angels', but checked myself, aware of Sire

Raymond's presence.

A man always full of surprises. 'So the angels might have sung,' he said, 'leaning down from Heaven over a humble stable.'

Emma smiled at me.

We all strained to listen, but the voices broke off and we heard a phrase or two on a lute and another instrument, perhaps a small viol, then the music stopped.

Bringing us back to the matter under discussion, Peter sat down and leaned forward, his hands on his knees.

'Now that I hold the manor of Leighton, I want to show the people of Leighton village that they have nothing to fear from me. I cannot bring back the de Veres, but I want to make it clear to them that, although I too am a merchant, I am not made of the same stuff as the fellow Gilbert Mordon, of whom I have heard so many sorry tales.'

'He did a great deal of harm in his short time here,' Edmond said. 'I think the wounds are mostly healed, though the scars remain.'

Peter nodded. 'I know there was a claim that a certain free man was of villein rank. I have had my lawyer draw up a document for him, stating that he is freeborn. The matter of your mill stream, Edmond, is in hand. I also intend to make it clear to all my tenants that those who wish to pay rent in coin or kind, instead of customary labour and boon days, may do so, and if I should need additional labour for ploughing and sowing, or at harvest time, it will be paid for. Have I forgot aught?'

Maud and Emma remained silent, for they were new to the village, and knew nothing of these matters.

'Gleaning,' Susanna said. 'The village women used to be permitted to glean in the manor fields after harvest, but Mordon forbade it.'

'That right shall be restored. Anything further?'

'I seem to remember,' Jordain said, 'that when we were here last, there was some dispute over rabbits.'

'Aye,' I agreed. 'The manor holds rights of warren,

but over the years many of the rabbits have escaped and bred in the wild. They can ravage the villagers' vegetable plots. Yves de Vere always turned a blind eye if one of them snared a coney on his own land, but Mordon threatened to fine and punish any who did so.'

'I do not believe I have rights of warren over *wild* rabbits,' Peter said. 'So there shall be no such threats on my part. What of pannage? Do the villagers have the customary right for their pigs to forage in my woods?'

'In the past, they did,' Sire Raymond said. 'None dared take their pigs into Wychwood in Mordon's time, for fear he would seize them. Of course, the season for fattening the pigs before Michaelmas, on the fallen nuts and acorns in the forest, was the very time the manor stood empty again. I believe some men took advantage of that, with their swine.'

'It was their right,' Peter said simply. 'That right also shall be restored. If you think of any other wrongs or grievances, bring them to me, and I shall do what I may to set them right. My own early life was not wealthy, and I know how small distresses may become a threat to life itself, if you are poor. The villagers will of course have the customary right to gather firewood, by hook or by crook. There should be an abundance for all in Wychwood.'

I thought that now Peter had consulted us over these village affairs, he would have done, but it seemed he had further matters on his mind.

'When I was a boy, over in the Herefordshire border land near Wales, there was always a great feast held by the lord once the harvest was gathered in. I shall do the same, but I am not minded to wait some nine months to greet my tenants and villagers. What do you say to a great feast for Christmas, to which all shall be invited?'

He sat back, looking expectant. Margaret and Susanna exchanged a glance. Maud opened her mouth to say something, then closed it again. She was the visitor here. Emma was watching Peter with a look of lively interest. The women already had matters well in hand for our own Christmas celebrations, although we had not yet heard from Peter whether we should receive a portion of the deer we had helped to bring down. I was not sure whether they would like this idea of a great feast for all, in place of our household meal. I kept my tongue behind my teeth and waited to see what they would say.

'Can you explain what you have in mind, Peter?' Margaret asked cautiously. I could see that she thought it awkward for Susanna to ask, as mistress of our family farm and thus Peter's neighbour.

'There are two places it might be held.' He fixed his gaze on her, with all the eagerness of a boy. 'Like a harvest feast, it might be held in my biggest barn. I have already enlarged it with two further bays at the far end, for my purpose is to use it as a weaving shed. At the moment, it stands empty. It would provide room aplenty for all. However, the weather may prove too cold, even with braziers inside and large fires in the yard, in which case we could use the great hall of the manor. It is smaller, but might be made to serve.'

'I recall when I was a boy,' Sire Raymond said, 'that Yves de Vere's father once held the harvest dinner there. We managed to save the crops just in time before the weather broke. Terrible storms we had that year, and more than usual reason to celebrate and give thanks, for it seemed like a second Flood! It would have been impossible to hold the feast outside in the usual way, so Sir Everard held it in the hall here. We were crowded, but it was possible. Now, since the plague, the village is barely half the size. I am sure the hall would prove large enough.'

Peter looked pleased at this, but turned again to where Margaret and Susanna sat regarding him thoughtfully.

'It is not my wish to give offence to anyone,' he said, 'and I suppose each family will be planning its own Christmas celebrations, but do you think the village would look favourably on my suggestion? Tell me at once, if you think I am quite mistaken.'

Susanna answered slowly. 'I cannot speak for the whole village. For ourselves, we have been preparing for our own Christmastide.' She glanced aside at Margaret, who gave a small nod. 'But I think we might rearrange matters. I suppose it might be best if we spoke to some of the village women. Was it your thought to hold this feast on the Nativity, or on Twelfth Day?'

'Here,' Peter said, 'I must be guided by Sire Raymond.'

The priest gave his sweet, unassuming smile.

'I shall hold the usual services. A Mass at midnight on the Eve, to herald the birth of the Christ Child. Then on the Nativity, the full canonical hours. For myself, I should have little time for feasting on the Nativity. Most of the villagers come to the midnight Mass and to some of the services on the Nativity.'

'That is what I suspected,' Peter said. 'So the Nativity might not be the best choice. What say you to Twelfth Day?'

'Epiphany? There will be a service, of course, but Epiphany is traditionally a day for joyous celebration and the giving of gifts. Some aspects may even be traced back to our forefathers' days, in pagan time.'

He laughed apologetically.

'Nicholas may have told you of this hobby of mine, studying the old customs. The turning of the year from the darkest day to the gradual coming of light has been celebrated for as long as men have lived. And the holly and the ivy, which we take to be the symbols of Christ's blood and everlasting life, were believed even in those ancient times to promise the renewal of life. The Magi brought gifts to the new born Babe on Epiphany, and we give gifts in His memory, but I believe some kind of gift giving may have been associated with the winter festival even before Christ's coming.'

He gave a little cough.

'Forgive me. I am carried away by my enthusiasms, and talk too much.'

'I think you talk a great deal of sense,' Peter said, 'and to the point. Let it be Twelfth Day, then, and let it mark a new beginning for Leighton Manor and the village, after the recent dark years.'

It seemed we were all agreed that, if the feast for the whole village were to be held, then it should be Twelfth Day. Margaret and Susanna were adamant, however, that the women of the village – at least those with the highest status and loudest voices – must be consulted before a final decision could be made. Maud laughed at this choice of counsellors, but agreed that it was wisest.

'There is one further matter,' Peter said. 'And I hesitate to ask it, but the scheme cannot go ahead without. My daughter Birgit is a good girl and tries hard to fill her mother's place in organising my household, yet she is but sixteen. To manage such an undertaking would be beyond her, I fear, though I know she would strive her best.'

He smiled winningly at the women. 'Could I prevail upon you to take it in hand?'

'Birgit would not be offended?' Margaret asked.

'She would be relieved, beyond measure. She likes the idea of inviting all the village, to show how we mean the manor to be managed from now on, but she fears her capabilities. It was she who suggested you.'

Margaret and Susanna looked at each other, then consulted with Emma and Maud in low voices.

'In that case,' Margaret said, 'should the plan go ahead, we shall be glad to help.'

We did not see the troubadours again before we left the manor, although snatches of their music drifted down, tantalising us. The boys were nowhere to be seen, but Peter promised to send James and Thomas home as soon as they returned from their ride. Extracting the children from Birgit's chamber was rather more difficult, and they emerged each clutching toys she had given them. They all elected to travel in the cart, driven by Maud, so that they might examine their trophies more easily than on horse back.

'You were very quiet during the discussion with Peter,' I said to Emma, who was riding down the lane to the village beside me.

'It was not my place to say anything,' she said. 'This is my first time in Leighton, so I can know nothing of village affairs, or how the people would react to his suggestion of a Twelfth Day feast.'

'Do you not think it a good plan, then?'

'Oh, indeed I do!' she said. 'When I was a child, before the plague, before my father died and my mother married again, we lived at my grandfather's manor. He used to give a feast for his tenants on Twelfth Day. It was a joyous time, and very exciting for a small girl. Then everything changed. I do not think he has done so since.'

'So you are in favour? Why did you not say so?'

'Not my place,' she repeated. 'Those troubadours – such beautiful voices! Did you ever hear the like?'

I turned over in my mind such singing as I had heard in my life.

'There are some wonderful choirs in Oxford,' I said, 'but of course they sing ecclesiastical music. The boys' voices are very pure, but that girl's voice . . . it made me shiver.'

She gave me a teasing smile. 'Ah, but she sang of love. And not the love of God!'

'You could hear and understand the words?'

'I did not need to.'

At that she laughed and rode ahead, where she was soon deep in conversation with Margaret.

Susanna decided to stop in the village, so that she might begin at once to sound out the views of the women. Their opinions might swing either way. A great feast for their families might be welcome, but they might still be suspicious of the new lord of the manor, after their brief but unpleasant experience of Gilbert Mordon. And, just as likely, they might not care to have their own carefully laid plans for the season disrupted. Susanna asked Margaret to go with her, so they left us to call on Joan Carter, Beth Wodville, and Martha Godsmith, all being women of some standing amongst the other villagers. The rest of us continued to the farm, where we found my mother rested and supervising the servants, some of whom had once been her own servants.

'The beasts are fed,' she said to Edmond, 'the afternoon milking finished, and the poultry shut away for the night, since it is not long till dark. I was not certain how much you would have eaten, since you seem to have been gone a good while, but there is a thick vegetable soup, and bread baked this morning.'

'We have not been eating this whole while, Mother,' I said, picking her up by the waist and whirling her about as she used to do to me when I was a child.

'Put me down, you foolish boy!' she cried. 'What are you about?'

'What do you say to the idea of a vast Twelfth Day feast for the whole village?' I said, setting her carefully on her feet. 'Held in the great hall of the manor house?'

'I say it will mean a great deal of cooking,' she said dryly.

Although we sat for some time after the children were abed, discussing all of Peter's plans for the manor and for a Twelfth Day feast, we were not late ourselves to retire. Before I blew out my candle, I opened the shutters and looked out, for it had grown dark early, with increasing cloud. Yesterday that had meant snow in the night, and now I saw that the pattern was repeating. Already the snow was falling quite heavily. We should need to dig our way to the barns and stable tomorrow, if it continued all night.

I slept soundly until a disturbance woke me and I groped for my strike-a-light. The candle did not catch at once, and when it did, I looked about blearily. It could not be dawn yet, there was still that feeling of deep darkness, but not the silence of the middle of the night. I realised I had been woken by a voice calling, and now there were more voices, and doors closing, feet thudding down the stairs.

It was difficult to drag myself out from the warmth of my bed, for the chamber was bitterly cold, but I flung my cloak over my night shift and, picking up my candle, went to the top of the stairs. There was nothing to be seen but a faint wash of light from below, so I made my way down as quietly as I might, clutching my cloak about me for warmth and hoping not to disturb any more of the sleepers. In the kitchen I found Edmond and Jordain, and, to my astonishment, Hans Winchingham. All looked worried.

'What's afoot?' I said. 'Hans, what are you doing here, in the middle of the night?'

'We have been attacked,' he said, his carefree bravado quite vanished away. 'The manor has been attacked. My father sent me to warn you that there are men roaming the village and to take measures to protect yourselves. And indeed,' he pointed to the door, 'your door was not even locked. I walked straight in.'

'Come you and sit down,' Edmond said, pulling out a stool by the table. After his first moment of shock, he spoke calmly. 'Tell us exactly what has happened.'

We seated ourselves at the table, then Edmond got to his feet again and fetched a pitcher of ale and cups.

'We were abed,' Hans said, once he had drunk deeply, 'and settled for the night, when the hunting dogs – it must have been the alaunts – began to bark. That disturbed the horses. I do not think they were greatly frightened, but there was some kicking of the partitions of the stalls. I thought it might be a wolf got into the stable yard.'

Edmond shook his head. 'There have been no wolves hereabouts in my lifetime. Though I suppose there may be some living to the north, and driven this way by the winter weather.'

'Nay.' Hans shook his head. 'These wolves walked upon two legs. They had broken into the barn where the troubadours have stored their cart. Then, the next we knew, one was scrambling up the ivy on the house wall, trying to reach a window, though God be thanked all were tight shuttered. My father and I saw him as we came outside and my father shouted and the man fell, but landed soft, for the snow is so thick. Then he took to his heels.'

'Was he alone?' I asked.

'There were four of them. Or at least we saw four. There might have been more. My father roused the men, and we searched. Their horses had been left in the lane, for we found the signs, but by then they were gone.'

'It was dangerous for you to come riding over here alone,' Jordain chided him, and I thought how careful he was for the safety of the students in his charge, all the more since the death of Emma's cousin, William Farringdon.

'I was not alone, most of the way,' Hans said. 'Others have gone to warn Sire Raymond and the men of the village. I was alone only riding up your lane. We were afeared there might be a general attack on Leighton, and all should stand prepared.'

I looked at Edmond and Jordain, and saw that they thought as I did.

'Hans,' I said quietly, 'it was good advice to warn us, but does it not seem to you, and to your father, that this is no general attack? Surely it is the troubadours once again who are sought.'

'We could not be sure,' he said. 'Certainly, the rogues went first to the barn where the troubadours have stored their cart, but their intention might have been to steal something else. In the dark, they may even have mistaken it for the stable and been intent on our horses.'

I did not pursue this, but thought it noteworthy that the thieves – if that was what they were – had known where to find that humble cart, which had provoked such interest.

'Which window did it seem that the man was seeking?' I said. 'The man who climbed the ivy?'

Hans shrugged. 'The first he would have reached is an empty bed chamber. Most of the bed chambers face that way.'

So, I thought, they might have discovered where the troubadours were lodged, or it might have been mere chance. It was possible that the man was simply seeking a way into the house.

'Their horses had been left in the lane, did you say?' Jordain asked.

'Aye, there were clear signs. The snow churned up, and horse droppings.'

Jordain looked at me. 'Nicholas, did the men who attacked the troubadours in Wychwood not come down the forest ride?'

I nodded. I too had noticed this discrepancy.

'They did. Whereas tonight's intruders seem to have come up the lane, from the opposite direction, from the village.'

'So you think it is some other enemy?' Hans said.

'Nay.' I shook my head. 'What I think is that they have remained somewhere in the neighbourhood and have scouted out the different ways to reach the manor. I do not like this. And I very much doubt whether we are in danger here on the farm, or the rest of the village.'

'You cannot be certain,' Hans said.

'We cannot,' Edmond said, 'but I think Nicholas has the right of it. For some reason, some person, or some people, are pursuing your musicians, and are mighty keen to lay hands on them.'

'On them,' I said, 'or on something they have in their possession. Have you seen anything to cause you to wonder, Hans?'

He shook his head. 'Everything seems quite open and innocent. Since Gaston is still somewhat enfeebled, I and one of our men helped Falquet unload the cart and carry everything withindoors. He made no attempt to hide anything. Nor have they kept anyone from their bed chambers. The maids have been in and out. There is nothing concealed. How can there be aught to interest these rogues?'

'I do not know,' I said.

Except, I thought, perhaps a message that one of them has memorised. But for whom could it be intended?

Edmond rose from his stool.

'I think we should dress and ride back with Hans to the manor. Perhaps we can give Peter some reassurance. Or more may have been discovered.'

'I agree,' I said.

'And I shall come.' Jordain rose. 'I could not sleep after this.'

Edmond nodded. 'Susanna woke when we heard Hans arrive, but I bade her remain in bed. I will tell her to bolt the door after us. You have the right of it, Hans. Here in the village we are apt to forget that these are lawless times. It is a sad judgement on the world that we cannot sleep safe unless we lock our doors, but until this matter is settled, 'tis best we should do so. Sad days.'

And, I thought, but did not say, if these rogues have been keeping a watch, they may know that we have visited the manor several times. That might give them the idea that something, this mysterious object, might have been passed to one of us. It was not a pleasant thought, particularly since such a thing might have been slipped into a pocket without our knowing. What in the name of all the saints could it be?

We were soon dressed and mounted, and Susanna had duly bolted the door after us. James had woken before we left, and demanded to accompany us, but Edmond had instructed him, as the oldest man left on the farm, that he must take charge of the women and children. In all the pride of his eighteen years, James had accepted.

It was still snowing, and full dark. We had all equipped ourselves with candle lanterns, but even so it was slow and treacherous going, despite the familiarity of the road. In the village we found people astir, slivers of light showing along window shutters, two women with their heads together at the Carters' doorway, a cluster of men outside Bertred Godsmith's forge. The huntsman Alan was there amongst them, and I rode over to him.

'Any further sighting of these men?' I asked.

In the glow from my lantern, I could see him shake his head.

'Long gone,' he said. 'Though by the prints in the snow, it is certain they came this way, heading for the Burford road.'

'What do you make of it?' I said.

'Hard to say. After that affair in Wychwood, it would seem they are the same fellows, though it was too dark for any at the manor to say for sure. We hardly saw them in any case, the day of the hunt. Just their horses' hindquarters disappearing up the ride. And this time no one even saw their horses, only the traces of them.'

'Aye,' I said, 'for myself, I could not identify the men who were there in the wood, nor their mounts, though these fellows seem to be pursuing the same prey.'

'Have you any notion why?' he asked.

'None that makes any sense. And Peter Winchingham's boy says that everything is open and innocent about the troubadours. They are concealing nothing.'

'Perhaps it is a mistake, as they claimed when we first saw them on the ride.'

'Perhaps.' I knew that I did not sound convincing, for I could not convince myself.

I shivered unintentionally, and not from the cold.

'I mislike the thought that they have been lurking hereabouts, spying out the land and the manor house.'

He grunted in agreement.

Peter Winchingham rode over to me.

'I fear we have stirred up a wasps' nest unnecessarily,' he said apologetically. 'Had we been quicker, we might have called out the hue and cry, but we tumbled out of the house in our night shifts, half fuddled with sleep. And they were quick. By the time we were fully in our senses, they were gone – men, horses, and all.'

'But empty handed,' I said.

'So we believe. Else why would that fellow have been trying to climb into the house?'

'Very true. And what of the troubadours? Where are they now?'

'Still in the house,' he said. 'I bade them stay within and bolt the doors. So you think, as I do, that they are the source of the trouble?'

'They seem to draw trouble, as the tall tree draws the lightning.'

'I cannot see any reason why. Perhaps it is, in truth, all a tangle of misunderstanding.' He turned his horse about. 'I shall tell the men of the village to go back to their beds. There is little point in going in pursuit now. The rogues will be halfway to Burford by this. We could never catch them.'

Soon the villagers had dispersed, and one by one the candles and rush dips in the cottages began to go out. Only Alan remained with us, together with the two Winchinghams, and some of their men servants.

'In the morning,' Alan said, 'I can set one of the tracking dogs to pick up the scent, if this latest snow has not wiped out all trace of it. We know they left through the village, but where were they before?'

'Aye,' I said, 'it would be good to know whether they have friends in these parts.'

'Let us hope not,' Edmond said gravely. 'I do not like the sound of that.'

'Nor I,' said Peter. 'It worries me that I seem to have brought trouble to your peaceful village. I would not wish to do so.'

'I do not think you brought it,' I said. 'It was the troubadours.'

'Aye, and I brought the troubadours.'

'The blame lies with these rogues, and no one else,' Jordain said firmly.

'Aye.' Edmond turned his horse and began to ride toward the lane which led to the manor.

'Do you go home to your beds,' Peter said. 'There is

133

nothing we can do now.'

'I'll to mine,' Alan said, 'but I shall be with you soon after dawn.'

He turned and walked off to his cottage, but Jordain and I followed after Edmond.

'We will see you safely home,' I told Peter. 'And mere curiosity means we cannot rest without seeing the scene of this attack.'

'There is nothing to see,' Peter said, 'but come if you will.'

Peter had the right of it. The snow was already beginning to obliterate the disturbance in the lane where the intruders' horses had been left. We could just make out the churned area where they had stood, restive in the cold, and one pile of horse droppings, almost hidden by now.

When we reached the manor house, light showed round the shutters of windows both upstairs and downstairs, but they had been kept closed. There was a dull gleam also over the stables, where one of the lads who slept there must have been awake and keeping watch on the horses.

'Here is where they went first,' Peter said, as we dismounted.

He led us over to a small barn. The door stood ajar, splintered wood showing where it had been forced open. I held up my lantern and looked about. There was little of interest to see. The place was used for storage. There were two handcarts here, and a stack of barrels, and some discarded pieces of ox harness. Nearest the door stood the cart I recognised as the one belonging to the troubadours. I went to it and cast my eye over it.

The canvas hood had been peeled off the supporting hoops, rolled up neatly, and stowed on the floor beside the cart. The interior, as I had expected from what Hans had said, was quite empty, though the cupboard doors stood ajar, and the hatch to the instrument store had clearly been tossed roughly aside, not by the minstrels. It was a large compartment, larger than I had realised, reaching almost the entire length of the cart. I leaned over and peered inside. There was nothing there other than a bundle of broken strings, for a lute or some other instrument. Again, as Hans had said, all was open and innocent.

'There is certainly nothing here worth so much eagerness to steal,' I said. 'Can you show us where the man tried to climb in?'

Hans led us round the corner of one wing of the house. The snow, which had been falling quite softly ever since we had left the farm, seemed suddenly to take a malevolent turn as we faced into the north wind, so that I was forced to screw up my eyes.

'Here,' Hans said, pointing.

It was clear to see. The ivy clinging to the wall was well established, spreading out from a great thick stem, of some years growth, with solid branches reaching out from it, clinging with their deadly and insidious arms to the stone of the undercroft and the timbers and plaster of the upper storey. Gilbert Mordon had had some of the creepers cleared from the house, but this back wall had not been touched and the ivy here offered firm footholds and handholds for an agile man to climb. The thief – if such he was – had torn away some of the smaller tendrils as he climbed, or in his hasty descent, so that they hung down, broken.

'I cannot think what he hoped to gain by this,' I said. 'It would have been difficult to gain entrance through the shutters.' I turned to Peter. 'Are they bolted on the inside?'

'Some are, some aren't,' he said. 'All those on the ground floor, aye. Not all those above. It has not seemed to be the most pressing need, bolts on the upper windows.'

'You would not think so,' Jordain said, tilting back his head and looking up. We could see quite clearly how far the man had climbed. 'An intrepid climber. I should not care to attempt it myself.'

'And in the dark and snow,' Edmond said. 'Well, I suppose there is naught we can do more tonight. Let us hope Alan's dogs may pick up a scent tomorrow, despite the snow.' He pulled his cloak closely about his throat and turned his back to the wind. 'Yet I hold out little hope, after this latest fall.'

'Come you within and take something to warm you, before you set off home,' Peter urged. 'If I know my daughter, she will be up and about, waiting anxiously for us to return.'

Edmond looked at me, and I shook my head.

'Nay,' he said, 'I think we had best be on our way. Our own womenfolk will also be awake and waiting.'

We walked back to where the horses stood, heads down and shivering. I ran my hand apologetically down Rufus's shoulder.

'Not long, old fellow,' I said.

I turned to Peter. 'I agree with my cousin. There is little we can do until the morning.'

Peter nodded and turned to his son. 'Take our horses to the stable, Hans. I will try to persuade Birgit and the troubadours to unbolt the door for us, else we must join the horses in the straw.'

He dismissed his men, who had been standing, shivering like the horses, and they went off thankfully enough.

I mounted as we heard the heavy bolts on the back door of the manor house being drawn back. This back door was the way I had often come as a boy, to sample treats in the kitchen, or to join the de Vere children in some game. I had never known the door to be bolted before. As both Sire Raymond and Edmond had said, sad times.

I leaned down to speak to Peter, as Edmond and Jordain wheeled their horses and started down the lane.

'I shall come back tomorrow, Peter,' I said. 'After this night's work, I think we must speak seriously to these troubadours of yours. I do not believe they have been mistaken for someone else. The pursuers are much too determined. They need help and must confide in someone, and that surely must be you.'

'We shall try to gain their confidence,' he said, 'but

136

they have shown themselves very determined in their protested innocence and denials.'

'All three *must* be in on the secret,' I said. 'Else how could they keep up such a concerted pretence? Emma says that troubadours are partly players, and suspects they may take on a feigned role with ease.'

'She probably has the right of it.'

The door opened, and the light flooding out through the snow showed Birgit, with her hand holding the collar of one of the big hunting alaunts.

'Brave girl,' I murmured to Peter. 'They are chancy dogs, even with their own handlers.'

He shook his head. 'Brave perhaps, but perhaps also foolhardy. She may have wanted protection, but I shall see the beast returned to the kennels. Get you home to your bed, Nicholas, before you and your horse turn to ice in my yard.'

I waved a farewell to Birgit, tapped Peter lightly on the shoulder, and turned Rufus to follow the others down the lane. The candle in my lantern was nearly burnt out, and I hoped that between them the other two might have more light.

The ride back to the farm was dark, cold, and miserable. All our lanterns were out before we reached it, even though we had made them last by only using one at a time. We were caked with snow, as were our horses, and my hands were so cold, even inside my thick leather gloves, that I could barely feel the reins. Thankfully, Rufus knew the way without much guidance from me, and he was as anxious to reach the shelter of his stall as I was to reach my own warm bed.

Through the driving snow, which had gradually grown more and more dense, it was a relief to catch sight of the lantern Susanna had set outside the farmhouse door, and James ran out to help us with the horses. Rubbing Rufus down restored some life to my numb fingers, and he showed his thanks for the double blankets by butting me on the shoulder and blowing in my ear.

The farm kitchen was a warm and welcome haven, all the more so because Susanna and Margaret were both up and dressed, and had a pot of soup on the fire for us. At first my teeth chattered so much on the spoon that I could barely take a sup, but gradually I began to thaw, as if my very blood and bones were ice, melting in the heat of the fierce kitchen fire.

'Well?' Margaret said. 'What news? James thinks the whole village has been roused, armed with their pitchforks and billhooks, to repel an invading army.'

She spoke mockingly, but I could see that she was worried.

'I never said–' James protested.

'No sign of the intruders,' Edmond said, reassuringly, stretching out his wet hose to the fire, for the snow had penetrated even through our boots. 'No cause for alarm. Ridden away to Burford, for all we can tell.'

'God be thanked,' Susanna said.

'And tomorrow,' I said, with more firmness than I felt, 'the troubadours must be persuaded to tell us what trouble lies behind this.'

Chapter Seven

When I rode over to the manor house the following morning, it was to find Alan Wodville and his nephew Rob setting two of the most experienced lymers to the scent of the intruders, by leading them repeatedly to the spot where the horses had been left the previous night, and encouraging them to pick up the trail.

'Have you any hope of success, Alan?' I said, reining Rufus in.

He shook his head.

'As I feared, too much snow has fallen since. It stopped around dawn, but by then all traces of men and horses were buried deep. We cleared away the top layer, but apart from the horse droppings, there is nothing left, and these dogs are trained to seek out deer, not to follow a horse from the scent of his droppings.'

'Well,' I said, 'you have done your best, but I suppose there was never much chance of tracking them to where they came from. Have you asked in the village whether anyone saw strangers riding through, making for the manor?'

'Aye, I have that, but 'twas a cold night, and most folk were tucked up in bed early. 'Tis my guess that the rogues never came past until well after midnight.'

'I agree. They would not want to risk being seen. Had the alaunts not raised the alarm once they broke into the barn, it is possible no one would have been roused even in the manor house.'

'Do you think they could have broken into the house?' he said.

'I misdoubt it. Even had the man who climbed the ivy been able to find a window where the shutters were not bolted, they would still have been hooked together. The noise he would have made, breaking them open, would surely have roused the household.'

'Seems like desperate measures then, do you reckon?'

'Aye,' I said thoughtfully, 'it does.'

'We'll be off then, and return the dogs to the kennels. We can do no good here.'

'I am come to see Peter Winchingham. I shall tell him that you have done your best, but there is nothing for the dogs to follow. Since they rode away toward Burford, it may be that they came that way too.'

'Easy enough for them to hide themselves amongst the folk in the town.'

'Hmm.' I did not altogether agree with this. To the villagers of Leighton, Burford might seem a town, but it had never been a large one, and like everywhere else in England was much diminished since the Great Pestilence. Wayfarers travelling from London and Oxford along the main highway to Gloucester and Wales would regularly spend the night at one of Burford's inns, but they would be noticed, nonetheless. It might be worth making enquires there.

I rode on up the lane, Alan and the boy trudging through the snow behind me, while the dogs frisked about, seeing this outing in the snow as an occasion for play.

One of the maids showed me into the small parlour, where I found Peter writing letters.

'Working even at Christmastide?' I said. ''Tis but two days until Christmas Eve.'

He grinned, motioning me to a chair, as he sealed his last letter and stamped it with an engraved gem stone mounted on a handle.

'We merchants must always be thinking ahead. I am

ordering some light weight silk brocade and samite from my son at Bruges. By the time they reach here, it will be late spring. And a merchant I deal with in Danzig has written asking the price of my various cloths of good Cotswold wool. For the moment I must buy in my bolts from Witney, but soon, God willing, I shall be making my own.'

'I thought you planned only coarse goods, for blankets and the like.'

'That was my first plan, but one of the master weavers in Bruges is an Englishman, and like me he wants to return home, now that the king is establishing the Staple in England. Also like me, he took a Flemish wife, and she would not at first be persuaded, but now he has written to say that they are to come, once the winter is past and the sea crossing bearable. I shall employ him.'

'Soon you will be rivalling the weavers of Witney.'

He laughed. 'They have nothing to fear from me.' He glanced toward the window. 'The snow has ceased for a time, I see.'

'Aye, but Alan had a hopeless task. His dogs could pick up no scent. I passed them in the lane, and the dogs thought it was nothing but sport.'

'I feared it would be so.'

He set aside his writing materials. 'Shall we try our luck with the troubadours? After what happened in the night, I cannot believe they will still keep up their pretence that nothing is amiss.'

'I am not so sure. It must be something of the gravest import, to occasion two attacks, or attempts at searching. They must have been told to keep silent, I think. What do you suppose can lie at the centre of this?'

He shrugged. 'Could they be carrying some object of great value, which they were asked to deliver while on their travels? Perhaps a reliquary of gold and jewels, containing a precious bone of some saint?'

I thought about various reliquaries I had seen in the Oxford churches, and shook my head.

'Surely a reliquary would be far too large? Whatever it is, it must be small enough to be concealed about their persons, for Hans told us that the contents of their cart and of their bed chambers have been open for all to see.'

'Aye, there is truth in that. Though I have seen one very small reliquary in a church in France. It contained a nail clipping of St Sebastian, and the reliquary was not much longer than my middle finger and about twice as wide.'

'I wonder,' I said, momentarily diverted, 'why the saint was careless enough to leave his nail clippings lying about, and who had the foresight to pick one up.'

'Nicholas!' He sounded partly shocked and partly amused. 'Have a care! Such thoughts might count as blasphemy.'

'Well, I know a fellow in Oxford, a great scholar of philosophy, John Wycliffe, who would raise many worse questions which might count as blasphemy.'

'Sounds a dangerous fellow.'

'He does need to learn to be more cautious in speaking aloud thoughts which wiser men keep to themselves. However, this question of a reliquary . . . it is possible, I suppose. One as small as you describe might be slipped down inside a man's shirt. He would not carry it in his purse or his scrip – too easily stolen.'

'Then it cannot have been carried by Gaston,' Peter pointed out, 'for after he was injured, he was stripped nearly naked, while he was unconscious and unable to conceal anything.'

'Of course,' I said, 'that is very true. Therefore, if there is some such small object that these fellows are seeking, Falquet must be carrying it. Or the girl.'

'Surely not the girl! Would they entrust something of such value to a woman?'

'Perhaps the very unlikelihood would be the reason for doing so.'

I thought, with some amusement, that Emma would scorn this disparagement of women.

'We should remember,' I added, 'that they took great care to hide the girl when they were set upon in Wychwood.'

'But that was for her protection. They feared the brutes might defile her.'

'That too. But perhaps there was more than one reason.'

'We may speculate from now until Doomsday,' he said, 'but we shall draw no nearer an answer. The only way to discover the truth is to question them.'

'Do you think they will be prepared to confide in us?'

'They were very subdued when we all broke our fast this morning. I think the events of last night frightened them.'

'And so they should,' I said. 'Will you send for them?'

He rose, and went to the door. 'They are practising again, but I will send word to Gaston, say that I need to discuss the Christmas entertainments with him. If I reveal my true purpose, he may not come.'

'Very wise,' I said, 'but I think you should send for all three of them.'

'Do you think that necessary?'

'I do, especially if one of the others is carrying this object of mystery. Their demeanour might give them away. Gaston, I should say, is the strongest character, the least likely to be persuaded.'

Peter opened the parlour door and called to one of the maid servants, telling her to fetch the troubadours so that they might discuss with him the arrangements for the Christmas music.

The troubadours arrived shortly, Gaston carrying his lute, Falquet a vielle (not the one, I think, which had been broken), and Azalais a sheaf of pages on which songs and music had been written. I tried to read them, even upside down, but did not want to appear unduly curious. It was a large bundle, and might, at a stroke, solve the problem of my book of songs.

'We have drawn up a list for your approval, Master Winchingham,' Gaston said, taking the papers from Azalais. He flipped through them until he found the sheet he wanted, then drew it out and laid it before Peter.

'For the Eve and the morning of the Nativity, we thought mostly holy songs, and carols on the birth of the Christ Child.' He pointed to the place on the paper. 'But perhaps during the evening of the Nativity, a more general concert, songs of many kinds.'

Azalais and Falquet stood quietly behind him, and I studied the girl carefully for the first time. It was she who possessed that remarkable voice, and although she stood with her hands clasped at her waist and her head slightly bent, she was watching us all with eyes unusually shrewd for such a young woman. Peter did wrong to underestimate her, I thought.

Gaston turned over his paper. 'For the great feast on Twelfth Day, I have written down some simple songs for the time folk are eating, then afterwards there will be dancing, no? Music, but not songs, I think, for the words would not be heard for the stamping of the feet! We have also a hurdy-gurdy which Azalais plays. That will be good for the dancing.'

As he became more immersed in his plans, I noticed that his accent grew stronger, and I understood what Peter had told me before. I had not the same ear for language as he had, but I caught something in Gaston's voice which could be a trace of Castilian.

'And between the Nativity and Twelfth Day?' Peter asked, leaning over the paper, quite engaged. 'What then?'

'Then it shall be as you wish. We have a great repertoire.' Gaston tapped the pile of song sheets with his fingernail, left long for plucking the lute strings. 'Whatever you wish. Songs of love. Songs of war. Songs of heroic deeds. Songs of humour or pathos or grandeur, we have them all.'

In someone else, it would have sounded boastful, but in Gaston I saw that it was simple truth.

144

'It sounds remarkable to me,' I ventured. 'I look forward with great pleasure to your performances. Even the fragments we have overheard are beautiful.'

Azalais flashed me a sudden smile, and Falquet grinned. Gaston bowed with dignity.

'I thank you, Master Elyot. We shall strive to give of our best. We have not forgotten how you came to our aid in the woods.'

I bowed in return, and glanced at Peter. This seemed too apt an opening to miss. He took the hint.

'Come,' he said, 'sit down, all of you. Let us drink a glass of wine to our plans.'

He sent a servant to fetch wine and some of the Christmas comfits, and soon we were all seated in comfort about the small table. I had managed a glance at the top sheet of Azalais's papers. The music I could read, for I had studied it both as a boy with Sire Raymond, and later as a student at Oxford, but the words conveyed nothing, for they were in some strange language, which I took to be Occitan, although it seemed almost like something halfway between Latin and French. Given time, perhaps I could make it out, at least on the page, though I doubted I should understand the spoken tongue.

'Now, Gaston,' Peter said, somehow slipping effortlessly from easy-going patron to determined lord of the manor, 'Master Elyot and I think that it is time you stopped playing the innocent with us. You have spoken of your rescue in Wychwood, and you know what occurred here last night. You cannot any longer maintain the pretence that the men who beat you, smashed one of your instruments, and turned the contents of your cart upside down, had mistaken you for someone else. Impossible after this second attempt.'

I was watching all of them as Peter thus called their bluff. Gaston's face remained blank, but a look of panic came into Falquet's eyes. Azalais's hands had been resting on the table. They convulsed involuntarily, although she too managed to keep most emotion out of her face. Only the eyes widened, as if in fear.

No one spoke.

'We wish you no harm,' I said at last, 'but it is clear that you need help and you need friends. We would be those friends and provide that help, but it is very difficult in a state of ignorance. Have you considered what danger you will be in, once you leave Leighton? I believe you head for London. There are many miles between here and London. Many miles, and many a dark avenue under trees or on bleak upland, where these men would have no trouble in falling upon you. Have you thought that you could all be killed?'

Azalais gave a slight gasp, and caught her lower lip between her teeth. Falquet began to pleat the fabric of his cotte between his fingers. Gaston still said nothing, but the look in his eyes changed. They were no longer blank. Instead, he looked like a cornered animal.

'These men,' Peter said, 'they are seeking something in your possession, something of value. Perhaps you have been asked to convey it to . . . someone . . . somewhere. A small object. Like a jewel. Or a reliquary.'

For the first time since being challenged, Gaston spoke. With a sharp bark of laughter, he said, 'I carry no reliquary.'

'That was merely an example,' Peter said mildly. 'Do you not wish to avail yourselves of our offer of help? You have known me for a time. I think you also know me for an honest man. And I can speak for Nicholas Elyot, for the man saved my life.'

He paused. 'And indeed, he saved the life of the Prince of Wales, Edward of Woodstock, him they call the Black Prince.'

At this last revelation of Peter's, all three of the troubadours turned and stared at me, as if they had not truly seen me before.

'Is it true?' Azalais whispered. 'You saved the life of the Black Prince?'

I flushed. It sounded more dramatic than I

remembered it.

'In a sense,' I said, 'we saved each other's lives. Then we sat on the villain who attempted the assassination. That was most satisfying.'

I was seeing it again in my mind's eye – Edward of Woodstock sitting with me on the Frenchman in the dark meadow beyond the Priory of St Frideswide, and both of us laughing.

Even Gaston smiled, and seemed to relax his wary stiffness a little.

'It is true,' he admitted, 'that these men are in pursuit of us. We lied. But we could not tell, at first . . . everything happened so quickly. We were not sure that we were safe, or amongst friends. They rode away, though by then I was out of my wits and Falquet and Azalais must think quickly what to do. Once those rogues were gone, it seemed safest to continue with the deception. Until last night.'

He ran the fingers of both hands through his thick, dark hair.

'After what happened last night, it was folly to think we could continue to pretend. Besides, we had brought the rest of your household into peril. But we could not reveal our mission. It is not for us to say. We have orders . . .'

He broke off, and glanced at the other two musicians.

'It is I,' Azalais said quietly, 'who carry this precious object which our enemies are so determined to seize.' She smiled gravely. 'It is no reliquary of gold and gems, nothing but a letter. Yet a letter on whose contents, we understand, men's lives might hang.'

So I had been right. It was the girl. I saw her hand stir and almost rise to the front of her bodice. A letter. It must be slipped down within the breast of her gown. It was not only to protect her person that the men had hidden her.

Peter was thinking carefully. 'From here you go to London. You are to deliver this letter to someone in London?'

As Gaston set his mouth hard, Peter added, 'Never fear. I do not ask to whom you are to deliver this letter.'

147

It was Falquet who spoke in haste now, his words tumbling over each other.

'Everything has gone awry. Before we set out, and it was known that we were to come to Leighton Manor, we were instructed to meet one here to whom the letter could safely be entrusted, to carry it onward. But he is not here!'

'One Reginald Le Soten,' Gaston said.

Peter looked puzzled. To him the name meant nothing.

To me, it meant much. I gave an involuntary groan.

'Le Soten? But Le Soten is dead!'

The troubadours exchanged looks of consternation. 'You knew him?' Gaston asked.

'Only briefly,' I said. 'When we were here at harvest time, he was attached to the household of Gilbert Mordon, but he had been sent here by the king, who had his suspicions about Mordon and his unlawful dealings. And there was the matter of Lady Edith . . . but that is somewhat apart. Le Soten acted as an intelligencer for the king, and was discovered. He was murdered in the very orchard here.'

Peter turned somewhat pale. 'I knew there had been trouble here, and that Mordon was killed by his faithless wife and her lover, but I had not heard of this other death.'

'It was in his role as intelligencer,' Azalais said, forestalling Gaston, who had been about to speak, 'that were we instructed to hand over the letter to Le Soten. Now what are we to do?'

For once Gaston, generally so sure of himself, seemed at a loss. Falquet looked to him, and I could see that he thought his brother-in-law should take the lead. Only Azalais, having asked the question, now tried to answer it.

'Le Soten was surely to have taken the letter to the king's court. Since he is not here, we must do it ourselves.'

I turned my wine cup around and around in my hands.

'As we have already pointed out, there are many

miles between Leighton and London, and what defence have you against armed and determined men? I would not predict you could travel safely twenty miles.'

It occurred to me that one important question had neither been asked nor answered.

'Who are these men who pursue you? Do you know?'

'Their names, nay,' Gaston said. 'Their nation, aye. They are Frenchmen.'

'Ah,' I said. I was beginning to suspect the nature of this letter Azalais had concealed beneath her gown.

'There is, perhaps, another way,' I said. 'When Reginald Le Soten was here, he was not the only royal intelligencer at Leighton Manor. Another had taken a position as waiting gentlewoman to Mordon's wife, the Lady Edith. Nor was she only an intelligencer, she was also Le Soten's cousin. Her name is Alice Walsea.'

'Mistress Walsea!' Peter exclaimed. 'That I met at St Frideswide's Fair? Who borrowed my barge to go to Westminster?'

'The same,' I said. 'I do not know where she is now, but most likely at Court. If we could get word to her, she could send a royal messenger, or even come herself, should you be willing to entrust the message to her.'

The three of them exchanged looks.

'It might be the answer,' Gaston said slowly. 'We cannot deliver the letter to Le Soten, since he is dead. As Azalais says, it was to be taken by him to the king's court. If this Mistress Walsea can arrange that . . .' He let his voice die away, but there was a gleam of hope in his eyes.

'But, Nicholas,' Peter said, 'how are we to reach Mistress Walsea? And she would surely not undertake the journey here herself, in this foul winter.'

'It will not be easy,' I said. I was thinking hard. 'There is a reliable carrier service that runs from Burford to Oxford, and then from Oxford to London. There may be delays over this Christmastide.' I turned to Gaston. 'But if you can remain here at Leighton Manor until a letter can reach London and bring an answer . . .'

'Not the letter we carry!' Gaston exclaimed.

'Nay, a letter I shall write to Mistress Walsea, seeking her help. She is a most resourceful woman, and well placed at Court. If she thinks it necessary, she will be able to send a troop of armed horsemen.'

'But can we know that she is in London?' Peter said.

'She will most likely be wherever the Court is. I will give instructions that the letter must be conveyed to the royal Court. They will surely be somewhere about London for Christmas, at one of the royal palaces. Easier to catch them at this time of year than almost any other, for the king moves constantly about the kingdom.'

'When he isn't fighting the French,' Peter said dryly.

'Had you any instructions to give to Le Soten?' I said. 'Does the letter bear a direction? Or were you to tell him who should receive it?'

They looked at each other again, then Azalais spoke. 'There is no written direction on the letter, it was thought safer that way. Master Le Soten was to hand it to King Edward himself, or else to the Black Prince.'

'You know of the Black Prince?' I said curiously, 'even in Provence – or should I say Occitaine?'

'Of course!' she said fiercely. 'He is an enemy of the French, as we are, and even as a boy, he defeated them in battle!'

'Aye, at Crécy.' I smiled at her. 'We too think him a great hero.'

'And he will defeat them again.' Her voice was passionate. 'And avenge our wrongs.' She reached out and took her brother's hand. 'The French bastards killed our grandfather's grandfather, who was court troubadour to the lord of Bézieres. He was no Cathar, nor was his lord, but they were slain most brutally, and the whole town put to the sword. His wife fled with her children, and we have kept the name of Bézieres in our family ever since, and kept alive the songs of our grandfather's grandfather.'

She laid her other hand on the pile of music. It was trembling.

'Some of them are here. And I will do anything. *Anything*. To defeat the French, even if it cost me my life.'

Her words seemed to echo from wall to wall in the silence of the room.

At last I said, 'Then I shall do my utmost to help you, mistress. And we shall begin this very day.'

She smiled at me through the tears which had filled her eyes.

'You had the right of it, Master Elyot. We need help, and we need friends. I am glad we have found them.'

I borrowed paper, quill, and ink from Peter, and sat down to compose my letter to Alice Walsea at once. The troubadours, who were both relieved by sharing their burden, but distressed after Azalais's outburst, were sent off by Peter to take dinner with Birgit and Hans, and then to practise their music.

'It will calm them,' he said to me. 'You had the right of it, Nicholas. That girl is worth any ten Frenchmen! And now I will have food sent to us here in the parlour while you write your letter and we decide what steps it were best for us to take until we can hear back from the Court, for I do not believe these French scoundrels will abandon their attempts to lay hands on that letter.'

I looked up from sharpening my quill.

'I wonder what it contains. I must confess to a great curiosity to know!'

'Matters of state, I should judge.'

'Aye, but from whom?'

'Someone who, like our king, is an enemy of France.'

We ate a light early dinner together, while I composed my letter to Alice. I kept it brief and gave few details, only that a letter had come to my attention that must reach the king or the Prince of Wales without delay, but that there was no secure means of sending it from Leighton-under-Wychwood to the Court. I asked that she might despatch a suitable messenger, amply provided with an armed escort, to fetch the said document.

Having written my first version of the letter, I decided that it might be wiser not to mention Leighton by name, lest my letter should fall into the wrong hands. Therefore I rewrote it, substituting for Leighton the words: 'at the house where we first met'. Few people would understand the meaning of that, and those would only be our friends.

'I shall be able to take your letters also,' I said to Peter, 'so that it seems quite natural that I should convey several to be taken by the carrier. And I have addressed the one to Mistress Walsea "to be found at the king's court", so that it should reach her, wherever the king is. I believe the king and his family often favour Windsor or Eltham at Christmastide.'

'Windsor I know,' Peter said. 'Eltham is in London?'

'I think it is near Greenwich,' I said, 'although I am not quite sure where.'

'Then it should not be difficult for the carrier to find, but I fear the journey from here to London will be much delayed by the snow.'

'It will, and all the more reason why I should set off at once for Burford. There is time to ride there and back today if I make haste.'

'It will be dark before you can return,' he said.

'Dusk, perhaps,' I said. 'But I will set a good pace. Will you send word to my cousin, where I have gone? I would not have them worry, but I cannot delay by going back to the farm before I leave.'

'I will send a servant at once. Have a care, Nicholas. These Frenchmen may still be lurking about, on the road to Burford, awaiting their chance.'

'They will have no interest in me. But best if the troubadours stay withindoors and out of sight.'

'I will see to it,' he said.

Rufus was soon saddled and I was on my way. Fortunately, for the last few days it had snowed only at night, so although the wind was cold there was no other trouble from the weather. The village street was cleared down the middle, and when I reached the lane leading to the Burford road, I found that the labourers had again been set to work, for it was passable nearly half the way, so that I was able to set Rufus to a brisk canter.

After I overtook the men, however, I was forced to go more slowly, picking our way through the drifts. We had already passed the place where we had been obliged to shift the fallen branch on our way to the farm several days before, but I kept a sharp lookout for others until I reached the road. As an important thoroughfare, linking Oxfordshire to the west, the road carried frequent traffic even this close to Christmas, and despite the recent blizzards the snow was packed down by passing horses and carts. I was able to move more quickly again, and soon fell in with a party in ecclesiastical dress. I did not ask their business, nor they mine, but I rode with them a way, until I felt I could make better speed on my own.

Riding once again at a steady canter, which Rufus can keep up for long stretches without seeming to tire, I reached the turn to Burford. The town does not lie directly on the high road, which runs along a raised ridge of ground, where I suspect men have trodden out a path since ancient times. To reach Burford, I turned to the right and headed along the main street, which leads quite steeply down to the crossing of the river Windrush, lying in a valley at the bottom of the town, just past the church. The street is lined with handsome stone-built houses, for Burford has grown wealthy on the wool trade.

About halfway down, I turned into the yard of the White Hart inn, and gave my horse over to an ostler, to be stabled and fed while I spoke to the innkeeper, a man I had known ever since I had come here with my father, when he brought his fleeces to the wool dealer in town.

'Master Elyot!' the innkeeper cried. 'Why 'tis a long time since us have seen ye in Burford. Why be ye here?'

'I need to send letters by the carrier, Master Townley,' I said. 'Is he still working, these winter days?'

'Aye, ye've just caught him. He will be setting off for Oxford early on the morrow. Are your letters for Oxford?'

'Nay, for London and beyond. One for Bruges and one for Danzig, but they must go to London first.'

He opened his eyes wide. 'Those be terrible strange places, Master Elyot.'

'Just business, for a merchant friend. And one letter of my own, to someone at Court, wherever the Court may be this Christmastide.'

'That I can tell ye, sir, for 'tis at Eltham Palace. We had some travellers stayed the night here, two or three days ago, and they told how 'twas all the talk of London, the mock jousts to be held for the royal princes, and mummeries, and I know not what other fooleries. Aye, 'twas to be at Eltham.'

'Then I may make the direction on my letter all the clearer,' I said, 'if I may borrow ink and quill of you?'

'Come this way,' he said, wiping his hands on his apron and opening the door to a small back parlour. 'Ink there,' he said, pointing, 'and some uncut quills. Will you be needing paper?'

He looked anxious, for I do not suppose he kept much of it, but now I knew that the royal princes were certain to be at Court for Christmas, I decided that I would also write briefly to Edward of Woodstock, in case my letter to Alice should go astray.

'Can you spare me one sheet?' I said. 'I will gladly pay for it.'

'Nay, nay,' he said, handing me a single sheet of coarse paper. 'I am afraid 'tis not such as gentlemen use. Now, what will ye take, sir? Hippocras, to warm ye after a cold ride? Something to eat?'

Truly, I needed nothing, but I did not want Master Townley to lose the cost of his paper and gain nothing in return.

'I cannot wait for a meal,' I said, apologetically, 'for I want to return to Leighton today. But a cup of hippocras would be welcome. And have you any of your wife's excellent pasties?'

He beamed. 'Certainly. Mutton or rabbit? Or one of each?'

'One of each,' I said, thinking I could put one in my scrip to eat on the ride home.

I added 'at Eltham Palace' to the direction on Alice's letter, then began the other, thankful that Sire Raymond had made it one of the lessons of my boyhood to learn the correct mode of address for everyone from the Pope or an emperor down to a landless churl. I never expect to address his Holiness, but then when I was a boy I had never expected to write to the firstborn prince of the blood royal.

Master Townley brought me the spiced wine and the two pasties himself, then left me to my letter. I ate the mutton one with my left hand, while endeavouring to keep the crumbs of pastry from falling on my writing. I reminded the prince briefly of our encounter in Oxford, then set out much the same information as I had written to Alice Walsea, though in this case I was obliged to mention Leighton Manor by name, as I had no sideways means of referring to it. I explained that I was also sending to her, and urged that it seemed the letter in question, carried by the troubadours, must contain urgent and perhaps perilous information which was intended either for him or for his father, the king. I added that there had already been two attempts made to steal it, by armed men believed to be French. I concluded with all the necessary humble words to His Gracious Highness, and signed my name with more than the usual flourish.

The innkeeper had some difficulty finding me wax to seal my letter, since his only use of paper was for his occasional accounts and bills, but he came back at last triumphant, having visited the town notary two doors away, and borrowed wax from him. After I had sealed the letter and written the direction, he peered curiously over my shoulder, and his eyes widened.

'Ye write to Prince Edward, Master Elyot? Do ye move in Court circles now?'

I laughed. ''Tis but another matter of business, but I would take it kindly if you would keep the matter to yourself. The carrier – who is it now? – is he a man to be trusted?'

'John Hayward, son of Thomas Hayward as used to be carrier to Oxford when ye came here with yer father when ye were but a boy. Father and son both men of discretion, ye need have no fear on that score. I'll take ye to him, he has a chamber upstairs.'

I returned the ink pot and used quill to their places, put the rabbit pasty in my scrip, and followed the innkeeper to the carrier's chamber.

John Hayward might have been his father grown young again, a man of about my own age, whom I had known slightly when we were boys.

'The letters concern urgent matters of business,' I said, 'in especial the two addressed to the Court. 'Tis bitter weather for travelling, but I shall owe you a debt of gratitude if you can speed them on their way.'

'I'll do my best, maister,' he said.

'Who drives the route from Oxford to London?' I asked.

'Why, normally, 'tis Ned of Wallingford,' he said, 'but the man has been sick these two weeks. I said I would take the London run this time, and he'll pay me back when he is well, driving the Oxford to Burford route.'

'It will be a long cold drive,' I said, but I was cheered by the thought that the letters could be entrusted to one man for the whole journey, instead of passing from hand to hand.

'I have a fur lined cloak and capuchon,' he said. ''Tis nobbut coney fur, but grand in this winter cold. And I'm well used to driving in all weathers. If the blizzards come on again, I must make a halt, but otherwise I can keep on my way.'

'The letters for Bruges and Danzig should be taken to the Drapers' Company for forwarding,' I said, 'for they concern the cloth merchant's business. The other two are for the Court, which Master Townley tells me will be at Eltham Palace, near Greenwich.'

'I shall see them safely delivered,' he promised. 'I have other deliveries on the way, and no doubt there will be more waiting for me in Oxford, but if all goes well, they should arrive within the week. Certainly by Three Kings Day.'

A week. Well, I could hardly hope for better.

'You will be on the road at Christmas,' I said.

'I'll find somewhere for midnight Mass on the Eve. I might even reach Oxford by then. And I shall spend Three Kings Day in London. There will be rare goings-on there, I'll be bound.'

I smiled. 'I daresay there will. We are planning a great feast that day in Leighton.'

'A new lord of the manor,' the innkeeper said. 'He stayed here, back a few months, when he was searching out a manor to buy. Came from Bruges, but did not speak like a foreigner.'

'He is as English as you or I,' I said, 'come home again, now the Wool Staple is returned to England.'

Both men nodded sagely. There is not a soul in this Cotswold country who does not understand every aspect of the wool trade. Having the Staple here would almost certainly mean greater prosperity for all, from the shepherds who tended the flocks to the spinsters and weavers, right up to the international merchants like Peter Winchingham.

I paid John Hayward the cost of carrying the four letters, with some coin over to buy a Christmas drink or two on the way. He did not look to me like a man who would overindulge and drive his cart into a ditch, or he would never have won the right to this profitable route. Our business done, I followed Master Townley downstairs.

''Tis growing dark early again,' he said over his shoulder. 'Snow again tonight, I judge.'

'Aye.' I peered worriedly out of the window of the main parlour as we entered. It faced on to the street and the few passersby hurried along, heads down against the wind, making for home before the blizzard began once more.

'I must be on my way,' I said, as the innkeeper brought me my cloak from the small parlour, where I had left it. The cloak was good English broadcloth, quite able to keep out a moderate wind, though not the wind I was going to face on my ride home. I wished it were lined with coney fur, like the carrier's.

Master Townley stared out of the window as well and frowned.

'I mislike the look of that sky. Will ye not stay overnight, and ride back in the morning? I have chambers enough. I'd not care to ride out into that myself. See that queer light in the sky? That is a bad sign.'

He had the right of it, no doubt, but I was anxious to get back. The family would expect me, and I did not want to find myself snowed up in Burford for the Christmas season, so I thanked the innkeeper, but said I would hasten on my way.

I could not leave at once, however, for the ostler had taken himself off somewhere, and it took me a time to find where he had stored my saddle and bridle. At last, however, Rufus was ready, and I led him out into the yard. As I was mounting, the innkeeper's wife came hurrying across, her face creased with concern.

'Master Elyot, ye should not be setting off in this, but if ye must, I have brought food and drink.'

She insisted on giving me half a dozen currant cakes, which I added to the pasty in my scrip, and I buckled the leather jack of ale to my saddle. I was not sure whether I should be able to free the buckle, once my fingers grew numb with the cold, and I deliberately left the buckles of my scrip undone, so I could at least reach out the food at need. The light in the sky was a streaky blend of sickly mustard yellow and grey, certain sign of heavy snow on the way, so I thanked Mistress Townley hastily, and headed out of the inn yard to the sloping street up between the Burford houses.

Even in the time since I had looked out of the parlour, the last of the people in the street had disappeared. The glow from the windows of the houses on either side was painfully tempting, but I resolutely urged Rufus up the hill to the main road. It was certain that I would be caught in the snow before I reached Leighton, but the further we could go before that happened, the better.

Once on the main road, I leaned forward over Rufus's neck and spurred him on first to a canter and then a gallop. The surface was still firm here, as it had been when I arrived, and we flew along, the only living creatures to be seen in that frozen landscape. All people of sense were safe by their firesides, and the creatures of the wild had resorted to their burrows and nests, curled down against the cold. Only that madman, Nicholas Elyot, was abroad. I should never have come. Or I should have stayed for the night at the White Hart. If I did not return tonight, my family would surely realise why.

For a brief moment I considered turning around and retracing my steps to Burford. The yellow light had gone from the sky and the first flakes of snow were drifting down, only the scantiest of drifts, nothing to worry us. I knew that this mild beginning was deceptive. However, Rufus had his own views on the matter, and it seemed that he was as keen to reach Leighton as I was. We pressed on.

By the time we reached the turn into the Leighton lane, it was snowing heavily. I had allowed myself to eat the rabbit pasty, though every mouthful came with a garnish of snow. The food, I thought, though cold itself, might help to keep out some of the cold all the better in my stomach than out of it. I would leave the currant cakes for later. As I had foreseen, I could not manage the ale jack. I hoped Rufus had been fed at the inn, for my own survival depended on him.

It was clear that the men from the village had not reached this outer portion of the lane, for the drifts of recent snow were untouched, and as the wind rose in howling fury, and the snow nearly blinded me, the drifts were growing ever deeper. It was hopeless. We could not continue at this pace or Rufus would founder, or stumble and break a leg. I reined him in, and we picked our way up the lane at an agonisingly slow pace. The drifts reached up to his knees, in places even higher. Several times he stopped, as if confused. Where was he to go? How could he make his way through this?

At one point a drift blocking the entire lane rose to his chest, and he stopped dead. There was nothing for it. I dismounted into snow which reached almost to my neck, and began scooping away a narrow cleft through it, tugging the reluctant horse after me, step by step. Soon my cloak, my hose, my long winter cotte, were all caked with snow. Every few minutes I had to wipe my face clear. At last we were through the blockage, and I reckoned Rufus could make his way forward.

I was so numb, I could barely lift my foot to the stirrup, or seize hold of the saddle to raise myself on to the horse's back. Twice I fell back, with barely the strength of a newborn kitten in my arms. I was almost weeping with frustration. If I could not mount and ride on, I would perish here in the blizzard, just a few miles from the farm.

This thought galvanised me to a final effort, and I managed to heave myself clumsily across the saddle, sprawled like a dead fish, so that Rufus shifted uneasily beneath me. Somehow I was able to right myself and slid my feet into the stirrups. Rufus needed no further invitation, but began ploughing slowly onwards.

If the blizzard continued as fiercely as this, I thought, the carrier would not be able to make the journey to London. He would go first, if he could, to Oxford, but that in itself would be difficult, if not impossible. Would conditions be worse or better, from Oxford to London?

Then a thought struck me, and I nearly shouted out at my stupidity. Why had I not sent the two letters addressed to the Court enclosed within a letter to Cedric Walden at Oxford castle? He could have despatched a fast rider directly to Eltham Palace, and saved several days, compared with the slow and roundabout route of the carrier. I cursed myself for not thinking of this in time. I had been so absorbed in following up the carrier from Burford, so readily available, that I had given no thought to any other means. Well, it was too late now.

While I had been blaming myself for my failure to think the matter through, Rufus had reached the point at which the men from the village must have abandoned their work of clearing the lane. More snow had accumulated since they had left, but even through the snow clouds, I could see that the way was clearer. Without any need of encouragement from me, Rufus broke into a slow and careful canter.

'Good fellow,' I said, leaning forward and patting his neck, through its crust of snow, with my gloved hand.

I was so intent on what little I could see of the way ahead, that I was paying no heed to the woods on either side of the lane, so that my heart gave a leap of shock when dark shadows crowded in on me from left and right, and a voice shouted 'Stop!'

Instinctively, I pulled Rufus to a halt. At first I thought it must be men from the village, come to warn me of a fallen tree or some other danger on the road ahead.

Then as the curtain of snow billowed and parted, I saw the gleam of swords.

And they were all pointed unwaveringly at me.

Chapter Eight

I suppose I was half stupid with the cold, and exhausted from my labours of clearing the way through the great drift with nothing save my hands, but I simply stared at the men, while my frozen brain – which up to that moment could only think of reaching the farm – tried to make sense of what I saw.

Through the snow, I could make out six men, three on each side of the lane, where they must have been waiting in ambush. Unless the neighbourhood of Leighton was a-swarm with outlaws, these must be the same men who had twice made an attempt on the troubadours. Hans thought that he had seen four men at the manor the previous night, but had said there might have been more. Difficult for him to judge in the dark. Were these the same fellows? They must be.

Certainly, they were not to be trifled with. All wore half armour, breastplates and light helmets. All but one had drawn swords in their hands, and there was a solitary bowman. He too wore a sword at his belt. I had nothing but a small dagger, useless against the length of a sword, even a single sword in the hands of one man, never mind five. I doubted whether I could even draw and wield my dagger, for my frozen fingers were clamped about the reins as though permanently curved, like some statue in marble.

I could not fight them. I could only bluff.

'What do you want of me?' I said, and was relieved that my voice came out steady, and not in the frightened

162

squeak I expected.

'We want what you carry.' It was a big, bearded man who spoke.

No Englishman under fifty wore a beard in that fashion, which betrayed him as a foreigner, even without the strong French accent, for he was no more than thirty.

'What I carry? I carry nothing, no more than a few coins. You waste your time on me, sir.'

Outlaws living rough in the woods would probably kill for those few coins I carried, but these were no landless men, poor and desperate.

The man, who must be in some sort their leader, sneered at my words.

'We do not want your coins, fellow. We want the letter you carry.'

There could be no further doubt. These were the men who were pursuing the troubadours.

'I carry no letters.'

I allowed my voice to sound exasperated, and was thankful that this was true. I began to flex my stiff fingers. Had I been ambushed on my way to Burford, they would have found my letter to Alice Walsea. It would have revealed my connection with someone at Court, which might have made me valuable to them as a hostage.

'See,' I said, flipping back the flap of my scrip and holding it half open. 'No letters.'

He frowned, then signed to the other men to move back a pace as he edged his horse nearer to me, to examine my scrip.

I saw my chance.

'I carry nothing but these,' I said, seizing one of Mistress Townley's currant cakes and flinging it full in his face as I dug my heels into Rufus's flanks.

Taken by surprise, the horse leapt forward, bursting through the men.

I felt a sword catch in a fold of my cloak and rip it, but I crouched low on the horse's back, urging him to a gallop, though it was dangerous ground, even here where the lane had been partly cleared.

Before we had gone more than a few yards, an arrow whistled past my shoulder, but missed its mark. It would be difficult for the bowman, with the dark and the snow, to take aim, and the wind would play havoc with the flight of his arrows. Another passed me, closer this time. Rufus must feel my fear, for he stretched out his head and galloped as I had never known him gallop before. But the men would not stay idle in the lane, they would be after us at once.

A third arrow caught Rufus on the shoulder, but only served to spur him on, and now I could see the first lights of the village.

Would they dare to follow me there? I knew that the men of the village could present little threat to half a dozen armed men, but these men had fled when confronted by Peter and Hans in their night shifts. Perhaps they were anxious to guard their identity, fearing that it might be revealed if even one of them were to be caught and questioned.

These thoughts flashed through my mind as we galloped the last stretch of the lane. If we could just reach the village . . .

There loomed up ahead of me, silhouetted against the lighted windows of the first houses, another body of horsemen. So there were more of them! I was trapped between them, before and behind.

I drew a gasping breath and began to slow Rufus from his heedless pace. There was no point in risking him breaking a leg now, whatever happened to me.

'Nicholas!' a familiar voice called out. 'Is that you? We were worried, with the blizzard, that you might fall foul of the drifts.'

'Edmond!' I shouted, careering up to him and halting Rufus in a whirlwind of snow. 'God be thanked. Have a care. Those Frenchmen are behind me, and they are armed.'

'So are we,' he said quietly.

And now I saw that besides Edmond and James there was a cluster of men, grim faced and carrying swords –

Peter and Hans Winchingham, Alan Wodville, Bertred Godsmith, even Geoffrey Carter, and more of the men from Leighton.

I swung Rufus round, so that I could look up the lane. There was nothing to be seen of the men who had accosted me, except the rumps of their horses, disappearing through the snow, just as we had seen them vanish in Wychwood.

'They are mighty keen not to meet an equal force,' I said, 'only to prey on those unarmed and in smaller numbers. Do you suppose they are reluctant to be identified?'

After my panicked escape, I was growing calmer, though my stomach still churned with fear.

'They are French, do you think?' Edmond said.

'They are French, never doubt it. It seems this truce of ours with the French king serves no purpose but to let Frenchman into England to work what evil they will.'

Having no desire to pursue the men and engage in a battle, we turned our horses in relief and made our way back into the village, where the others parted from us. I promised Peter that I would come to the manor the next day.

'Your letters are safely despatched by carrier to London,' I assured him.

Edmond, James, and I rode up to the farm together.

'How did you fare in Burford?' Edmond asked as we dismounted and led the horses into the stable.

'I will give you a full account when I may tell the others as well,' I said. 'No need to tell it twice. But I need to give Rufus some care, he has had a bad time of it.'

I turned to James. 'When you have seen to your horse, will you bring me a warm bran mash for Rufus? And ask Margaret for her wound salve? He caught an arrow on his shoulder.'

Edmond and James had soon seen to their horses. Alone now in the stable, I removed Rufus's tack, and began to rub him down. After our bitter journey through the blizzard, the stable was warm from the other horses and

Edmond's yoke of oxen, settled sleepily in the furthest stall. James brought the bran and the salve, but left again, with word that his mother would soon have supper ready.

Rufus stood drooping, his head hanging down, and I feared that he might have done himself some injury in that desperate gallop. The wound in his right shoulder, I was relieved to see, was not much more than a graze. The arrow had not penetrated. It had sliced a groove in the flesh, long but not deep. I smeared it liberally with the salve, which I knew from my own use was soothing. Margaret made it herself from cooling and healing herbs. Rufus seemed to be aware of it, for he raised his head, stood straighter, and began to eat the bran, which he had ignored at first.

I buckled on the double blankets, then threw my arm over his neck and pressed my forehead against the soft hair in the hollow between his neck and his left shoulder. Although I knew I was safe now, my hands were still shaking. How terrified those troubadours must have been, with their horse injured, who had no chance to ride away.

'You're a grand fellow, Rufus,' I murmured. 'Without you, I would probably lie under a snow drift in the lane now, a chilly corpse.'

The horse paused in his eating, and nudged my side, leaving a smear of the soggy bran on my cloak. As he continued to eat, I remained leaning against him. I could feel the slow, steady beat of his heart, and gradually my own slowed and kept time with it.

I do not know how long I stood there, simply holding on to the horse, my mind drained even of thought. Then I heard the stable door open, and light footsteps on the cobbled floor. I patted Rufus and turned round.

Emma stood there, holding a candle lantern aloft, which lit only her head and shoulders, the rest lost in darkness, where the lantern left by Edmond near the door could not reach. Her face was blanched pale, and her eyes were wide and shocked.

Without a word, she hung the lantern on a nail and stepped forward.

'When you did not come in, I wondered . . .'

Her voice shook, and she reached both hands out to me.

'I was afraid . . .'

I stepped forward and took her hands in mine.

'I am unhurt. But Rufus was a little injured, and I must see to him. He saved my life. If he had not galloped at a speed I never saw before, they would have caught me.'

'God be thanked for Rufus.'

'Aye, God be thanked for Rufus,' I tried to smile, but I fear it was somewhat weak.

'Your cloak is torn.'

'Nothing to matter,' I said. 'The arrow did not touch me.'

'There were at least half a dozen men, Edmond told us.'

'How did he know they would be there? And how did he come to be in the lane? And the Winchinghams also? I don't understand,' I said.

'Did he not tell you? Peter and Hans were here at the farm – quite by chance, or at least they came because they wondered if you had returned from Burford. They had taken Hans's horse to the smithy for a shoe, and came on to us. Then your cousin's shepherd – Godfrid, is he called? – came with a tale. Some of the sheep had broken out and he was herding them back through the woods near the lane. He saw men lurking there, and brought word of it. From what he said, they thought it must be these same men who attacked the troubadours. Knowing you must come that way, they rode out to meet you, with some of the village men. Though Edmond says they came too late.'

'I wondered that they should be there,' I said. 'And although they were too late to catch the men before they first stopped me, I am sure the sight of them turned the rogues away at the last.'

'But I do not understand how you escaped them yourself. You and Rufus.'

She drew one of her hands from mine and laid it on

the horse's neck. He lifted his head briefly from the bucket and looked at her, then resumed eating.

She smiled. 'He seems very calm.'

'Aye, he does now, but they alarmed him, or I do not think he would have shown such a turn of speed.'

'But how could you escape?' she said. 'Six men surrounding you. They must have been armed.'

'With swords. And one bowman.'

'And you unarmed.'

'Not quite,' I said. 'I had my secret weapon.'

I reached into my scrip and drew out another of Mistress Townley's currant cakes.

'My secret weapon.'

I laid it in her hand. 'I threw one hard into their leader's face.' I laughed, perhaps a little wildly, for unlike Rufus, I was not quite calm.

'A cake?' she said. 'But surely–'

She raised it to her lips, as though she would take a bite.

'Have a care!' I said. 'Lest you break a tooth.'

Startled, she peered at it in the gleam from the lantern.

'She is famous for them,' I said, 'Mistress Townley. A wonderful light hand with pastry, she has, but her cakes would serve as cannon balls for the king's new guns. She pressed them on me as I left the White Hart. Had I found myself stranded in the blizzard, I might have tried to soften one in the snow rather than starve. As it was, it gave me a weapon that the men were not expecting.'

'I hope you gave him a black eye, or broke his jaw!' she said fiercely.

'At any rate, it gave him pause.'

I took the cake back from her and returned it to my scrip.

'I should not like Rufus to break his teeth on it, were we to leave it here.'

'Nicholas Elyot,' she said, 'you may jest, but you could have been killed.'

168

She looked at me, her eyes bleak.

'You would care?' I whispered.

'Do you not know?'

I put my arms around her then, and held her close. She pressed her face against my shoulder, as I had pressed mine against Rufus, and she was weeping. I stroked her hair gently, for her hood had fallen back, and it gleamed gold in the lantern light. Her tonsure as a novice was quite gone, and her hair, which she never dressed in the elaborate fashions of the day, fell to her shoulders in soft, loose curls. I saw that my hand was shaking, but now it was from a different kind of fear.

'Promise me,' she said, her voice muffled in the folds of my cloak, 'that you will not run heedless into such danger again.'

'My love,' I said, greatly daring, 'I had no means of knowing that I was running into danger, save from the blizzard. I am no knight errant, from one of the ancient romances of Arthur. I do not seek out danger.'

She made an odd sound, half gasp, half laugh.

'Nay, it seems that danger seeks you out, like lightning to the tallest tree.'

I remembered that I had said the same thing of the troubadours.

'I suppose that you must be forgiven this time.'

She stood back and wiped her eyes on the edge of her trailing sleeve.

'We must go in, else they will all be wondering what is afoot.'

'Aye,' I said, with a broad grin, 'so they will.'

I took her face between my hands, and kissed her, very lightly, on the mouth. She did not draw away, but she blushed and lowered her head.

'Come,' she said, taking up the lantern in one hand and reaching out the other to me. 'We must indeed go in.'

I blew out Edmond's lantern, and bolted the door behind us.

As we entered the kitchen, everyone looked up, but

we had composed our faces and withdrawn our hands. Emma blew out the lantern and hung her cloak on a peg beside the door.

'Nicholas!' Margaret said. 'What has come to your cloak?'

'An arrow,' I said, 'but it did me no harm.'

'That is excellent to hear,' she said dryly, 'but it is your best cloak, and however carefully I mend it, the tear cannot be hidden.'

I smiled at her absently as I took it off and handed it to her. I was suddenly very tired and hungry, and did not look forward to recounting the day's events, but I must.

My mother gave me a shrewd look.

'Do not scold the boy, Margaret. He is exhausted. Let him eat and warm himself, and later he may tell us all that has happened today.'

In the present circumstances, I did not even object to being called a boy, as I supposed I always would be in my mother's eyes, and I was glad to enjoy my supper without being pressed with questions. Afterwards the children were sent to bed, though Alysoun demanded that I should tell her my whole adventure the next day.

When the remaining company gathered about the fire, I gave an account of all that had occurred, trying to keep it brief, but stopping necessarily when someone asked for more detail. Although Peter had been here earlier, he had only managed to tell them that the troubadours had revealed a little of their mission. Before he could say more, Godfrid had arrived with the news of the strangers he had seen in the forest, and the men had ridden out at once.

'So, although we have no idea of the contents of the letter the troubadours are carrying,' I said, 'the conduct of these Frenchmen has made it quite clear that it is something of grave import. We must suppose that it is some kind of threat to France, but who has sent the message, the troubadours either cannot or will not say.'

'And that is why you have sent to Alice Walsea,' Jordain prompted.

'I thought at once of her, when I heard that the letter was to have been delivered to her cousin, Reginald Le Soten. Failing him, Mistress Walsea, who also acts as an intelligencer for the king, seemed the best person to approach. While I was at the manor, I wrote a letter to her, asking that she send someone – or even an armed body of men – to fetch this missive and carry it to the king. Clearly it is too dangerous to be trusted to any ordinary carrier.'

'Peter told us this much,' Margaret said, 'and that you took the letter, with two of his, dealing with his business affairs, to the carrier at Burford.'

'Aye, and there was no difficulty with that. 'Tis John Hayward is carrier now, son of Thomas Hayward that we used to know. He will take the whole route to London, for the sake of a fellow who is ill. But I learned more.'

I paused and drank some of the ale that Edmond had served us.

'Master Townley of the White Hart had word that the Court celebrates Christmas at Eltham Palace this year, and all the royal princes are to be there. They are planning some joust and a whole host of lavish entertainments. Since the letter carried by the troubadours is intended either for the king, or for Edward of Woodstock, I thought it best to have another string to my bow.'

'An unfortunate analogy,' Emma said dryly.

I grinned. 'Perhaps. In any case, I borrowed paper from the innkeeper and wrote also to Prince Edward. I cannot think what he will make of a letter written on the kind of paper which might have been used to wrap a couple of mutton collops from the butcher, but I made mention of matters only he and I know of, so that he will be sure it comes from me, and is not some trick.'

'You did not ask the Black Prince to come himself!' Susanna looked shocked.

'Never fear. I am sure he is too much occupied with the Christmas mummeries. But if my letter to Alice Walsea should go astray, or should she have difficulty sending someone to fetch the letter, then the prince may provide the authority.'

I turned to my mother. 'It was writing this extra letter that delayed me, so that I was caught by the blizzard. I am sorry if I have given you cause to worry.'

'Aye, we were worried,' she said, 'but I daresay those men would have been lying in wait even had you come earlier. And in that case, we might not have had Godfrid's warning.'

I nodded. 'You speak very true, Mother. And without Edmond's rescue party, I might not have reached here in safety.'

'What I do not understand,' Emma said, 'is why these men were set to waylay you at all. Why should they do so? The troubadours, I can understand. Somehow they have discovered that Gaston and the others are carrying a letter which – so we are guessing – means trouble or danger for France. Someone has ordered these Frenchmen to obtain it by whatever means, and hence they attacked the musicians on their way to the manor. Had they been following them? And then they searched the cart and tried to break into the manor. All that makes sense. But why waylay Nicholas?'

It was something which had been worrying me, once I had time to think. The bearded fellow had demanded the letter I was carrying.

'I cannot say.' I shrugged. 'They seemed to think I was carrying a letter – *the* letter, we must assume. But, as Emma says, why me? I am not one of the troubadours.'

'You have been often at the manor since they arrived,' Edmond said slowly.

'Aye.' Jordain leaned forward. 'And you were one of those who rescued the troubadours in Wychwood. Since they found no trace of the letter when they searched the cart at the manor, perhaps they imagine that the letter has been passed to you.'

I frowned. 'It seems unlikely.'

'It makes me very uncomfortable,' Margaret said, 'to think that these men, who are clearly dangerous, are lurking nearby and spying out the village.'

Juliana was sitting on a rug at her mother's feet, with her arms clasped about her knees. She gave me a troubled look now.

'Do you think it is safe for us to go about the village, Master Elyot? I have promised Birgit to go to the manor tomorrow, to help her arrange the festive greenery, but I do not like the idea that it may not be safe.'

'I must go to the manor myself, tomorrow,' I said, 'to tell Peter Winchingham all that passed in Burford. I can see you safely there.'

Maud said nothing, but laid a reassuring hand on Juliana's shoulder.

'I have said I will come too,' Emma said. 'We shall all be safe in company.'

'We have still to fetch in our own holly and greenery from the wood,' Susanna said. 'We are behind times with it this year. I shall expect you all to help with that in the afternoon tomorrow.'

'Let us hope the storm will have subsided by then,' Edmond said, getting up and going to the window.

He opened it a crack and peered out.

'Still snowing, but I think the wind is not so fierce.'

'Nay,' Susanna said, 'for I noticed that it is not howling as loud in the kitchen chimney. Earlier, we could barely hear ourselves speak.'

Edmond closed and latched the shutter.

'After such a day, I think it is time we were all abed. I will smoor down the fire.'

It was clearly dismissal, and I was glad to take it as such. I had revived briefly with food, but the warmth of the fire, while welcome, was making me sleepy. It seemed like a week ago, not merely this morning, that I had sat in the parlour at the manor with Peter and persuaded the troubadours to trust us.

I lit a candle from the one standing on the coffer, and took myself off to bed.

I fell asleep at once in my narrow bed, and must have slept

an hour or two, but began to be troubled by dark dreams, in which I tried to run, but could not move. I felt myself falling and woke with a start, to find myself having tumbled out of bed in a tangle of bed clothes. Groping about in the dark, I managed to restore some order to the bed, but by now I was thoroughly awake.

Ever since I had been waylaid by the Frenchmen, I had been so occupied, and so tired, that I had hardly allowed myself time to think about it, but now I found myself shivering with horror at the memory. I had been in very serious danger, hopelessly outnumbered by the men, armed and determined that I was in possession of something they had come near to killing Gaston to obtain.

What moment of madness had prompted me to throw a cake in their leader's face? It was hardly the stuff of one of the heroic tales in the collection Roger was scribing. Perhaps not out of place in one of Walter's comic tales, when an innocent lad, little more than a fool, outwits a giant by some absurd means. For absurd it was.

But fortunate.

It had served its purpose.

I thought, if I should ever meet Edward of Woodstock again, I could hardly match his exploits on the battlefields of France. *Well, Your Highness, I felled my enemy with one of Mistress Townley's currant cakes.*

Nay, best stay silent.

I wondered whether our deductions about why I had been waylaid were correct. It seemed a little farfetched. Why should the troubadours have entrusted their dangerous letter to me? And why should I be riding about the countryside with it in my possession?

This led me to another worrying thought. If the Frenchmen thought I had had the letter in my possession, and they discovered that I had despatched letters with the carrier while I was in Burford, would their next victim be John Hayward? He would set off in all innocence for Oxford tomorrow morning, provided the snow permitted, and they might attack him on the way.

I tossed restlessly. There was no way we could get a warning to him in time. Well, if they did seize the letters he was carrying, and read mine to Alice Walsea and the prince, then they would know that the letter they sought was still in Leighton. But it also meant that my request for help would never reach the Court.

There was nothing, however, that I could do about it. If my letters went astray, or were stolen, we would simply wait in vain, and no one would come.

This vital news, contained in the letter the troubadours carried . . . was the timing of it important? They had not said that it must reach the king before a certain date, but perhaps they did not know. They had been told – we still did not know by whom – to deliver it to Reginald Le Soten. The matter would then have been out of their hands. They had expected to find him here and to hand over the letter at Christmastide. Or as soon as they reached the manor, which was several days ago. If Le Soten had then set off directly for London, he would be nearly there by now.

If so, and if the news was urgent, whoever had sent it would expect it to reach the king well before the Christmas festivities were over. But now . . . by carrier . . . travelling through blizzards . . . how long before it could reach him?

Would it be too late? Too late for whatever news or warning it contained to reach the king, and for him to act on it?

My thoughts continue to whirl in my head like the snow flakes still whirling outside. Somehow, eventually, I fell asleep again.

I was the last down to breakfast in the morning, but I suppose I was forgiven on the grounds of the previous night's disturbances. Edmond and his sons had already gone out to the beasts. The maid Elga had finished the milking, and Margaret, Susanna, and Maud had a row of fresh loaves cooling on the coffer. My mother had taken charge of mending my cloak, and while I ate a hasty meal,

Juliana and Emma fidgeted around me, making it clear that they had been ready for some time to leave for the manor.

'Why do you not harness one of our Oxford cart horses to Edmond's cart?' I said. 'Then you can both ride in the cart and I will accompany you on Rufus.'

Clearly this was a welcome suggestion, better than walking to the manor, an undemanding distance in the summer, but a trial in heavy snow.

Hilda shovelled two more loaves out of the bread oven with the long handled bread paddle and slid them on to the coffer to join the others.

'May I go to see Birgit too, Mother?' she asked.

Susanna looked up from beating cake batter in a deep bowl, and pushed a loose strand of hair back from her face.

'Very well, but – mind! – I want you all back here this afternoon to gather our own greenery. There are some good holly berries in the woods this year. Mother Nature has provided for the birds.'

Rafe tugged at my sleeve. 'We will leave some berries for the birds, won't we?' he whispered.

'Never fear,' I said, tousling his hair. 'There will be plenty and to spare. There is a great holly thicket up behind the farm. You will see.'

I was glad that Hilda was to be allowed to come with us. Susanna worked her very hard, but then, her brothers also worked as hard as their father.

We were soon on our way, the three girls bright as birds in their winter cloaks and hoods. Juliana started to sing, her breath steaming in the frosty air, and soon they were all singing winter carols in rounds. It was no longer snowing, and the sharp cold made the sound chime like bells.

I halted briefly at Alan Wodville's cottage, where he was chopping firewood.

'No sign of those men this morning, I suppose?' I called.

He rested his axe on the ground and wiped his hot face on his sleeve.

176

'None that anyone has seen. Mind, they seem to prefer to do their business at night.'

'Very true,' I said. 'You have the right of it. However, if anything should be seen, send word of it, will you? To the farm and to the manor?'

'Aye.' He lifted the axe. ''Tis to be hoped they will try nothing at Christmastide.'

'Indeed,' I said, urging Rufus on again, to catch up with the cart. Though I had little confidence in any respect the Frenchmen might have for the season.

At the manor I left the girls to their labours with Birgit, whom we found standing dismayed beside an enormous heap of ivy, evergreen branches, and berried holly twigs carried into the great hall by the manor servants.

'Mary and Jesus be praised that you are come,' she was saying, as I headed for the small parlour. 'I do not know what to do with all this!'

It did not take long for me to recount to Peter everything that had happened after I had left him the previous day.

'It was a good plan,' he said, 'to send a letter to the Prince of Wales, as well as to Mistress Walsea. How long do you suppose it will take, before they reach the Court?'

I shook my head. 'Not quickly, I fear. The carrier said about a week, perhaps Twelfth Day, but that was before the latest snow fall. There will be little traffic along the roads over Christmas, so the snow will not be beaten down. It could be much longer.'

'So I feared. I have persuaded the troubadours that their wisest plan is to remain here with me until someone comes from Court, rather than risking themselves, and their precious letter, on the road to London. They have no pressing engagement in London, only that they hoped to find employment when they reached there.'

'I am glad they have seen the sense, at last, in trusting us to help them,' I said. 'Perhaps now we may turn our minds to the Christ Child's birth, and to your Twelfth Day feast.'

'Indeed. Some of your party have come to help my daughter decorate the hall for the season, have they not?'

'They are there now.'

He rose from his chair. 'Perhaps we should lend a hand. It will be good to celebrate an English Christmas again. I hear some of the manor people speaking of Twelfth Day as Three Kings Day.'

'Aye, 'tis often called that hereabouts. Or Little Christmas.'

'Or,' he said, 'as Sire Raymond named it, correctly, Epiphany.'

We found the four girls busy draping the winter harvest from Wychwood about the panelled walls and arranging wreathes of holly in the window embrasures.

Emma was sucking a pierced thumb. 'Ah,' she said, 'the gentlemen come when the most painful part of the work is done.'

Hilda looked a little shocked that Emma should address the lord of the manor so, but Birgit merely laughed.

'My father can twist the garlands of holly and ivy for the hallway and the stairs,' she said. 'Then he will know the pain of the holly leaves.'

'And I shall have the good sense to wear thick leather gloves to do it,' he said, patting her cheek. 'I can see we are hardly needed here, Nicholas.'

Nevertheless, we spent the rest of the morning decorating the manor, before I chivvied the girls away, mindful that we were expected to gather our own festive greenery in the afternoon.

'You have helped me so much,' Birgit said, 'that I shall come and help you – if I may, Father?'

'Of course, why not take Hans as well. You can ride pillion behind him, and will need only one horse.'

Altogether, we made quite a party, riding back to the farm.

In the afternoon we were a veritable army, setting out on

our expedition, for everyone but the women went from the farm (they being busy still about their festive cookery), and our numbers were augmented by the two from the manor. Even the youngest came. Although the small children could be of little help in cutting branches, they would remember this, as I remembered such expeditions in my own early childhood.

Part of the farmland had been assarted from Wychwood in my grandfather's day, but just beyond these newer fields, the woods began again, and it was to this part of the forest that we made our way, following along the headland at the edge of one of the fields, where the hedge had kept the snow to a minimum. Once we were within the forest itself, the great trees had held back some of the snow, although the branches were layered deep. Every so often a clump of snow would slide down without warning, causing us to jump out of the way, but we did not always escape a dowsing.

Thomas was trundling a handcart to carry home our spoils, and kept cursing as it became wedged amongst protruding roots, or threatened to tip over, taking him with it. The girls laughed at him and refused to help. I watched Emma covertly. Her eyes were sparkling and her cheeks were reddened by the cold, so she looked no older than the younger girls. Perhaps she could now forget the unhappiness of her time as a forced novice, and the terror of pursuit by her murderous stepfather.

She is so young, I thought. I am seven years older, but more than that. I am older through widowhood and fatherhood. I should leave her to enjoy her youth, with Juliana and Hilda, and now Birgit. She is much closer to them in age than to me.

'Are we not nearly at the holly thicket, Nicholas?' Edmond had stopped and was looking about him.

'Bear further to the right,' I called. 'But first, see that hawthorn behind you? There's a fine cladding of ivy on the trunk, with large leaves. Let us harvest some of that.'

We dragged it down with billhooks, and chopped the

flexible vines away from the solid central stem, then coiled it up as best we could, into the handcart.

'I shall make myself a crown!' Alysoun said, and began twisting a fallen tendril into a garland, but it sprang apart again.

'Like this,' Birgit said, tying two soft ends together. 'Your Majesty's crown.'

Nothing would do then but for Maysant, Lora, and Mega to have crowns. I could see Rafe debating whether such frippery might be suitable only for girls, but then he found a fallen branch to serve him as a sword.

Hans seized another, and parried Rafe's weapon with his own, pretending terrible defeat when Rafe thrust at him, collapsing into the snow, clutching his chest.

'I should have beaten those Frenchmen with this,' Rafe told me, 'if I had been with you.'

'One day,' I promised, 'I shall teach you to use a sword, although I am no great hand at it.'

'Sadly neglected,' Jordain said, 'in the Oxford course of study.'

'I think we have enough ivy,' Edmond said. 'Lead us to the holly thicket, Nicholas, if you can remember where it is.'

It was further than I remembered, and we gathered a load of evergreen as we went, but it was worth the walk, for the red berries shone out in great clusters.

'Oh, this is very fine!' Birgit exclaimed. 'Much better than we have in our part of the wood.'

'The painful part,' Emma said, 'is in the gathering of it.'

However, we had equipped ourselves with hedging shears as well as billhooks, so we managed to keep the injuries to a minimum.

'I can see why holly is taken as a symbol for Christ's crown of thorns,' I said, with feeling.

Even through the thick leather gloves Edmond had lent me, the spines had pierced me, and I was driven to sucking two bleeding fingers. A drop of my blood fell on the snow, and Rafe gazed at it with a worried frown.

'Are you badly hurt, Papa?' he said.

'Not at all,' I said, with manly bravery, and Emma grinned at me.

'Now we have everything,' James said, 'save mistletoe. And there is some on the apple trees in the orchard, if we go back that way.'

'Time we went back in any case,' I said, 'for it is getting dark.'

We had been so absorbed in our hunt for the Christmas greenery, that the dusk had crept up on us. The smaller children were suddenly tired, and needed to be carried, so we made somewhat slow progress back to the farm. Once we were out of the woods it did not seem quite so dark, but the snow was deep as we trudged toward the orchard, and a few flakes drifted down, as though the weather sought to tease us as to its intentions.

There were some great balls of mistletoe on a few of the older apple trees, more than twice the size of my head. It is strong, mistletoe, rooting itself in its host tree and feeding off it, very reluctant to leave its stolen home, but we managed to hack down two bunches, having sent the younger children ahead to the farm, with Thomas and the handcart. We came into the kitchen in a wave of icy air, to the smell of gingerbread.

'You should be away,' Susanna said to Hans and Birgit, 'if you are to be home before full dark.'

'But we are here to help you decorate!' Birgit protested. 'We will go when it is done.'

I saw Edmond and Susanna exchange a glance.

'James and I will ride over with them,' he said quietly. 'Let the young ones enjoy the festive season and put other worries out of mind.'

'The more hands to the work, the quicker it will be done,' Margaret said.

Although life in the farm revolved almost entirely around the kitchen, the oldest part of the house was the hall, with its great curved roof beams, reaching as high as

181

the bedchambers in the newer parts of the building, which had grown over the generations, almost like one of the great yew trees in the wood, which throw out peripheral trunks just as the house had thrown out additional wings.

As it was so large, and so high, the hall was difficult to heat, but we always celebrated Christmas here. The Yule log already lay in the vast hearth, and would be lit on the Eve, but for the present we kept warm pinning up our garlands around the walls, framing the narrow windows with ivy, and filling every remaining space with our abundant, glistening holly branches, their berries as red as the blood I had shed on the snow.

'Enough!' Susanna said at last.

'But the mistletoe,' Alysoun said.

'That must be woven into a kissing ring,' Susanna said, 'and it is too cold to do that here. We shall make it after supper, and you shall help me.'

She herded us back to the kitchen, leaving the old hall mysterious and silent behind us. I wondered how many Christmases it had seen, and how many of my ancestors had garlanded its walls.

Realising just how late it had grown, Hans and Birgit would not stay to eat with us, but fetched their horse and rode off to the manor, escorted by Edmond and James. I could see that Edmond was concerned, as I was, that anyone from the manor might be in danger, if the Frenchmen were still about, but he and James returned soon after, having met with no trouble.

'No more snow either,' James said. 'God be thanked.'

After supper, true to her word, Susanna laid out the mistletoe on the kitchen table, together with a few of the ivy tendrils she had kept back, and some lengths of farm wire.

'Now,' she said to Alysoun, 'you shall learn how to make a Christmas kissing ring, for every woman must master the art.'

'I am afraid I do not know how to make one,' Emma said. 'One of my grandmother's waiting women always made ours at my grandfather's home, and later, my stepfather did not like such things.'

'Then you shall help as well,' Susanna said.

Helga and Juliana exchanged smiles, confident in their own skills, and instead sat near the fire with their knitting. I watched the work for a time, then joined my mother, setting a stool near her cushioned chair.

'Thank you for mending my cloak, Mother,' I said.

She clicked her tongue and shook her head.

'You cannot always depend on Margaret to care for you. What if she should wed again?'

I looked at her, startled.

'I do not suppose she thinks of such a thing.'

'Perhaps she may. One day.'

'Well,' I said, relieved that she did not seem to have anything specific in mind, 'for now, let us enjoy the present.'

'Aye. It is good to see so many young people about the farm. And I like the new people at the manor.'

I nodded. I found I was growing sleepy in the warmth of the fire, after our hard work in the woods and in the hall. I yawned.

'Christmas Eve tomorrow,' I said.

Chapter Nine

The Eve of Christ's Nativity dawned very quiet and still. The house was silent when I woke, and for a time I lay with the bedclothes drawn up to my chin, remembering other Eves when I had woken in this room, my mother and father in the largest bed chamber which Edmond and Susanna now occupied, my brother John directly below my attic room, and Margaret, before she was sent off to be married, in a small chamber next to my parents, which Hilda was presently sharing with Juliana.

My parents had had other children, but they had not lived past birth or infancy. I was blessed, I knew, that both my children had survived, even Rafe, whose mother had been taken by the plague so soon after his birth. He was such a little scrap of a thing, when I held him cupped in my two hands, not much bigger than a kitten, it seemed at the time. And the terrible risk of finding a wet nurse, who might herself carry the plague. Even now he was small and slight for his age. How fragile, too, must that Child have seemed, born in a rough stable, bedded on straw. How cold and unwelcoming the world. Yet He had lived to change that very world.

It seemed almost a sacrilege to make any sound on this holy morning, so that I found myself turning back the blankets quietly and tiptoeing to the window. I opened the shutters carefully, hoping they would not squeak, for the whole house was wrapped in silence. Outside, not a branch stirred, not a bird hopped on the ground, no mouse or squirrel scurried across field or yard. I felt as though I was the only living soul awake on this bright morning.

For it was bright. The sun had just risen and the sky was a perfect dome of pale azure. More snow had fallen in the night, but there were no snow clouds to be seen now. The unmarked white crust stretched away across the farmland, all the way to the woods, and the low beams of the sun set it dazzling in crystal brilliance, so that it seemed as though nothing in Creation could look more pure, more perfect.

I dressed quickly, took up my boots in my hand, and went softly down the stairs to the kitchen. The fire was almost burnt out, so I laid a few logs on the embers, but did not stir it up, for fear the noise would wake the girl Elga, who slept in a little room beside the pantry. Then I laced on my boots and slipped outside.

I hesitated to mar that unblemished carpet of crystalline white, so I skirted around the edge of the yard, and then along the headland of the field beyond, and here I saw that I was not the only creature awake, for there was the delicate feathering of bird tracks, criss-crossing the snow. Something drew me to the wood shore, but I did not go further than a yard or two into the trees, then brushed the snow off a fallen trunk and sat down. I had been there no more than a few minutes when a robin flew down beside my feet, and studied me with interest, then a wood mouse peeped out from beneath a bush of broom, and studied me likewise, and retreated. In some way they reminded me of my children, the robin like Alysoun, bold and curious, the mouse like Rafe, cautious and shy. I nearly laughed aloud at my absurd analogy, but did not want to scare away the bird.

Then suddenly the robin launched itself into the air and was gone. Something had startled it, though I had not moved. I turned my head carefully. Was there some other creature about? They came bursting out of the undergrowth, three of them, half grown fox cubs, tumbling and playing in the snow like children, tasting it, rolling over

185

and over, mock fighting then breaking off to leap straight up into the air and chase each other round and round the broom bush. I hoped the mouse had dived down into a safe burrow.

I struggled to keep silent, for they were comical in the sheer joy of their play, and I did not want to frighten them. Then there was a short bark away to my right, a fox's bark. The cubs paused in their play, one with his foot on his brother's tail. They looked at each other, as if to say, 'Ah, well, we had best go home', then they scampered off, in the direction of the adult fox. Well trained children indeed.

As I made my way slowly back to the farmhouse, I could tell from the steady plume of smoke rising straight into the sky from the kitchen chimney, that at least one other person was about by now. Margaret or Susanna, probably, shaping last night's risen dough into loaves. I marvelled how they could make bread, day after day, with what seemed such little effort, yet it was all planned and timed so that we never went without.

Instead of going straight into the house, I visited the stable first, and on my way to Rufus's stall I scooped up a measure of oats for him from the barrel where they were stored. After his extraordinary gallop in escaping the Frenchmen, I felt he deserved more cosseting. Besides, it was the Eve of Christmas. If Rufus was surprised at this early morning treat, he did not show it, so I left him to his oats, and went back to the kitchen.

Maud was shovelling the hot embers out of the bread oven, ready for sliding the loaves inside, while Susanna shaped a sixth loaf, five already sitting on the table, ready for baking.

'By the saints, Nicholas!' Susanna pressed a floury hand to her breast. 'You startled me, coming in like that. Whyever are you abroad so early?'

'I woke,' I said simply. 'And it is very beautiful outside. Very quiet, as though the whole world is holding its breath, waiting for Christ's Nativity.'

I looked around. 'Can I do aught to help?'

'Aye, you may fetch us in more firewood. You know where it is stored?'

I smiled. 'I know where it is stored. Where it was stored in my father's time, in my grandfather's time, in my grandfather's father's time . . .'

She laughed. 'Well, fetch us that basket full, then. Tip those last logs on to the fire.

I did as I was bid. Outside, the day no longer had that perfect tranquillity I had felt when I first woke, but I sensed still the feeling that everything was waiting. After what had been afoot in recent days, such a sense of waiting might have seemed ominous, but it did not. Somehow I was convinced that nothing evil could happen this day, nor the next, for the air of holiness was palpable. Perhaps I was moved by some blind naïve faith, but I felt that even the Frenchmen lurking somewhere nearby could not harm us. It was difficult to explain, even to myself, what I felt, but the men seemed to have faded into nothing more than mist, a ghostly illusion. I could not even begin to believe in their reality.

The woodpile stood, as it had always done, against the outside wall of one wing of the house. This had been forever its chosen place, because the upper storey of this wing jettied out over the lower by a good yard or more, a style of building you see more often in towns than in the country, for in towns space at ground level is scarce and costly, and the only way to extend your house is out over the lower storey. In the country there is generally space enough to build wide at the start. Why this part of the farmhouse was built like this, no one knew or could remember. Perhaps one of my ancestors had changed his mind in the course of building this wing. Or perhaps the upper storey had been added later, and a larger room was wanted than the one below.

Whatever the reason, the protruding upper floor provided excellent protection for the wood store, where the logs were stacked up neatly, row upon row. I had never known the entire stock of logs to be used up, so I was certain that the bottom layers were as old as I, and perhaps a good deal older.

I filled the basket until I could cram no more in, then swung it up on to my shoulder, the more easily to carry it into the kitchen.

'Ah, I thank you, Nicholas,' Susanna said. 'Put it over in its place, and add another log to the fire. This cold weather, we need a good blaze.'

'Why is Margaret not about?' I said, dusting the scraps of bark from my hands.

'Let her sleep,' Maud said. 'She has worked harder than any of us.'

I knew it was true. I hardly ever saw Margaret rest. Even if she sat down of an evening, her hands were never idle – sewing or spinning or mending or knitting.

Without being asked, I began to lay the table for breakfast, and was met by raised eyebrows from Edmond as he and his sons passed through the kitchen on their way to feed the animals, but he made no comment on my domestic chores.

Susanna tapped on the door of Elga's room, and the girl came out, yawning and rubbing her eyes. Without a word, she flung a shawl around her shoulders, picked up two milking buckets, and trudged outside after my cousin.

It was a morning like any other morning on the farm, yet still that sense of expectancy hung in the air.

One by one, the rest of the household gathered. Emma took over shaping loaves from Susanna, while Hilda and Juliana dressed the small children in the warmth of the kitchen fire. Jordain went out to the barn, and reappeared carrying two buckets of milk for Elga, who was bringing a third.

'Look, mistress!' she said. 'So much milk for wintertime! How can it be?'

'Perhaps an offering of the kine for the Christ Child's birth,' Jordain said, smiling at her.

She clasped her hands together. 'Do you really think so, Master Brinkylsworth?'

'Why not? There have been greater miracles. The Birth itself the greatest of them.'

Her eyes were shining, as though she herself had helped the miracle to happen. I was glad to see the child quite unscarred, after her vile treatment at the hands of Gilbert Mordon. She took up a broom and began to sweep the ashes which had fallen from the bread oven on to the hearth.

'Why did no one wake me?'

Margaret appeared at the foot of the stairs, as immaculately tidy as ever, but a look of astonishment on her face.

'You were sleeping so peacefully when I woke,' Emma said, 'that I thought I would let you lie. It will be a busy time, today and tomorrow, and all the days to this great feast of Master Winchingham's on Three Kings Day.'

'I am here to work now,' Margaret said briskly, reaching for an apron. 'What needs to be done, Susanna?'

'Nothing for now,' Susanna said. 'But you might call to the men. I am making an oatmeal and gravy stir-about for this cold morning, and they should come while it is hot.'

The day continued in that strangely quiet, almost sleepy mood, shot through with a feeling of expectancy. In the late morning, Alysoun sought me out, her eyes bright with excitement.

'Cousin James says that when he was my age, he used to go sledding on the high field below the wood. The one they call Edwin's Piece. Can we go sledding? Will you take me? Please?'

I knew the place. I had gone sledding there myself as a boy. I looked over Alysoun's head at James, who was grinning.

'This was your doing, James,' I said. 'What do you intend to do about it?'

'Why should my cousin not sled, if she wishes?' he said innocently. 'Or is she too ladylike, with her Oxford manners?'

'Too ladylike?' I said dryly. 'Never that.'

Alysoun's lower lip had begun to quiver, and Emma took her hand.

'I am certainly not too ladylike, Alysoun,' she said. 'I have not been sledding . . . Oh, these ten years and more. My cousin William and I used to slide down a hill on my grandfather's manor. Shall we see what we can use?'

My mother was listening, her face solemn, but her eyes sparkling.

'The tray you used for a sled, Nicholas, is still here, in the apple store. And John's as well. They took such punishment they were never good for their proper purpose again.'

'Aye,' James said. 'Thomas and I used them as well.'

'There is a broken door from the henhouse would make another,' Thomas volunteered. 'I will fetch it from the barn.'

In the end, there were quite a few of us, climbing up to the far top of Edwin's Piece, one of the earliest fields cleared from the woodland, so my grandfather used to say, around the time the first part of the farmhouse was built. It was somewhat steep, and so mostly used to pasture the sheep nowadays, since there was better arable land lower down. I took possession of my old tray, which was a little small for me now, and took Rafe on my knees. We set off first, flying down the unmarked snow with that heart stopping sense combined of exhilaration and fear. Rafe clung to me at first, then as we slowed smoothly on the more level ground at the bottom of the field, he crowed with joy.

'Can we do it again, Papa? Please?'

'Aye, but we must climb all the way up again. Slow for the climb, swift for the drop.'

Like a courtier, I thought.

'Have a care!' I pulled Rafe out of the way as John's tray flew down toward us, Emma and Alysoun looking much of an age, their eyes bright, their hair whipped out by the wind of their flight, their mouths open as they shrieked with delight.

'Not ladylike at all,' I said with a laugh, as they slewed sideways and stopped at my feet.

'Who cares for that!' Emma said eagerly. 'Come Alysoun, we shall race them to the top.' And they were off, narrowly missing Thomas and Juliana, who came hurtling down almost together. James and Hilda followed more circumspectly, Hilda holding Lora, though little Megan had shaken her head when invited to join us, and chose to stay in the warm kitchen.

I had forgotten the sense of freedom it imparted, that wild careering descent of the snowy field. As fast as a galloping horse, without the control of reins or stirrups. The only way to guide or stop the tray was by digging your heels into the snow, and, if done injudiciously, it could hurtle you face down into a drift and deliver you a sharp blow from the heavy wooden tray.

With the speed and the excitement and the laughter, we might all have been children again, until at last the cold and our stiffening fingers drove us inside to thaw.

Hilda looked guiltily at the pot simmering over the fire, and the dishes ready laid on the table.

'I am sorry, Mother,' she said, 'I should have come sooner to help.'

Susanna laid her hand on her daughter's rosy cheek.

'Nay, child, 'tis right for you to have some fun. Years enough ahead for you to spend your days at the cooking.'

As we gathered for our plain Advent midday dinner of vegetable potage, I caught a wistful look on the girl Elga's face. She, too, deserved to be a child sometimes, maid servant though she was.

After dinner, Hilda and Juliana took the small children down to the village, to see whether the pond had frozen hard enough yet for skating, and to keep them from under the feet of those making the final preparations for the family feast on the next day.

191

'Let them take Elga, too,' I murmured to Susanna. ''Tis Christmastide and the girl has worked as hard as Hilda, as hard as a grown woman. Let her too have her fun, though there may be little to do at the pond.'

Susanna looked surprised at my suggestion, but nodded.

'Aye, the girl may go, if she wishes.' She turned to Elga, who was leaning over the table, peeling onions and chopping cabbage.

'Would you like to go down to the village with Hilda and the others, Elga?'

The sudden brightness of the girl's face was answer in itself, and she ran into her little cupboard of a room to fetch cloak and boots.

On the threshold she paused. 'If you are sure you do not need me, mistress?'

'Nay, be off with you,' Susanna said, flapping her apron as if she were shooing hens.

Jordain had gone out to help with the stock, saying that he wanted to visit Sire Raymond later, and Emma had been told her help was not needed in the kitchen.

'I shall make a start on Walter's book of his mother's stories,' she told me. 'I have done nothing to it since we arrived, and had no time before we left Oxford. I thought I would sort them into an order which seems right to me, as I suggested when you gave them to me, then ask you what you think before I begin to scribe. If that pleases you?'

'Aye,' I said with a smile. 'That pleases me. I shall like to see what you make of his stories.'

'I have heard him tell some of them, but certainly not all.'

'You will find that some are very curious, I think possibly very ancient. When the book is made, I think Sire Raymond will like to see it. He has a great interest in such ancient things.'

I was not wanted for the scribing, or in the kitchen, or about the farm. I considered saddling Rufus and riding over to the manor, but a kind of lassitude had come over me, after my early morning burst of energy and our sledding in Edwin's Piece. I went up to my bed chamber, and although it was very cold I lay down on my bed, and fell asleep.

Perhaps I had woken too early in the morning, for I slept deeply, and when I woke I could tell from the change in the light that at least a couple of hours had passed. Feeling an idle wretch, I made my way downstairs again, expecting to be chided for my absence, but there was no one in the kitchen but Margaret, who sat in the cushioned chair usually occupied by my mother. She was darning a pair of Rafe's hose.

'The house seems deserted,' I said, sitting on my heels before the kitchen hearth and stretching out my hands to the fire, for they were frozen. It must have been the cold in my garret that had woken me.

'Our mother is resting,' she said, 'and Emma is working on her book. Susanna and Maud have gone down to the village to visit old Goody Taylor, who cannot easily leave her cottage nowadays. The others, I think, are still down by the pond, making sure Alysoun does not fall through the ice. Some of the village lads have been skating around the edges, but Edmond thinks it is too soft in the middle to bear their weight.'

'And Alysoun cannot be relied on to stay away from it,' I finished for her.

I brought a stool over to the fireside and sat down.

My mother's words had lingered at the back of my mind, vaguely troubling me ever since she had spoken them.

'Meg,' I said, studying her face closely, which – to tell truth – I rarely did. 'Do you think you might ever marry again?'

It was not so unreasonable to ask. She was but thirty, still of child bearing age. Although she never spoke of them, I knew she had never ceased to mourn the loss of her two boys to the Pestilence. For all of us it is difficult to speak to those times and those deaths.

She laid her mending in her lap, and looked at me,

her eyes wide.

'What a curious thing to ask me, Nicholas!' she said. 'What has put that into your head?'

'Something our mother said. She thought you might wish to marry again, that you would not care to spend all your life caring for me and my children.'

She picked up her mending again, and kept her eyes on her needle, as it flashed in and out. It has always amazed me, how quickly she sews, even when she is working on a complicated piece of embroidery.

'I wonder what might have prompted her to say such a thing.' Her voice was calm and detached.

'I think perhaps she does not like to see you wasting your life on us,' I said slowly, 'when you might be mistress of your own house. Yet I have always felt that you are mistress of our shared family home.'

Still keeping her eyes averted from me, she said quietly, 'My experience of marriage was not such as would spur me into another.'

'Not all men are the monsters that Elias Makepeace was,' I said. 'You might find a good husband yet, and have children of your own.'

'I love Alysoun and Rafe as much as if they were my own.'

'I know. And without you, I do not know how I could have reared them so well. Nor could I have kept house, or fed us.' I smiled. 'You have but to look at John Baker and how he struggles to rear his son. We widowers are poor, helpless fellows.'

'Aye, that you are.' She held up Rafe's hose. 'Could you have mended these?'

'Indeed, I could not. Nor baked fresh bread every morning.'

'Nor mopped up the puddles when that puppy Rowan was small.'

'Now that,' I said, 'I might have managed.'

She laughed, and rolled up the hose. 'That is all the mending I propose for Christmas Eve, though I wager that when Rafe and Alysoun come in from their visit to the village pond, there will be more rents, or buttons missing. To say nothing of how fast they outgrow their clothes.'

She rose from the chair and shook out her skirts, tucking the hose into the basket of her mending, which never seemed to grow any less.

'I told our mother I would wake her after an hour, and it has surely been longer than that.'

She walked to the bottom of the stairs, then turned toward me. 'Never fear, Nicholas. You will not be abandoned to bake your own loaves. Should I ever find myself a new husband – and Jesu knows, I am not seeking one – then I will give you fair warning, so that you may find some other woman to bake your bread and mend your children's clothes.'

At that, she smiled broadly, and went away up the stairs to wake our mother from her rest.

I was pondering whether to see how Emma fared with her work on Walter's tales, or whether she would prefer to bring them to me later, when there came a tap on the door, followed immediately by the entrance of Godfrid, the farm's elderly shepherd. As usual in winter, he was clad in a miscellaneous mixture of coarse woollen garments and dressed sheepskins, one of which he was wearing today like a kind of sleeveless tabard, belted in at the waist with a leather belt from which hung several tools of his trade – a small pair of shears (for cutting away brambles caught in a sheep's fleece), a curved spike with a wooden handle which I had seen him use to clean a hoof, a horn he used to call his dog, when he was too far away for a whistle, and a rubbed and ancient leather scrip. His crook had a handle of carved ram's horn, and he wore loose trousers over his hose, bound criss-cross with leather garters. His tan and white dog slipped in quietly at his heels, assessed the kitchen with his bright, intelligent eyes, and – finding no other canine occupants – lay down close to the fire.

'Master not here, then?' Godfrid said.

'Gone down to the village,' I said. 'The children

wanted to see the skating.'

'There will be none in the middle of the pond yet.'

I nodded. Godfrid was the most weather-wise man in Leighton.

'Is there a problem with the sheep?' I asked.

He shook his head. 'All's well with the beasts. 'Tis fellows on two legs is the problem.'

It was Godfrid, I remembered, who had spotted the Frenchmen in the woods when I was on my way back from Burford. I sprang to my feet.

'They are here?'

My children and the others, gone blithely down to the village, never thinking of danger lurking nearby.

'Not here, nay, but signs of them. Come ye.'

He jerked his head imperiously toward the door. I snatched up my cloak and followed, the dog padding at my heels.

Godfrid led the way out of the farm at his long loping pace, perfected over the years to accompany a moving flock. My strides were shorter, and I had nearly to scramble to keep up. He headed for the part of the wood where we had gathered greenery just the day before, and my heart lurched at the thought that the children had been so close to danger.

Godfrid, however, headed deeper into the wood and veered off to the left, along a track barely visible amongst the trees, made by something smaller than deer. Badgers, perhaps. It was crossed with low branches and spiked tendrils of bramble, so we were forced to duck or thrust the impediments aside.

'They cannot have come this way on horseback,' I said.

He stopped to hold a vicious blackberry vine away from my face.

'Nay, they came t'other way. There's a path through to the manor you could just get a horse along.'

'Wait a moment,' I said. 'I know where we are now. Isn't this the way to old Goody Fairburn's cottage? I haven't been this way since I was a boy.'

'Aye. She's been gone these eight years and more.'

'They used to call her a witch in the village,' I said nervously. 'And we lads would dare each other to go up to her cottage, but never did. She was probably nothing but a poor old woman.'

'Poor she was. Witch she was not, though she was a wise woman for the herbs.'

'And who has the cottage now?'

'No one. Stands empty. Who would want to live out here, now there are empty cottages in the village, since the Death?' He paused. 'Or at least it *was* empty.'

We pushed our way through the last of the undergrowth – for the badger track had petered out – and there was the cottage in a small area of cleared ground. That is, it had once been cleared ground, but already the wood was taking back its own. And the cottage could hardly be called a cottage. It was a one room hovel, its roof of thatch badly decayed, its door hanging askew.

'They have been here,' I said, 'the Frenchmen?'

'Aye.'

He thrust the door fully open with his shoulder and we peered inside. Certainly someone had been here. Rough beds had been made of piled up bracken, which was still partially green, so it had not long been gathered. There was an earthenware cup with a broken handle, with a few dregs of ale still in the bottom, and a riding glove, too good to have been discarded. It must have been dropped.

'More than one man,' I said, 'by the number of beds.'

'Aye.'

I poked at the hearth, no more than a circle of stones set in the centre of the floor, leaving the smoke of the fire to find its way out through the thatch. It held fresh ashes. I knew some people in the village still preferred this arrangement to a chimney, saying the smoke in the thatch killed the fleas and bed bugs, which would proliferate in a house with the luxury of a modern fireplace.

I picked up the glove and studied it. It was made of

fine leather and embroidered.

'It was the Frenchmen who were here?' I said, though I thought the glove was evidence enough.

'Aye, I saw them riding away, this morning. I would have come to Master sooner, but I had a sick ewe to attend, one of my best. And I reckoned, since they was riding away, 'twas not urgent.'

'Where were they going, could you tell?'

'They headed for the Burford road, not for anywhere hereabouts, so I thought good riddance.'

'If they stay way.'

I was thinking hard. Why would the men leave, when their mission was certainly not accomplished? Perhaps the rough life in the forest hut had proved too much for them in the intense cold of recent days. The occupation of Goody Fairburn's cottage explained why they had been nearby, able to descend on the manor at night, and wait in ambush for me.

We stepped outside, and I thrust the glove into my scrip.

'I think they will be back,' I said, 'wherever they have gone now, and for what purpose. Will you keep your eyes and ears open, Godfrid?'

'I will that, Master Nicholas. We want no filthy foreigners creeping round our woods.'

'We do not,' I agreed. 'Not, at least, if they are French.'

We walked back to the farm in silence. I could not think what to make of the men's departure, though their bivouac in the woods made sense enough. At the farm we parted, Godfrid to the paddock beside the barns, where he turned out the sheep in the daytime, and where they could scrape aside the snow to find the grass beneath. I went thoughtfully back to the kitchen, deciding that for the moment I would say nothing of Godfrid's discovery. The Frenchmen were gone and I had no wish to mar the tranquillity of Christmas Eve.

The others returned soon afterwards, their faces rosy with the cold. Alysoun, I was not surprised to discover, had soaked her boots, hose, and the bottom of her gown to at least a foot's depth.

'You did not go into the middle of the pond!' I said, momentarily shocked.

She was here, and safe, but what peril had she put herself in this time?

'Nay, I did not,' she said demurely. 'Cousin Edmond told me I must not, but the village boys were very rude when I said I wanted to skate. They said girls may not skate. That is not true, is it? Cousin James says he will make me a pair of skates out of mutton bones, and soon the pond will be quite frozen. It is much better for skating here than in Oxford.'

'Indeed,' I said, thinking with a shudder of the treacherous waterways of the Cherwell and the Thames. 'But that does not explain why you look as though someone has taken you by the armpits and dipped you in the middle of the pond.'

She giggled. 'Oh, it was not the pond. We came back past Cousin Edmond's mill, and I tried the ice at the edge of the mill stream. I stamped on it hard, to be sure it was strong enough.'

I shut my eyes in resignation. 'And it was not.'

'Nay, it smashed at once.'

'Did you not realise how dangerous that was?'

'It wasn't a bit dangerous. Cousin James caught me before I could fall in.'

I opened my eyes and looked accusingly at Edmond and James, who were somewhat sheepish.

'She was too quick for us,' Edmond explained. 'I never thought she would try the mill stream.'

I took Alysoun between my knees and gripped her hard by the shoulders.

'Now, pay me mind, my pet,' I said. 'You must *never* go on to the ice where there is fast flowing water beneath. It will always be treacherous, even in a cold winter like this. We only skate on still water, like the village pond, and you may only go on to the ice after it has been judged safe, and someone much heavier than you has tested its strength. You must promise me, or I will tell Cousin James not to make you any skates.'

'I promise,' she said cheerfully. 'It was very, very cold in the mill stream.'

'Aye,' I said dryly, 'it would be. Now go and change your wet clothes before you take the lung fever.'

Juliana held out her hand to Alysoun. 'Come with me. I will help you.'

'She can dress herself,' I said severely.

'Of course she can,' Juliana said, 'but we must make ourselves pretty for the midnight service, Alysoun. That is, if you are allowed to stay up so late?'

'On this one night of the year,' I conceded.

We ate a light supper, appropriate to the last evening of Advent – salted fish, rinsed of the preserving salt, and cooked simply with a little butter and eaten with cabbage, onions, and bread. All the children were put down to sleep, that they might stay awake for the service. The rest of us gathered quietly beside the fire, while Jordain read aloud the account in the Gospels of Mary and Joseph coming to Bethlehem to be taxed, during the reign of Herod the Great. As Emma and I were the only ones who understood the Latin, he also retold it in simple English for the others, although Juliana said to me afterwards that she could follow most of it.

'Although perhaps that is because I know the story so well,' she admitted.

As it grew towards midnight, the children were fetched downstairs, yawning and fuddled with sleep, and given a cup of milk and a Christmas gingerbread to sustain them. I smiled at my mother as she handed out the gingerbreads, which had been shaped in a mould to resemble the star that rose over Bethlehem. I had been given the same milk and the same gingerbreads, made in the same mould, when I was a boy.

I wrapped my mother's cloak about her, for she had insisted that she would attend the midnight Mass with the rest of us.

'I have never missed it yet,' she said, 'and I shall not miss it now, not so long as I have two feet to walk on.'

'Except that you shall not walk to church,' I said. 'I have sent Thomas to hitch up the cart, and I shall drive you there, like a queen.'

'Aye,' she said with a laugh, 'in the farm cart, like a very queen!'

Edmond covered the fire, and we set off, the others walking. I brought an arm-load of blankets and tucked them around my mother, for it seemed the coldest night yet.

'So many stars,' she murmured, as we drove down the farm lane. 'So many. How could the Kings have known which one to follow?'

'I suppose it must have been especially bright,' I said, looking up.

The sky was clear of any cloud, and the moon cast a silver light so bright and hard that it put to shame the soft yellow glow of the lantern I had hung from the front of the cart. And my mother was right. So very clear was the sky that there seemed more stars in the heavens than I had ever seen before. But it was cold. Bitterly cold.

'Here,' my mother said, working a hand out from beneath the blankets. 'I kept this for you.'

She handed me one of the gingerbreads.

'You always loved these as a boy,' she said.

'I do still,' I said, biting into it, and relishing the familiar combination of honey and spices on my tongue. Why should that bring tears to my eyes, a grown man, who could lift his mother as easily as if she were a little child?

As we reached the village street, we joined the throng of villagers all heading toward the church, where light shone from the open door, and the small bell, with its sweet tone, had begun to ring. Sire Raymond and the verger, Geoffrey Carter's elder brother, awaited us.

201

'Good e'en to e'e, Mistress Bridget,' people called as we passed. 'Blessings on e'e, Mistress Elyot.'

Of course, I thought, she could not come to live with us in Oxford. Leighton was her place, where she had lived since birth. She would never leave it now.

'Did you hear about Alysoun and the ice?' I said. 'James has promised to make her some skates. The village lads teased her and said girls might not skate.'

I could not see her smile in the dark, but I heard it in her voice.

'I used to skate on the village pond,' she said. 'Sometimes it froze hard enough. The lads teased me as well. Times pass, but village lads will always be village lads.'

'Did my father tease you?'

'Aye, he did, at first.' She gave a soft chuckle. 'Until I stuffed a handful of snow down his back and threatened to fight him. After that, he treated me with more respect.'

'Mother!' This was a side of her I did not know. 'I think you must have been like Alysoun.'

'I think I was.'

I heard – could it be? – a note of satisfaction in her voice.

I halted the cart beside the lych gate and climbed out, reaching up to help my mother down.'

'Well,' I said, tucking her arm under mine, 'I ask only that you do not encourage her. She needs no encouragement.'

'I promise nothing,' she said cheerfully, and squeezed my arm. 'Do not fret, Nicholas. Alysoun will fall into scrapes all her life, but her life will be the richer for it.'

We followed the crowd into the church, and took our place at the front on the right. That on the left was reserved for the manor, but my family had always held the second highest place in Leighton. For my mother's sake, I sent up a prayer of thankfulness to Yves de Vere, who lay at rest before the altar. His ancestors had embellished the church with fine monuments and its one window of coloured glass, but Yves de Vere had embraced the new custom of providing benches so that the congregation might sit through the long services. Some of the villagers who clung to the old ways had disapproved at first, but I think everyone had come to appreciate them now. Even in Oxford, few of the churches possessed this modern luxury.

The party from the manor arrived, Master Winchingham and his children taking the front bench to our left, while behind them his steward and reeve and other senior servants took their place. They were joined, to my surprise, by the three troubadours. I had thought that they might not dare to venture out of the manor house, but they slipped in along the second bench with quiet composure. The lesser servants would find room at the back of the nave.

The rest of our own party came in close behind those from the manor, and Rafe climbed on to my lap, still half asleep. Alysoun took her place demurely by my side, neatly dressed in clean (and dry) clothes, with her hair cleverly braided with coloured ribbons in two clusters on either side of her face, like a grown lady. Juliana's work, I guessed. Emma sat on the other side of Alysoun, reaching out briefly to touch my hand. I felt a sudden sharp sense of joy that she had come with us to Leighton, and that we could sit thus together to welcome the Christ Child's birth.

Sire Raymond had left just the two candles on the altar burning, after the verger had extinguished those near the door, which had been lit to guide the village people through the dark. Now he closed the door and Sire Raymond began to speak the words of the Mass, or rather to chant them in his sweet musical voice.

Rafe burrowed his head into the folds of my cloak, and I closed my eyes, feeling the familiar Latin flow around me and lift me up, until I seemed to leave my body and float above the tight packed crowd in the little church. There was a scent of homely country herbs, from the simple incense Sire Raymond used in the censer, though tonight I could also pick out the rich perfume of frankincense, so rare and costly that it was only used at special services, such as this. I thought the candles must be scented as well, for their smoke coiled through my imaginings, as I found myself whispering the words of the Mass along with the priest.

As the service drew toward its end, I opened my eyes again. Rafe was asleep against my chest. My mother was sitting very still, but with a soft smile playing about her lips. Alysoun was leaning forward, her lips parted. She regularly attended Mass, but the darkness, the exotic scents, the whole aura of strangeness had her transfixed. I reached behind her and took Emma's hand. She kept her face turned toward the priest, but she smiled and slipped her fingers through mine.

Now the altar boys, Alan's nephew Rob, and Goody Taylor's grandson, lit tapers at the altar candles. The church bell began to ring out joyously, and the boys walked through the nave, lighting candles as they went.

'Christ is born!' we cried. 'Christ is born in Bethlehem!'

As the light sprang up and spread throughout the church, we looked at each other, and the cry rose to a triumphant shout.

'Christ is born in Bethlehem!'

All over England, nay, all over Christendom, the shout would be rising up, shaking the very stars in their courses. In Oxford, I knew, all the fine bells from all the great churches and the college chapels would be ringing out in a vast jumble of joyous sound. People would be out on the streets, laughing and calling to each other, but there was the same joy, the same excitement, in this little church in a humble Wychwood village.

And whereas in most churches of Christendom, the end of the Mass and the ringing of the bells would mark the closing of the service, this was not the practice here in Leighton-under-Wychwood, for Sire Raymond understood very well that all that pent up joy swelling the hearts of his congregation needed to burst out. Here in Leighton, we sang.

The priest approved the singing of holy carols, those that celebrate the birth of Our Lord. There are many carols, for many seasons of the year, some religious, some, certainly, purely secular, for dancing in a ring on May day, or at harvest time – songs which were old and treasured, and had their place in the cycle of our lives, but their place was not here, not now. We would sing of the Child's birth, of his Virgin Mother, of kings and shepherds, of angels bowing down from Heaven, and an evil king who slaughtered the innocents, sadly born at the same time as their Saviour.

Sire Raymond gave us the note, and we began.
Lullay, myn lykyng, my dere sone, myn swetyng,
Lullay, my dere herte, myn owyn dere derlyng.

The whole congregation was singing now, filling the church with joyous song – men, women, and children, some with fine voices, some who croaked like frogs. We sang with a sense of relief. Midnight had come. The Child was born again. Then suddenly the sound was lifted, enriched, by voices beyond anything the village could offer. A high sweet treble extemporised a descant, a pure tenor woke echoes from the stone arches overhead, and a rich bass made the very air tremble. The troubadours were singing.

For a moment the village voices faltered, as if in awe at what they had awakened. Then, emboldened, the people of Leighton filled their lungs and sang of a young Mother's tenderness toward her newborn Son.

I saw a fayr maydyn syttyn and synge.
Sche lullyd a lytyl chyld, a swete lordyng.
Lullay, myn lykyng, my dere sone, myn swetyng,
Lullay, my dere herte, myn owyn dere derlyng.
That eche lord is that that made alle thinge.
Of alle lordis he is lord, of alle kynges kyng.
Lullay, myn lykyng, my dere sone, myn swetyng,
Lullay, my dere herte, myn owyn dere derlyng.
Ther was mekyl melody at that chyldes berthe,

Alle tho wern in hevene blys their made mekyl merthe.

Lullay, myn lykyng, my dere sone, myn swetyng,
Lullay, my dere herte, myn owyn dere derlyng.

Aungelebryt thei song that nyt and seydyn to that chyld,
'Blyssid be thou, and so be sche that is bothe mek and myld'.

Lullay, myn lykyng, my dere sone, myn swetyng,
Lullay, my dere herte, myn owyn dere derlyng.

Prey we now to that chyld, and to his moder dere,
Grawnt hem his blyssyng that now makyn chere.

Lullay, myn lykyng, my dere sone, myn swetyng,
Lullay, my dere herte, myn owyn dere derlyng.

The day of Christ's Nativity had begun.

Chapter Ten

The morning of the Nativity was another bright, clear, cold day, like the day before. Despite the midnight service and the consequent short hours of sleep, I woke strangely full of energy, and almost an excitement, although why I should feel excited, I could not imagine. We would eat our festive dinner at midday, over which all the women had been slaving for hours, and I knew better than to hinder them. I would stay well clear of the kitchen until I was summoned. In the late afternoon we were to go to the manor, where Peter Winchingham had planned a Christmas meal for a few friends and the manor's own servants. This would be on a much smaller scale than the great feast on Twelfth Day, to which every tenant of the manor was invited, and every cottager for at least five miles around.

We were bidden to this supper, as well as to the festivities on Twelfth Day, and although I feared I could scarcely do it justice, after the heaped delicates planned for our own Christmas dinner, yet I would not have missed it for the world. The company was to be entertained by music during the meal, provided by the troubadours, and afterwards by a full concert of songs. I had still not ventured to ask whether the musicians would be willing to share some of their precious lyrics and music with me for the song book, but I intended to make a note this evening of those I thought might be suitable, so that when I did come to ask, I could make my request specific, instead of asking for everything, like a greedy child confronted with a box of comfits.

From what I had seen of the troubadours as we had come out of church last night, they seemed calmer and less troubled than at any time since we had first found them stranded in the wood. Perhaps having handed over responsibility for delivering their dangerous letter to the king, they felt more secure, yet I could not myself feel confident of their personal safety. I had been surprised to see them at the midnight Mass, although when they left amidst a large crowd of manor servants and farm labourers, they looked well protected.

I did, however, take Peter Winchingham aside as we came out of the church.

'I do not think the danger is passed from the Frenchmen,' I said. 'I believe they are not in the neighbourhood at the moment, but they have been.'

I told him what Godfrid had discovered at the old cottage in the woods.

'It might have been anyone there,' I said. 'Any masterless men or outlaws living rough, had Godfrid not himself seen them leaving, and had I not found this.'

I drew the embroidered glove out of my scrip, and we looked at it together in the light from the flaming torches the verger had set either side of the church door.

Peter took it from me and examined it closely, tilting it to gain the best of the light.

'Aye, certainly French, I agree. And not a poor man's glove, either. Did you notice any such on the men who waylaid you?'

I gave a rueful grin. 'I had other things on my mind at the time. Besides, it was dark and snowing heavily. However, I think it simply bears out what Godfrid saw. Our men were there, bedded overnight, though for how long, it is impossible to tell.'

He handed the glove back to me. 'At any rate, they are gone for the present.'

'Aye, but for how long? And where have they gone?'

'Mayhap merely to find warmer lodgings. I should not care to sleep rough in a forest hovel myself this winter.'

'And one of them, at least, a gentleman. You may have the right of it. They may simply have sought warm beds in an inn, at Burford or Witney. But what if they have friends hereabouts?'

He looked at me, startled. 'Do you think so?'

'I do not know what to think. I should not have said there were any traitors in this rural countryside, but we live in strange times. The world has gone awry since the plague. Men have lost homes and families and any hope for the future. Some might be ready to practice treason merely for coin in the hand today, never mind tomorrow. Think of what we saw in Oxford, just short months ago – the traitor Hamo Belancer.'

'And he paid for it with his life, at the hands of his vile collaborator.'

'But how many would even take such a possibility into account?' I said.

'You think these men may have allies nearby?'

I sighed. 'Truly, Peter, I do not know. Perhaps these Frenchmen have but found themselves an inn for Christmas.' I smiled grimly. 'Perhaps they even wished to worship at a midnight Mass, like good Christian folk.'

Today my thoughts were no clearer than they had been when I talked to Peter last night. Probably the men had merely sought more comfortable lodgings, but the possibility that they might have an ally in the neighbourhood made me uneasy. Then something else occurred to me. We still did not known their full number, but probably the six who had waylaid me was the entire group. Six. Now it was true that a truce of sorts existed at the moment between England and France, but we had been at war, off and on, with France, since before our present king came to his throne.

Should six armed Frenchmen, clearly not harmless merchants or suchlike travellers, arrive at a Cotswold inn all together and demand lodgings, most innkeepers would be very wary. I was certain Master Townley at the White Hart in Burford would be. And it was unlikely that the men would split up, some to one inn, some to another. They themselves must be wary, here in a hostile country. They would stay together. After all, they had made off when seen by the Winchinghams at the manor, and again when Edmond and the others rode out to meet me on my way home from Burford. They were being mighty careful not to be identified. Why was that?

I wished I knew what was in the letter the troubadours carried.

I needed a quiet place to think, and there would be nowhere quiet about the farm today. Sire Raymond had said that he would celebrate the whole cycle of canonical hours on the day of the Nativity. There was no obligation on a parish priest to do so, but Sire Raymond went his own way. If he felt it right to celebrate all the services today, then he would do so, even if his congregations were small or non-existent. This morning the church beckoned me, a sanctuary of peace, where my thoughts might find their way through the confusion. I could walk down to the church, attend Terce, and still return to the farm in time for the Christmas dinner. Two geese were dressed and ready for the spit, a vast ham, already cooked, stood upon the largest trencher the farm possessed, and I would not be forgiven, should I keep them waiting.

I had donned my winter boots and was just fetching my cloak, when I met Emma coming down the stairs.

'You are going out?' she said.

'I was. Did you want me to come and discuss Walter's book with you?'

'Nay, today is not the day for work. We will leave it until after the Nativity.' She smiled tentatively. 'May I come with you? I am banned from the kitchen today. Only the senior cooks are permitted to preside.'

'I was on my way to the church,' I said. 'I thought I would join Sire Raymond for Terce. He will have few other celebrants. And I felt a need for a place of quiet and reflection.'

'That would suit me very well,' she said. 'Will you wait while I fetch my cloak?'

A few minutes later we were walking together down the lane to the village, her arm through mine.

'I know the weather is bitter cold,' she said, 'and it is a hard time for the poor, and for the wild creatures, but do you not think it is beautiful? Not with the soft beauty of the budding spring, nor the lavish beauty of summer, but with something magnificent and enduring. I love to see the trees, stripped to their bones, standing so defiant against the winter winds.'

'There is something in me,' I said, 'that always responds to a world of ice and snow. Aye, it is magnificent but remote. It calls out to our strengths, not our weaknesses. It does not offer solace, but demands endurance, yet at the same time the beauty of the winter world is so . . . so strange, so unearthly.'

I broke off, fearing she would find me absurd, but she nodded.

'That is it exactly, Nicholas. Demanding, strange, and unearthly.'

The village was in a state of eager preparation, and the wonderful scents of Christmas dinners floated out from every house. We are, by and large, a kindly village. We have our petty squabbles, our temporary fallings-out, but no one goes in real need, if it can be helped. I saw the Carters' children solemnly carrying baskets and covered dishes to Goody Taylor's cottage, where she lived alone with only her young grandson. She was bent with the bone troubles of old age, so that she and the boy found it difficult to cook, and her vegetable plot was only as much as a boy of ten could manage. They would eat well on the Nativity, sharing the Carters' dinner.

At the forge, we could see through the window that Bertred Godsmith's lad, who never spoke, was turning the spit for Martha. The boy's parents had been taken by the plague and he had found work with Bertred, sleeping in the loft over the smithy, no longer homeless.

As we neared the church, I saw that we should not quite be the only celebrants at Terce. A few of the important dames of the village, those who had daughters or sons' wives to cook for them, were making their stately way to the church. All were clad in their finest clothes, mostly of old-fashioned cut, which would have been the fashion in Burford twenty years ago, and in Oxford thirty years since, as I pointed out.

'And none the worse for that,' I murmured to Emma.

She smiled at me. 'I did not know you were a scholar of ladies' fashions, Nicholas.'

'You forget,' I said. 'Many of my customers come from the university, students and masters alike. But my lay customers are frequently women, and women of fashion. I cannot help but notice their changing styles of gown, and hair, and headdress.'

She laughed. 'I see I shall need to take more care of my clothes.'

'Nay,' I said quietly, 'do not change. I would have you stay just as you are.'

'Everyone changes.' She was serious now. 'When I am an old woman, if I live so long, I will be much changed from the girl you see now.'

'Then I hope I shall live to see it.'

Before we could say more, we had reached the door of the church. I was anxious to talk to her further, but Sire Raymond was welcoming us in with delight.

'Christ's blessing on you, this day of His birth,' he said. 'I had not thought to see you young people here today!

'That was a beautiful service last night,' Emma said, reaching out and taking both his hands in hers. 'I never knew a more joyous celebration on the Eve. The singing – it was wonderful!'

He beamed at her. 'Ah, we dearly love to sing in Leighton, we have always done so, but last night . . . such voices those three musicians are blessed with! I have never heard the like.'

'Nor I. Shall you be there to hear them tonight?'

'Perhaps, after Compline I might slip along to the manor, if the music lasts so long.'

'Oh, I am sure it will!' she said. 'You must come, a lover of music such as you are.'

We entered the church, made our reverence to the altar, and took our places on the family bench at the front. As I knelt again, I felt the brush of Emma's skirts as she knelt beside me, and my thoughts, which should have been occupied elsewhere, turned to her. How would it be, to spend the rest of my life with her always beside me? Part of me yearned for it, but that voice in my head warned me, as it had warned me ever since Elizabeth's death. Love was dangerous. It could only end in tragedy and loss. Even my children could be taken from me. I must harden my heart. Besides, I argued with myself, rationally, she is much younger. Those seven years younger than I, on the threshold of life, while I have known marriage and children and widowing. I am tarnished already by life. She is of an age with James, and I think of James as a boy still.

Another voice argued, But she has known her own tragedies – at the hands of her stepfather, and the murder of her cousin.

With a wrench, I brought my thoughts back to the matter in hand.

I prayed for guidance in the present tangle of affairs surrounding the troubadours and what I had begun to regard as their accursed letter. I should have been able to let the matter rest. I had played my part, written for help to Alice Walsea and Prince Edward of Woodstock, and seen the letters on their way. Although the Frenchmen had lain in waiting for me, I had come to no harm. The letters must take their chance in the dire weather conditions for the carrier, but even if they reached the Court safely, we could expect no response yet. Even Twelfth Day must surely be too soon. I must contain my impatience.

The troubadours and their letter were safe for now at

the manor, and by all the signs, the Frenchmen had left their temporary camp near the village. Perhaps they were gone for good, and I should put a stop to this foolish speculation.

Yet had they gone for good? Why should they do so, when they had not succeeded in stealing the letter which so concerned them?

What fateful news did it contain?

And why were they so anxious not to be identified?

I tried to thrust these questions from my mind, but what most troubled me was the fresh idea that had come to me when I was talking to Peter after Mass last night. Could these men have an ally in the neighbourhood, some English traitor, who had taken them in?

I heard the church door close, opened my eyes, and resumed my seat on the bench. Sire Raymond walked forward to the altar and commenced the short service of Terce.

He began with the singing of *Nunc sancte nobis spiritus* which is customary at this service, then he invited us to join him in the singing of three psalms. The congregation had grown to a larger one than I had expected, so that our voices were not lost amongst the arches of the roof overhead. When we took our seats again, Sire Raymond opened his Bible, where it lay on the simple oak lectern.

'In honour of this day,' he said, 'the day of Christ's birth, the reading is taken from the Gospel according to St Luke, chapter 2.'

Factum est autem in diebus illis exiit edictum a Caesare Augusto ut describeretur universus orbis.

'For those who do not have the Latin tongue,' he said, 'I will render it into simple English.'

'It happened however in those days that an edict went out from Caesar Augustus that the whole world should be enrolled for a census.'

I smiled as I listened, and stole a glance around at the elderly matrons sitting with folded hands and attentive

214

looks. As I knew from current disputes hotly waged in Oxford, traditionalists in the Church believed that the unlearned lay people should simply accept the Latin of the Bible, and ask for no more than the parish priest's explanations. It was unnecessary for them to have the holy text given to them word for word in English. The ignorant commoners would misunderstand, impose their own interpretations on those words, deviate from the accepted interpretation laid down by the Church.

That clever but incautious older scholar John Wycliffe, whom I had known since first I came to Oxford as a student, was convinced that the Bible should be rendered into English, so that any man might read it for himself. His arguments were passionate, and often convincing, but had already brought him into head to head collision with some of the university's great men. If he did not learn to curb his tongue, he might lose his Oxford post.

Yet here was modest, self-effacing Sire Raymond presenting the gift of the Bible's exact words to his simple parishioners, without fuss, without dramatic preaching to gatherings of rebellious students. It was as well, perhaps, that the long noses of those Church and university authorities were unlikely to sniff him out here, under the ancient shelter of Wychwood.

> *et peperit filium suum primogenitum et pannis eum involvit et reclinavit eum in praesepio quia non erat eis locus in diversorio*
>> 'And she gave birth to her firstborn son and wrapped him in cloths and laid him down in a manger because there was no place in the inn.'
>
> *Et pastores erant in regione eadem vigilantes et custodientes vigilias noctis supra gregem suum*
>> 'And there were shepherds in that same country watching and guarding the night watch over their flock.'
>
> *et ecce angelus Domini stetit iuxta illos et claritas Dei circumfulsit illos et timuerunt timore magno*
>> 'And behold! An angel of the Lord stood next to

them and the brightness of God shone around them
and they were afraid with a great fear.'

Et dixit illis angelus nolite ecce enim evangelizo
vobis gaudium magnum quod erit omni populo

'And the angel said to them, Do not be afraid, for
behold! I bring you a message of great joy which
will be to all the people.'

quia natus est vobis hodie salvator qui est Christus
Dominus in civitate David

'Because today there is born to you a Saviour, who
is Christ the Lord, in the city of David.'

The familiar words, spoken in that familiar musical
voice, rolled about the church like the echo in a sea shell,
awakening memories, renewing a promise. All would be
well. Christ is born this day!

The service ended with a simple prayer and blessing,
and we came out from the tranquillity of the church to a
village full of boisterous children.

Emma and I walked in silence back to the farm, both
too uplifted by the service to waste our breath on trivial
words. I had not found, in the peace of the church, any
solution to the confused affair of the troubadours and the
elusive Frenchmen, but I felt calmer in spirit than I had felt
for days. Emma's arm was slipped through mine, but she
was absorbed in her own thoughts. Now was not the time to
speak to her of the future. That could wait. Enough, for
now, to be near her.

We returned to a house filled with such wonderful smells,
one could almost feast on the air itself. The geese were on
the spit before the fire, and the spit was so heavy the girl
Elga could not turn it, so that Thomas and James were
fulfilling the role of kitchen scullions, occasionally assisted
by Juliana and Helga turning it together. The goose fat was
dripping into a pan filled with all manner of vegetables –
onions, leeks, beans, carrots, I know not what – which Elga
basted from time to time with a long-handled ladle.

Susanna, flushed from the fire, stirred something in a great pot, which she swung out from the hearth on its hook in order to reach it, then returned it, bubbling, over the heat. Margaret and Maud had their heads together, concentrating on a small pan set over a brazier. Emma laid aside her cloak at once, seized an apron, and was absorbed into the culinary mysteries.

Edmond and Jordain came into the kitchen behind us. Edmond took one look around and began to retreat.

'We're not wanted here,' he said, jerking his head aside at me. 'We dine grandly today, in the old hall.'

This was a tradition in our family. Although day by day, the kitchen was the heart of the family life, it was the ancient hall, around which the house had been built, that served as the setting for all great occasions. Edmond, Jordain, and I withdrew tactfully to wait there, amongst the festive greenery. The Yule log was already lit, and burned with a steady glow.

Everything about that Christmas dinner is fixed in my mind, sharp and bright, like one of Emma's illuminations. During my childhood, this was where we had celebrated Christmas, and again whenever I had returned for the season from Oxford. Elizabeth and I had been here once when Alysoun was a baby. But never on any previous occasion had we been so large a company, or indeed so merry. The very abundance of our numbers seemed to burst forth in gaiety, and all the trials of the previous days – the blizzards, the hard journey from Oxford, the outlaws at Witney – all were forgotten. Even I forgot the troubling matter of the troubadours' letter and their hostile pursuers. It was, after all, no affair of mine. Instead, I plunged happily into games of hoodman-blind, and throwing walnuts into a bowl, and burned my fingers, along with everyone else, in snatching raisins in a hectic round of snapdragon.

Eventually, even the children grew tired after the hours of over excitement, and were chased off to rest before going to the manor for the evening's entertainment. I volunteered to do the afternoon milking, for the girl Elga was nearly asleep on her feet, and I was glad to exchange the heat and heavy scents of food in the house for the sharp tang of frost on the way to the cow barn. Within, the familiar sweet scent of hay and cows carried me back to my boyhood and learning to milk cows, taught by my father. There is something very soothing about milking a cow, your forehead against her warm side. Edmond kept his dairy cows in milk as long as possible after calving, for cheese was a staple in the farm diet. I was glad to see that I had garnered as much milk as Elga on her day of miracles.

We set out for the manor before dusk, and even my mother chose to come with us, for she was curious to hear these musicians about whom she had heard so much. The great hall of the manor had been laid out as it had been in the de Veres' day, and as it must have been for generations past. Between the swags of greenery we had helped to hang, torches had been fitted into the old iron sconces. At one end the dais had been set out with the lord's high table, while in the body of the hall trestle tables ran at right angles to it, almost filling the entire space. Although this evening only the upper ones would be occupied by the immediate manor servants, indoor and outdoor, the rest would be used on Twelfth Day, when the much greater number must be accommodated.

At the opposite end of the hall, over the door, there was a raised minstrels' gallery, where it seemed the troubadours were to perform. I hoped the sound would not be muffled there, high up and partially enclosed. I had sometimes been here as a boy, but there had never been music except from Yves de Vere's harper, who played in the body of the hall, not in the gallery. In my scrip I had brought the small tablet I used for making notes when I was away from quill and ink, and a couple of thin charcoal sticks for writing, like the ones Emma used for sketching her drawings before outlining in ink. I had no hope of writing down the unfamiliar words of the songs, but I hoped that I might make some kind of note which would help me to remember a song when I spoke to the troubadours later. If, that is, I could ever gain their confidence enough to ask for their songs.

It was difficult to do justice to the meal on top of the enormous dinner at the farm. Peter – or Birgit – must have taken account of the fact that most of their guests would already have dined lavishly that day, so the food was mostly light confections of cold meat in delicate sauces, with small pastries and compotes of fruit – apples and pears with the addition of slices of exotic oranges, dried figs, and redcurrants in syrup. The kitchen staff of the manor had been kept on by Peter, but some of the dishes suggested a foreign hand. Perhaps the Winchinghams had brought a Flemish cook with them.

While we ate, the musicians played a series of lively dances, and although I could not see them clearly I could pick out the sound of viols, double pipes, a tabor, and even a crumhorn. They must be keeping back the lute to accompany the singing. As the meal came to an end, the servants who had taken their seats to enjoy their own supper rose from their places at the trestle tables and cleared away the used dishes and the remains of the food, which I suspected would find their way to the poorest in the village.

There was a good deal of noise in the hall, with the clatter of the dishes, and people moving about and talking, but through it all I heard a new instrument, a portative organ. I had not realised the troubadours had one of these, for I did not think it usual – their delicate songs, whether they tell of love, or valour, or have the satirical sting of a *sirventes*, are more appropriately accompanied by an equally delicate instrument like a lute or a vielle. The full-throated voice of a portative organ is more suited to ecclesiastical music. Indeed, what it was playing now was a Nativity hymn. In its own right, it was very beautiful, but I was eager to hear the vocal music.

It seemed to take a long time for the company in the

hall to settle down in quiet again, and in the meantime the music had ceased altogether. I felt a pang of disappointment and glanced along the table to Peter, but he was deep in conversation with Sire Raymond, who must have slipped in to join us without my noticing. Space had been made for him between Peter and Susanna, and one of the serving men was setting before him a plate of choice foods and a cup of wine.

When I looked back again down the length of the hall, I saw the three troubadours coming in by the door under the gallery, Gaston carrying his lute, Falquet a vielle, and Azalais a pile of music sheets. They took their places just below the dais, facing us. The two men put their heads together, tuning the strings of their instruments, while Azalais laid out the music on a small table someone had set there for them.

Then they began.

I find it difficult to describe their songs, for they were unlike anything I had ever heard before. Jesu knows, we hear music a-plenty in Oxford. Every church and college has its choir, and music sounds through the town for every service, every saint's day. The streets ring with the boisterous songs of students and apprentices – often in competition with each other – and here in Leighton, under the influence of Sire Raymond, I had grown up both with his simple but pure church music, and his eager enthusiasm for the old songs sung by the country people, which were written by no one, but had grown as naturally as the trees in Wychwood, out of the labour on the land and with the beasts, out of the joys of new birth and marriage, and out of the sadness of farewell and death.

These songs were different. The music was as complex as church music, but it was a different complexity. Whereas ecclesiastical music is rooted in centuries of tradition, which gives it a sonorous dignity inspiring awe, the music of these songs was so unlike it that it dazzled the ear and both alarmed and delighted the mind. It was something so new, so fresh, I had difficulty in following it at first, as the three voices intertwined, chased and echoed each other, played tag with the lute, then came together in harmony. I know that this music of the troubadours was not, in truth, new, for it had dazzled the courts of Occitaine a century ago, but for me it was new. I was drunk with it, lost in it. And I forgot altogether to take note of anything.

For the most part they sang in Occitan, but some of the lyrics were in Latin, and these I could follow. Emma had been right when she said they sang mostly of love, and I understood now what she had meant by saying that she knew that from the music itself. I remembered that she had once told me that a troubadour had come to her grandfather's home when she was a young girl, so this was not the overwhelming revelation to her as it was for me, but I could not believe that a single man could achieve what those three voices in consort could achieve. And in the love songs, the music itself was the voice of love and longing.

Then there were the songs praising famous heroes. Some of these men were new to me, for they were probably those who had recently withstood the French armies, but names of ancient heroes stood out, even amongst the Occitan words – Hector, Aeneas, even Caesar. The music was stirring, but did not move me as deeply as the love songs.

They concluded with three of the satirical *sirventes*, and for our benefit had rendered the words into English. Two were attacks on the French, and one on the ruler of Aragon, King Pedro. That was intriguing, I thought. Aragon was a long-standing enemy of Castile, so this seemed to support Peter Winchingham's theory that Gaston was Castilian.

Then, suddenly, it was over. The three troubadours bowed, gathered up their music, and had slipped away through the door while the applause and cheering was still ringing throughout the hall. When it was quieter at last, Peter leaned forward over the table and smiled at me.

'Well, Nicholas,' he said, 'what do you think?'

'I have not the words,' I said. 'Unlike anything I have

ever heard before. Wonderful.'

Words, I felt, were inadequate.

It was inevitable, I suppose, that the days between the Nativity and Twelfth Day were taken up with preparations for the feast which would bring together all the tenants of Leighton Manor, the villagers, and even those who lived in the scattered isolated cottages, some in the cleared land at a short distance from the village, some in lonely assarts hacked out (not always legally) within the forest itself.

Although the manor had a head cook and (I had been right) a Flemish assistant, not to mention a full complement of kitchen maids and scullions, all the women of our party seemed to feel the need to be over at the manor for a large part of every day, apart from my mother, who remained in command of the farm kitchen which had once been hers.

Hilda and Juliana took charge of the children, and frequently carried them off also to the manor, where they could be entertained with Birgit's seemingly unending supply of toys. As well, Hans had rashly undertaken to teach Alysoun how to ride. The troubadours' pony had recovered from his injury, and Gaston had agreed that, in the interests of helping him exercise and regain his strength, he could be used as a mount for Alysoun. I suspected that it would not be long before Rafe was demanding a turn.

Jordain had shown an interest in the notes that Sire Raymond had been compiling for at least twenty years on the ancient customs of Wychwood and its villages, so he went off every day to plunge into eager discussions on such matters as seasonal rituals, agricultural chants, and I know not what else. I helped around the farm when I was needed, but apart from the day-to-day care of the animals, there is not a great deal one can do in December and January, save mend harness and tools, and take a rest before the gruelling labour of the farming year begins again.

Everything seemed now to be directed toward the festivities of Twelfth Day, but in the meantime I felt myself redundant and restless. We were no nearer to discovering what had become of the Frenchmen who had pursued the troubadours, for they seemed to have disappeared altogether. 'Good riddance,' Edmond said, but I was not so sure. I would rather an enemy I could see than one who had become invisible. I worried constantly about whether my two letters might have reached the Court by now. John Hayward had thought he might be there before Twelfth Day, and certainly we had had no further blizzards since shortly after my trip to Burford, though one could not tell what might have happened elsewhere in England. If he had not been badly held up by the weather or any other impediment, he might be there by now.

How long would it take for a body of men, riding directly here, without the carrier's errands, to reach us? A week? Perhaps less. I thought of Captain Beverley and his men. They could probably have covered in one day the distance which had taken us, with the slow cart, three days. My head went round and round with calculations.

Irritated by my enforced idleness, I decided I must do something positive. The day before Twelfth Day, I announced over breakfast, before everyone went about their usual affairs, that I would be out all day myself.

'If I am not needed,' I added, mindful that there might be some task I would be wanted for.

It seemed I would not be needed. No one appeared very interested in my plans.

'I thought,' I said, turning to Edmond, 'that I would ride over to Sir Henry Talbot's manor.'

My mother looked surprised. 'What do you want with Sir Henry, Nicholas?'

I realised that it might be wise not to reveal my true purpose and cause alarm, so I mumbled something about wanting to see an old friend while I was here in the country. I am not sure she quite believed me, but everyone was by then so caught up in all the tasks of the day that I was not questioned further. However, when I was saddling Rufus, Edmond leaned over the stall door.

'Why are you really going to Sir Henry?'

I opened the door and led Rufus out past him.

'It occurred to me that if those Frenchmen should have any friend in the neighbourhood, Sir Henry might know something to the point. He is a wise old bird, and as Justice of the Peace he must have his finger on most that happens in this part of Oxfordshire. If there has been any hint of treasonable activity, or any sightings of this group of foreigners, he will know of it.'

'Aye,' Edmond said, following me out into the yard. 'That is well thought on. And even if he has heard nothing, you may give him a warning to keep his ears open.'

'That too is what I thought.'

I swung myself up on to the horse's back.

'Give Sir Henry my good wishes for the season,' Edmond said. 'And remind him he has not visited us this many weeks. He was ever a good friend to your parents. Your mother is always glad to see him.'

'I will so,' I said, and set off down the lane.

Sir Henry's manor lay on the way to Burford, though to the south of the high road, while Leighton and Burford lay to the north. As there had not been a great deal of snow since I had ridden back from Burford, the night I was ambushed, the lane had been well cleared by the men from the village, all the way to the Burford road. There was still a deep covering underfoot, but it was packed down firm and hard, although in places somewhat slippery. I was in no great haste, so we made our way along the lane circumspectly, Rufus watching his feet, and I watching ahead for any more fallen branches. Fortunately there were none.

Once we reached the high road, the snow and ice had been hammered down by the passing traffic, rather than cleared, but it offered a similar surface, so I continued to take care until we reached the turn to Sir Henry's estate, about midway between the Leighton lane and the road down to Burford.

The lane to the Talbot property was quite short, and

sand had been scattered over the snow, creating a safer surface for both man and beast. I had not been here for some years, but nothing seemed to have changed. The house was more modest than Leighton Manor, very old, with a stone undercroft and timber upper storey throughout, very little altered throughout the centuries, apart from the addition of chimneys. A stranger seeing it might suppose that Sir Henry was a man of modest means, but he would be mistaken. The Talbots held property all over Oxfordshire and into the neighbouring counties, gradually acquired through judicious marriages down the generations with heiresses of comfortable if not grand estates. Sir Henry preferred to live mainly at this manor, for he had been born here. And as well, he enjoyed the hunting in Wychwood and the fishing in the rivers Evenlode and Windrush, in all of which he had rights, due to his various properties.

He was a widower now, with an elder son managing his own manor, a younger son who would be given one when he reached a suitable age, and three daughters well married. Sir Henry was one of the great men in this part of Oxfordshire, but a man who kept to the old ways and scorned what he called 'the high flown pretences of London'. His contempt for Gilbert Mordon had been deep seated, but concealed under his natural courtesy. I thought he would like Peter Winchingham, a man with as frank and open a nature as his own.

Sir Henry greeted me with a bear hug, refused to allow me to see to my horse, and bellowed to his son Giles to take Rufus. Giles, I had always thought, took after his mother, an elegant woman, who had brought with her a useful manor in Berkshire, while the older son, Edward, was the image of his father, without the bulk. I noticed now, as Giles led Rufus away, that he was growing more like his father.

'Come in, come in!' With his arm over my shoulder, Sir Henry steered me into the house, where the central hall was still used as the main room of the house for everyday living, unlike our farm or Leighton Manor. At one time they probably cooked at the huge fireplace, but Lady Talbot had secured one improvement to her home when a kitchen had been added to the back of the house.

'Said she could not abide the smell of boiling cabbage rising up to the bed chambers,' I had heard Sir Henry say more than once. 'Now what is amiss with the smell of boiling cabbage? Still, ladies must have their fancies.'

The poor woman had not succeeded in securing any other alterations to the house, and now that it was an entirely male preserve, there was a detritus of hunting gear, muddy boots, and – oddly – half a pair of hose scattered about the hall table, as well as two rather smelly dogs stretched out on the hearth.

Sir Henry swept a half mended bow, a cluster of bow strings, and a hunting knife off the end of the table with his arm, and shouted for ale, and would not heed me until he saw me settled with a huge tankard of ale at my elbow.

'I had heard you were here for Christmas, Nicholas,' he said, 'and I would have ridden over to Leighton but for this damnable weather. Always brings on a stiffness in my right knee. Been sitting nursing it by the fire like an ancient crone.'

'We should be glad to see you when you are recovered,' I said. 'Edmond sends you God's greeting for the season.'

'A good fellow, your cousin,' he said. 'I was grieved when you lost your father and brother, but Edmond has done well by the farm, and that's a good woman he's wed to.'

'And they have taken in my mother,' I said, 'so that she may not live alone in her cottage.'

He leaned forward, his face concerned. 'How does she fare, Mistress Bridget?'

'Very well. She was not fit to make the journey to Oxford, so that is why we are here. She would welcome a visit from you at any time. But now she is as busy about all these Christmas affairs as the younger women. There's to be a great celebration at Leighton Manor tomorrow.'

'Aye, I know. For Three Kings Day. I'm bidden.'

'I did not know you had met Peter Winchingham yet,' I said, surprised.

'No more I have, but I am invited all the same. Don't know whether my knee will allow me.'

I grinned. 'You could always be trundled there in a cart, wrapped in blankets.'

'Ha! Do not tease me, boy! I take that as a challenge. I see I shall have to come.'

'You will like Peter Winchingham.'

He grunted. 'I have heard nothing but good of him so far. Cloth merchant, is he?'

'Aye, but born a countryman. And you would have appreciated the shot with which he brought down a stag the other day.'

'So you have been hunting in Wychwood again, have you? Nasty business that was, last harvest time.'

'It was,' I said, 'and as it happens, our hunt this time threw up another mystery, though not a fatal one.'

He looked at me with those shrewd eyes of his, so at odds with his blunt country manner.

'And that is why you have come to see me. Now, what mystery have you dipped your toe into this time, Nicholas?'

'Not intentionally,' I said, 'but Leighton has found itself caught up in something odd, something involving the French, and I do not like the smell of it.'

As quickly and concisely as I could, I told him everything that had happened from the moment we had first encountered the troubadours stranded in their cart on the forest ride. I explained why I had despatched the two letters to Court, in the hope of assistance from that quarter, though as yet I had heard nothing.

'And then, as I rode back to Leighton from Burford that evening, I was caught first in a blizzard and then I was ambushed by this same group of Frenchmen.'

He continued to listen without interrupting, though his face grew more and more grave.

'So the last we know of them,' I finished, 'is the evidence of the hut in the woods, which our shepherd saw them leaving, and this glove I found there.'

I took it out of my scrip and laid it on the table, where the elaborate embroidery struck an odd note in the Spartan simplicity of the room.

Sir Henry poked the glove with a disdainful finger. 'French,' he said, in tones of the utmost disgust.

'It certainly looks French. The men have now disappeared. I thought to go on from here, to enquire whether such a group might be staying in one of the Burford inns, but I am sure that if such men are about, you would have heard of it.'

He shook his head. 'Certainly no fellows of the type you describe are staying in Burford. Someone from my household is in the town nearly every day. I would have heard.'

'They might have gone to Witney.'

'Further away. If they want to keep a watch on these musicians of yours, I'd say that is too far away.'

I nodded. 'That is what I think also.' I paused. 'There is another possibility.'

'You think they have found somewhere else to stay, out of the cold? Not at an inn?'

Again, I nodded. 'It may be farfetched, and I do not care even to contemplate the idea, but do you think they might have friends in the neighbourhood? You must hear everything that happens hereabouts. Can you think of anyone?'

He sipped slowly at his ale. I was surprised there was any left in his tankard, but he had been giving his full attention to my story.

'I can say nothing for certain, Nicholas. No one who has lived here for any time would be such a traitor to England as to welcome these men into his home. But there are a few incomers, not so well known to us. Since the

Death, some of the lands around here have passed through several hands – heirs, more heirs, false claimants. That fellow Mordon with his financial trickery was not the only man playing the game, hoping to rise by climbing on the bodies of dead men. Except he made the mistake of trying to cheat the king.'

'I know this is true,' I said, 'but treason is another matter, surely?'

'Hmph. Once a man sets his feet on the road to evil, what is to stop him? A little cheating here, a bigger crime there, a manor cozened out of a grieving widow. Why not treason against the king? I reckon that fellow Mordon would not have hesitated, if the reward was large enough.'

'What makes the whole matter so baffling,' I said, 'is not knowing either what is in this letter the troubadours are carrying, nor who has sent it. Only that it is vitally important, and must reach the king or Prince Edward. Whoever sent it must be an enemy of France.'

'Or of these particular Frenchmen,' he said.

'Aye,' I said, 'that is very true. And who is behind these particular Frenchmen? We talk as if it is the country France, or the king of France, who has despatched them to steal this letter, but that might not be so. I am sure there are factions in France, just as there were in England before our present king came into his own.'

'Well,' he said, draining his tankard and setting it back on the table with a thump. 'Leave the matter with me. There are a few questions I can ask. One or two people I can look into.'

He got up and slapped his knee.

'See, you have cured my bone ache! All it needed was the spur to action. There is most of the day still to be used. I think I shall come to your Master Winchingham's great feast tomorrow after all, and I will bring you whatever I have managed to discover. Let us hope there is no treason afoot, but if there is, better to root it out at once than let it grow.'

As I rode Rufus away from Sir Henry's manor, he

was already shouting to his stable lads to saddle his horse. He might discover nothing, but already I felt much of my burden lightened.

Chapter Eleven

It was Twelfth Day, the final day of the Christmas celebrations, the day of the Magi, those eastern kings, travelling from some mysterious land and guided by an unknown star – which some said was a fiery comet – who had come first to King Herod, believing he would know the birthplace of this Babe, who was to be king, not only of the Jews, but of all the world. Herod, insecure and in terror on his throne, spoke with his forked tongue, promising to come and worship the Child, instructing these foreign rulers to return and bring word of the birthplace. Twelve days old, and how close the Child came to death!

Twelfth Day. Three Kings Day. Little Christmas. Epiphany.

Gold for kingship. Frankincense for holiness. Myrrh for death.

A day weighted with so much of glory and terror.

Yet at Leighton Manor, there was nothing but riotous joy. And noise! We had made our way to the manor soon after dawn, once the animals had been seen to, leaving the farm deserted, although, given the troubles of recent days, Edmond locked the doors. Only Godfrid was left, still physicking his sick ewe.

'She be on the mend, Master,' he told Edmond. 'I'll likely come to the manor soon. 'Tis not often us has the taste of venison.'

The stag we had shot at that memorable hunt had been kept for today, and three days after the Nativity Alan

Wodville had taken the boys – Hans, James, and Thomas – out for another day's hunting, and to their delight they had secured another. Both deer were now turning slowly on spits over fire pits dug well away from the manor house and the barns, and would provide the principal meat for the feast, since it was a rare treat for most in the village. But there would be mutton as well, and beef joints (roasting over the kitchen fire), and hams stewed slowly with onions and dried peas, providing both meat to slice and soup to spoon.

Meat would be the central feature of the feast, for the cottagers saw little enough meat on their tables in the ordinary way, but there would be great bowls of vegetables roasted in the juices dripping from the meats turning on the spits. There were pies of every sort – savoury pies of pheasant and partridge, of fish from the mill stream, and of bacon, and sweet pies of apples and plums and pears and dried cherries. The cakes stuffed with currants and dates and more of the dried cherries promised better eating than Mistress Townley's cannon balls. And the profusion of comfits and sweetmeats piled up in pyramids a yard high made even my eyes dazzle. The children were beside themselves.

It was good to see how many children were running about the manor yard and in and out of the house. So many village children had perished in the Death, that for a time it had seemed that the village itself would die, having no future, but now young voices were heard again in the village lanes. Their very numbers seemed a kind of defiance in the face of that Death, and the other Death inflicted on the Innocents by the wrath and vengeance of Herod.

It was our normal custom on the day after the Nativity to present gifts to all those who had worked on the farm during the previous year, and also to the farm's two tenant families, who held cottages of Edmond. However, the weather being so bad, and the prospect of everyone gathering at the manor on Twelfth Day, meant that

Susanna, who was in charge of this gift giving, sent word round that this year she would be dispensing the gifts at the manor on the morning of Twelfth Day.

As a result, Jordain had driven to the manor, not the farm cart, but the large cart we had brought from Oxford. It was laden with these gifts, everything from parcels of food to wooden toys and knitted shawls, gifts for all the families, and from the youngest babe to the oldest granddam. And determined not to miss out on Peter's great celebration, they had all come. Some, like Goody Taylor, being trundled here by families or neighbours, in handcarts, or even wheelbarrows.

Our family's dispensing of gifts had begun as soon as we arrived, and I was pleased to see Alysoun, solemn for once, and stately as a matron, handing over the baskets and parcels from the back of our cart. It had been an inspired notion of Susanna's to choose Alysoun to help, although I knew that, inside the cart and out of sight, Hilda and Emma were sorting out which gifts were to go to which family. It would be good for Alysoun to know that Leighton was also her place, as well as her home in Oxford.

Along with the other men, I found that my tasks were mainly fetching and carrying heavy loads, following the example of Peter, who had rolled up the sleeves of his shirt and his cotte, laid aside his cloak to move more freely, and was working as hard as any of his men servants. I saw that his tenants and the cottagers had noticed it, too. He might not earn the awed respect Yves de Vere had commanded, but these were changed times. I caught some approving glances.

Our sheer numbers and the fact that the food was partly preparing inside, in the manor kitchen, while the venison was roasting outside, meant that the dinner was hardly a dignified affair. There was a constant coming and going of men servants with platters of slices from the venison, or meat from the kitchen, and maid servants with jugs of ale so heavy they could barely lift them. Then, as they too must be allowed to sit down and dine, others would jump up to take their place and the procession of food would start again.

Eventually I found time to take my own seat at the high table and eat a little of the roast venison and a slice of game pie.

'Do you think it is going well?' Peter asked anxiously, hovering behind his chair.

'Everything is indeed going well,' I said. 'Sit down and enjoy it yourself.'

'Aye.' It was Sire Raymond, rosy with pleasure to see so many of his poorest parishioners eating a meal such as they had never seen before. 'Sit down and look at the happiness you have brought to these people.'

I had not yet seen any sign of Sir Henry, so perhaps his knee had not permitted him to ride over to Leighton. Nor had I seen the troubadours, but they must be up in the minstrels' gallery again, for music could just be heard faintly over the noise.

When I commented on this to Peter, he grinned. 'Wait until the dancing begins!'

The feasting went on for several hours, but at last even the most voracious appetites were satisfied, and the time came to clear the hall for dancing, although, despite the cold, some of the younger boys and girls from the village declared that they would dance in the yard, for it had grown so powerfully hot in the hall.

The great advantage of trestle tables is that they can be dismantled and put aside quickly. A few of them were left standing, ranged along the front of the dais, with yet more jugs of ale to slake the thirst of the dancers (some of whom were already a little unsteady on their legs), and with slices of pie for those whose stomachs still had a corner unfilled.

The troubadours came down from the gallery and stationed themselves on the dais, in front of the lord's table, ready to play for the dancing. Azalais had the hurdy-gurdy which Gaston had spoken of earlier, while he himself had a crumhorn, and Falquet a pair of small drums. They struck up a loud and lively dance tune, and people began to form into rings, men in one circle, women in another, facing each other. The door to the hall was left open and beyond it the door to the yard, where the youngsters were also taking their places. At first I was not sure whether they would be able to hear the music from there, but once the musicians began to play, there was no doubt of it. This was no longer the elegant music of Occitaine, the refined lyrics and complex tunes of sophisticated troubadours. This was the rollicking simple thumping sound of village dances which must stretch from the cold north of Norway down to the sunny valleys of Italy and Spain.

'Come, Nicholas, you must join in the dance!' Emma grabbed my hand and pulled me to my feet.

I made no protest, and we were followed by others from our party, Susanna with Edmond, Juliana with Jordain, and – to her speechless delight – Alysoun with her big cousin James.

'We shall never hear the last of that,' Emma said, as James led Alysoun on to the floor.

'I fear my daughter will burst soon, with excitement.' I grinned at her. 'Come, you must join with the women, and I with the men.'

However, our country dances do not remain segregated for long. Soon men and women paired off, parted again, wove the simple steps in rounds and through the arches of raised arms. We have no such dances in serious Oxford, but once learned in childhood, you never forget the figures.

It was, in truth, very hot in the hall, and after a time Emma and I stepped into the yard for air. Sitting on the step of our cart we watched the youngsters cavorting in some version of the dance they were inventing as they went along. Very soon we cooled down, and then began to be cold, so I found some of the family cloaks which had been left in the cart, and we wrapped those around ourselves.

'Have you now arranged Walter's stories to your satisfaction?' I asked.

'I have done so at last,' she said. 'We might look at them tomorrow. I am afraid I have been very negligent of my duty, but much has been happening since we arrived in Leighton.'

'I am sorry you have been obliged to work as hard as a kitchen maid,' I said.

'But I have been happy!'

She worked her hand out from beneath the folds of her cloak and found mine.

'I am so glad I was able to come here, Nicholas. To know your home and your family. And your earliest teacher, Sire Raymond. You are blessed to have this place, and I think I know you better now, having been here.'

I pressed her hand, and looked about, at the old manor house, the orchard where I had scrumped apples as a boy, the fringes of Wychwood lying beyond.

'I love the place,' I said slowly. 'And I love the people. But I could not have stayed.'

'You could not. You would have been like a song bird, trapped in a cage, beating your wings against the bars, unable to sing.'

'Hardly that.' I could feel the colour rising in my cheeks. 'But it is true that Oxford has nourished something in me that Leighton never could.'

'And you see how fortunate that makes you? I wish I had that . . . that nourishment. Although I am glad to visit my grandfather, I cannot recapture what I once had there as a child. There was too great a severance when my mother married again. And I think there is some lack in me, that I could not accept what Godstow offered, what many women have found in a religious life.'

'You would have been like a song bird, trapped in a cage, beating your wings against the bars, unable to sing.' I said, echoing her words.

'Aye, that is probably true. Well, perhaps Oxford will nourish me as well, even though I may not drink from its wells of knowledge, guarded by dragons against my sex.'

For that, I had no answer.

236

I was on the point of suggesting we retreat into the warmth of the house again, as it was beginning to grow dark, when I caught sight of a mounted figure approaching up the lane. Nay, two mounted figures. I stood up.

'I think Sir Henry has come after all,' I said, 'though somewhat late for the feast. And someone with him. Not his son, I think.'

'Shall I leave you to speak to him?' Emma said.

'From his expression,' I said, 'I think it would be well if you could find Peter and tell him that Sir Henry is come. His face carries a burden of news.'

She ran off to the house and I walked forward to hold Sir Henry's horse steady while he dismounted. The other man I did not recognise.

'So you are come after all,' I said, more a question than a statement.

'Aye.' He dismounted with a grunt, rubbing his knee. 'I have news, and it is not pleasant.'

'Peter Winchingham will be here in a minute,' I said. 'Save your breath until then. I would bid you withindoors, save that you could barely hear your own thoughts. They are dancing now, inside and out.'

The young people, having stared for a few minutes at the newcomers, had resumed their own dance.

The other rider had also dismounted.

'And this is?'

Sir Henry drew him forward. 'John Allworthy, constable at Burford. We have worked together in my courts. He has information for you. We both have.'

We bowed to each other, but before more could be said, Peter had arrived. The further introductions were brief, all of us aware that lengthy courtesy would be out of place, with this urgent news the two men brought.

'We cannot speak inside the house,' I said, 'for the noise. Within our cart is likely as quiet as anywhere.'

I called over two of the village lads to take the horses to the stable, and led the way into the cart, where I found and lit a candle lantern. It was a strange place for a conference which must, I was sure, concern the rogue Frenchmen. The four of us found seats on the benches, amongst a scattering of leftovers from the earlier gift giving.

'You asked me yesterday, Nicholas,' Sir Henry began, 'whether there might be anywhere these Frenchmen could have found friends and refuge nearby. As I told you then, I could think only that some manors hereabouts have changed owners and fallen into the hands of strangers. There are three not too far from Leighton. I rode over to Burford yesterday afternoon to consult Allworthy here, to see whether he knew more of them than I.'

He indicated to the other man to continue.

'Of the three,' Allworthy said, 'I could rule out one man at once. He is a cousin by marriage to the de Veres who used to hold Leighton. As honest a man as you could wish. There would be no treason in his household. As for the other two, I was not so sure. One holds a manor over beyond Burford, across the Windrush, the other manor is back a piece in this direction, on the other side of the high road from your lane to Leighton, but not touching Sir Henry's land.'

'I think I know both,' I said, 'but 'tis some years since I lived here, and Master Winchingham is but new come.' For a moment I considered sending for Edmond, but thought it better not to delay.

'We went first to the manor nearest Burford,' Sir Henry said, 'as we were already in the town. There was no time to think of any particular subterfuge.'

I thought, with his blunt nature, Sir Henry was unlikely to show any great subtlety, but before I could put a question, Allworthy spoke again.

'We said we were making enquiries,' he said, 'about a valuable horse gone missing from Sir Henry's stable. No idea whether 'twas merely strayed, or stolen.' He grinned. 'It gave us a reason to check their stable. We would soon have noticed six horses more than should have been there.'

'Allworthy's idea,' Sir Henry said, 'too clever for me,

238

but it served very well. There was nothing amiss in that stable, and nothing amiss with the new owner either. Perfectly decent man, younger son, his elder brother to inherit the father's estate in Warwickshire, about to wed himself, taking advantage of the manor going for a song, like so many since the Pestilence. Even knows my son Edward. So of course he insists we must take supper with him, and 'twould have looked damned odd had we refused.'

'Which left us no time to visit the other manor last night,' Allworthy said.

'Had a bit of a problem with the old knee this morning,' Sir Henry said, slapping it in reproof, 'but when they finally managed to heave me on to my horse, went along to the other manor, the one south of here, and that was another story.'

'You found the Frenchmen?' I said, feeling my chest tighten.

He held up his hand. 'Told the same story, explained my manor only a few miles away – the horse could have strayed in this direction. By now I was quite convinced myself that I'd lost the poor beast, out wandering somewhere perhaps, in the snow. Mayhap injured. I was quite moved.'

He smiled dreamily.

'A chestnut gelding. Four years old. White blaze. A white sock on his off fore, reaching from the fetlock almost to the knee. Showing promise as a hunter. I truly regret losing him.'

'You looked in the stable?' Peter said.

'They were not so willing,' Allworthy said. 'No sign of the lord. We were told he was absent. The steward was a surly fellow, but Sir Henry looked down his nose at him, and he gave in at last.

I grinned. This fellow John Allworthy must be on very good terms with Sir Henry.

'And?' I said.

'The lord away, and every stall in the stable

239

occupied,' Allworthy said dryly. 'Curious, don't you think?'

'And never a sign of my missing nag.' Sir Henry shook his head sorrowfully. 'We examined every horse, to be quite sure, with that steward breathing down our necks every step of the way. Oh, those were your Frenchmen's horses, never doubt it.'

'So what did you do?' Peter said. 'You could not challenge him, the steward.'

'Nay, we could not. But I asked, was there none of the lord's family at home, and he admitted that the lady was. Well, 'twas quite in order for me to call on her, neighbourly, as they are new come to the manor, and I just a few miles away. So I called on her. A very beautiful woman she is, too. Lady Fanshawe.'

I frowned. 'A well born Englishwoman, her lord away. Have these Frenchmen frightened her into giving them refuge?'

Sir Henry smiled, as pleased as a terrier who has caught a rat.

'Lady Fanshawe,' he said, 'is French.'

In order to maintain the deception, Sir Henry had been obliged to accept Lady Fanshawe's invitation to midday dinner, leaving Allworthy to kick his heels at the stable.

'There was a general unease amongst the lads,' Allworthy said. 'Some have come new with the Fanshawes, and some worked at the manor before. I'd say there is no love between them. While Sir Henry was being gallant to the lady, I managed, in the end, to have a private word with one of the local lads, who has family in Burford and knows me by name. He admitted there had been strangers about during the last few days, "talking foreign". He didn't care for the look of them. Thought they might be mercenaries.'

'Hmm,' Peter said, 'and they might be, at that.'

I shook my head. 'I think they are some man's close attendants. Some nobleman who thinks himself endangered by the contents of that letter the troubadours are carrying.'

'That glove you found,' Sir Henry said. 'That was a gentleman's glove.'

'It was,' I said. 'Perhaps they are more than attendants. Perhaps there is no other who has sent them, but it concerns these men themselves.'

I shook my head, denying my own words. 'Nay, that will not serve either. The man who is their leader, I saw him, briefly. A gentleman, perhaps, but not–' I found it difficult to frame an elusive impression. 'The letter is meant for the king. It must concern high matters of state. That man was not of such a rank. He serves someone higher.'

I gave an impatient sigh. 'How I wish we knew who sent the letter and what it contains! We are like blind men, groping in a fog.'

'Aye,' said Sir Henry, 'you speak truth, Nicholas. As soon as I could leave Lady Fanshawe without arousing suspicion, we rode over to Leighton as quickly as we might, and now we must decide what to do.'

'It seems to me,' Peter said slowly, 'that there is little else we can do, until some word comes from the Court. Not knowing the contents of the letter carried by the troubadours, it is very difficult for us to act.'

'Do you think that they themselves know?' I asked.

'They keep close counsel,' Peter said. 'My impression is that they do not know the contents, but they know very well who entrusted it to them, so that perhaps may suggest what it concerns. I am, of course, merely guessing.'

'Then all we can do is keep the musicians safe until someone comes from the Court,' I said. 'Do you agree, Sir Henry?'

'I'd prefer to deal with these French scoundrels first,' he said, 'and ask questions afterwards, if we could but lay hands on them. The longer they roam freely about the countryside, the longer they are a danger to us all. Do not forget, Nicholas, that they also waylaid you, as well as these troubadours. Anyone of us could come to harm, should they take it into their heads, perhaps, to seize a hostage. Have you thought of that? Are the women and children safe?'

To tell truth, I had not thought of that. I should have done. Had Alysoun not been taken once, to force my hand?

'Have you thought of any way to "deal" with them?' I used his own words, not sure what he had in mind.

'Bait a trap for them,' he said promptly 'Let them think they have a chance to lay hands on this letter they are so anxious to seize, then surround them and seize them in their turn.'

It had the makings of a plan.

'I have brought a small armed body with me,' Peter said. 'In my travels as a merchant, I have often needed them.'

'And I have my men,' Sir Henry said. 'Between us–'

Soon they had their heads together, muttering about tactics. Allworthy looked at me, his eyebrows raised in query.

'You do not quite care for the idea, Master Elyot?'

'As a military tactic it is sound enough,' I said, 'but I should not care to be the bait in the trap. That would fall to one of the troubadours. Would they trust us enough to run so great a risk?'

He shrugged. 'Having not met them, I cannot say.'

'It is the girl who carries the letter, though the Frenchmen do not know that. I think they suspect it is Gaston, their leader, the girl's husband. I would say that he is no coward. He might be willing.'

The other two must have overheard me.

'We agree,' Peter said, 'that Gaston is the most suitable one to ask. We think that we might try the plan tomorrow, when we can place our two groups of armed men strategically, and by some means draw these rogues in. It needs more planning, but I must return to my guests now. Do you all come in and join me. Master Allworthy, it sounds to me that although Sir Henry dined with Lady Fanshawe, you did not. There is food a-plenty within.'

All of us realising that there was nothing we could do now, with the manor overrun with festive villagers and evening already upon us, we followed him into the house. While Peter led his two latest guests away to the high table, Emma caught my arm.

'Have you news?'

I told her briefly about the discovery of the horses in the stable of the French Lady Fanshawe, and of the plan Sir Henry and Peter were proposing to implement the next day.

'This Lady Fanshawe, she has an English husband?'

'Aye, but who is to say where her loyalties lie, or his?'

'You do not like this plan of the baited trap.'

I sighed. 'Somehow my heart misgives me. It sounds too simple. What if it fails, and the Frenchmen succeed in carrying Gaston off?'

'But they would not have the letter.'

'He could be used to bargain for it. You have said that Azalais is deeply in love with him. I suspect she would trade the letter, however important, for her husband's life.'

'I am sure you have the right of it. What would you do instead?' she said.

'Wait a little longer for word from the Court. If we are to hear at all, it must be soon. If we hear nothing, that will be the time to try some scheme of our own. In the meantime, I think our best course is simply to keep the troubadours safe, all three of them.'

We stopped at the door of the great hall, where the most indefatigable of the dancers still held the floor, although many were beginning to gather up their families, preparing to go home. The musicians continued to play, although they looked exhausted, and very hot, despite the winter weather outside.

'I must help Birgit,' Emma said. 'Susanna warned her that it might be difficult to send everyone home. We are to serve bowls of the ham pottage and bread, to warm people for the cold walk home. They will find it sharp, after the heat in here.'

She went off in search of Birgit and Susanna, and I sank down on a stool near the wall. It was some relief to know where the Frenchmen could be found, instead of imagining them behind every thicket in the forest, but this Lady Fanshawe presented a problem. Was her husband also a traitor? There were many marriages between English and French, especially amongst the nobility, for these families frequently held lands on both sides of the narrow waters separating the two countries. We were in dispute with France over Aquitaine, which the French had tried to steal from us, and we had taken opposing sides in the battle over the succession in Brittany. Above all, our King Edward had a sound claim to the very throne of France, which was the fountainhead of all the other disputes. There was a risk that there might be other pockets of treason in England, where such families as the Fanshawes might have greater possessions in France than in England and placed their loyalty where it could serve their own interests best.

I found that I was not altogether surprised at what Sir Henry and John Allworthy had discovered.

Under the supervision of Birgit and Susanna, the manor servants began to carry in the food intended to send the guests on their way. At a signal from Peter, the musicians ceased playing and – with some considerable relief, I thought – carried off their instruments out of the hall. They had had a long and tiring day. The last of the dancers, laughing and breathless, gathered for their share of the ham potage. There was a general rummaging for mislaid cloaks and missing children, some of whom were found curled up behind the stacks of trestles.

I helped to load our own family into the large cart, while Jordain and Thomas fetched the horses and backed them between the shafts. It was dark now, with the early darkness of January, but torches had been lit to provide some light to the milling crowd in the yard, where Margaret and Emma were handing out baskets of leftover food to any of the villagers who wanted them.

Finally, our own party left – apart from Edmond and

244

myself – along with most of the guests. A few of the villagers, too cup-shotten to walk home, were being bundled by the manor servants back into the hall, where they could sleep out their drunkenness in the warmth and carry their aching heads home in the morning. I went in search of Peter to say my farewells before saddling Rufus to ride back to the farm. I met Sir Henry and John Allworthy just coming out of the house.

'I am away home,' Sir Henry said, 'and John comes with me for the night. We shall be back tomorrow, to lay our plans for the trap, although we have had no chance to speak to this fellow Gaston yet.'

He was full of cheerful plans, so I decided to wait to voice my objections until the next day.

'God give you a good night, Sir Henry,' I said. 'You have done well to find where these fellows are hiding.'

'Like smoking out a den of foxes,' he said, 'who are preying on your geese.'

They went off, and I continued into the house in my search for Peter.

The first person I saw was Gaston de Sarlat. His face was white, and he grabbed me unceremoniously by the sleeve.

'Master Elyot,' he gasped, 'have you seen Azalais?'

'Not since you stopped playing and left the hall,' I said. 'Were you not all together?'

'We were, aye, but you understand, we had become very hot, very tired. Azalais, she said she would go outside for a little, she needed to breathe some air, she said. But I cannot find her.'

'Well,' I said, 'there has been a great crowd out there. It would be easy to miss her in the dark. Perhaps she has come back inside. Have you asked Mistress Birgit? You must all be very thirsty. Your wife may have gone to the kitchen for a drink.'

'I have been to the kitchen. I have been to our bed chamber. I have searched the house. She is nowhere.'

He looked sick with worry, and I began to feel

concerned, but I tried to reassure him.

'I am sure she can have come to no harm. There are only friends here.'

Even as I spoke, I wondered whether I spoke the truth. I had seen none but friends, but as it had grown darker and people milled about preparing to leave, it had become impossible to have a clear view of everyone.

'Come,' I said, taking him firmly by the arm and propelling him toward Peter's small parlour. 'It is vital that you do not go wandering about. Today we have ascertained that the men pursuing you have been staying at a manor not far away, just over beyond the Burford road. Do not run any risks. Where is Falquet?'

Gaston allowed himself to be steered into the parlour.

'He was putting our instruments away. We have kept them in his chamber, where there is more room. He has not seen Azalais since we finished playing for the dancing.'

'Then I will tell one of the servants to send him here to the parlour. Both of you should stay where we know you will be safe. I shall go myself to look for Mistress Azalais. Now that almost everyone has left, it should be easy to find her.'

As I came out of the parlour, I nearly collided with one of the maid servants who was carrying two empty ale flagons back to the kitchen. I bade her go at once and send Master Falquet down to the parlour, where he was to remain until sent for. I wasted no breath on explanations.

Surely, I thought, the girl Azalais could not be far, but I was increasingly uneasy – and angry, too. She knew the risks. Perhaps the presence of that merry crowd had made her forget the danger in which she stood. Or perhaps the sheer numbers had seemed like a shield against that danger.

I found Peter in the great hall, overseeing the clearance, and told him briefly what Gaston had said.

'Can you arrange a thorough search of the house?' I said. 'Gaston says he has hunted everywhere, but he may not know all the nooks and crannies. It is a complicated building. And I will search outside.'

'At once,' he said, his face creased with concern.

I could not remember where I had left my cloak, but did not stop to look for it. Outside the torches were burning low, and one had gone out. The yard was eerily quiet after all the bustle no more than half an hour before. Edmond came out of the stable, leading his horse.

'Are we for home then, Nicholas?' he called to me.

I ran across to him.

'Azalais has gone missing,' I said grimly. 'It may be nothing, but I do not like it. The other two musicians are safe in the house, but they have not seen her since they finished playing and she came outside for some air. Peter is having the house searched and I am going to hunt out here.'

I looked around at the empty yard. Nothing stirred.

'I will help you,' he said.

I could not decide what was best to do. 'Can you ride down the lane?' I said. 'It may be that she has walked that way to escape the crowds after their trying day's work. It may be no more than that. Ride as far as the village. If there is no sign of her, come back. In the meantime, I will search the gardens and orchard. I do not think she would go into the barns.'

'Unlikely.' He swung himself up on to his horse. 'Hand me up one of the smaller torches. It will help to have some light.'

I gave him one, then thought to equip myself, but remembered I had seen a row of candle lanterns on a shelf in the stable. A lantern would be easier to carry, though it meant a few minutes' delay.

Once I had equipped myself, I headed for the gardens. These were extensive. The de Veres had created a series of beautiful formal gardens, which had deteriorated after the death of the family. During the short period of Gilbert Mordon's lordship, a beginning had been made on their restoration, but the further one went from the house, the more overgrown they were. I did not think much had been done since the Winchinghams had come, but of course much of that time had been in winter weather.

As it was, the feeble light of my lantern showed up grotesque shapes covered with snow, which might be anything from a dormant bush to a body. There were tracks through the snow, but since there had been no fresh falls for some days, it was impossible to tell whether or not they were recent. For some reason I was hesitant to call out to Mistress Azalais, for my voice would be lost in those empty spaces. Later, perhaps, I would bring more people, and our voices together might sound less pitiful.

I could see no sign of any other person in the gardens, neither the formal gardens nor the kitchen and herb gardens, which I also searched. I made my way to the orchard. There were certain unpleasant memories associated with the orchard, from the events of a few months earlier. It was here that Reginald Le Soten had been found murdered. The very man the troubadours were to meant to pass their letter to.

As I came to the edge of the orchard, I heard a horse whicker.

The sound did not come from behind me, where the manor stable was, but ahead. I stopped. A horse had no business in the manor orchard at night.

Could Azalais be here? For a moment I was filled with suspicion. Was the girl herself a traitor, and had come to hand over the letter secretly to one of the very men who had pursued her and her companions, and beaten her husband? Then I dismissed the thought, remembering her furious passion when she had sworn her hatred of the French. That had rung with the truth.

I realised that I was standing still, with no cover, and with the lantern clearly illuminating me for anyone to see who should look this way. Fool! A poor soldier I would make, scouting out the enemy. For now I was sure that at least one of the enemy was there, in the orchard. Had he seized Azalais? And had he torn the letter from her? Was she even alive?

I blew out the lantern, and slipped sideways behind a

large bush of lavender, holding my breath, as if that would make it easier to listen, although the sound of my own heartbeat seemed to drum in my ears. Very faintly I could hear distant sounds from the house, but I tried to block them out and focus my attention on what was ahead of me in the orchard.

The horse was some distance away, of that I was sure, and now I could make out muffled sounds, of what seemed to be a struggle. Could this be where Azalais had gone? Or been taken? It might, of course, be no more than the drunken and amorous fumblings of some couple who had been at the feast and then taken themselves off for some privacy. But surely not on a bitter January night, in the snow!

I began to work my way deeper into the orchard. It was a place long familiar to me, but in the dark, not daring to use the lantern, I found myself colliding with trees and stumbling over hidden tussocks under the snow. Gradually I began to get my night vision, and whereas the lantern had given me a good sight of everything within the circle of its light, I found that the cold moonlight, although pale and deceptive, allowed me a wider scope.

And now I could make out moving shapes which were not trees. The horse was there, and two figures, struggling. One was a woman, for I could see the fullness of her skirts. If it was Azalais, and if it was one of those desperate rogues she was fighting, it was a wonder he had not already killed her. I began to run toward them, stumbling and awkward in the snow, and I shouted out – what words I know not. I was trying to create the illusion that there were many here, not one man alone. If it was a courting couple, I should look a fool indeed.

I was almost upon them when something flew past my head and hit a tree behind me with a heavy thud.

'I have disarmed him!' It was Azalais's voice.

In Jesu's name, how could any girl do that?

Now I was near enough to see them. It was the man I had encountered in the lane, the one I took to be their leader, and I could make out an empty scabbard swinging from his belt. Somehow Azalais had managed to seize the sword and send it flying, but the man was not disarmed. He held her about the waist, pressed before him like a shield, and he had his dagger at her throat.

'One more step,' he said, 'and I cut her throat.'

I stopped abruptly.

'I do not care!' the girl cried. 'Let him kill me, but kill him after.'

'No need for any killing,' I said, trying to keep my voice calm. 'You are very mistaken, sir, if you think you can escape. There is a body of armed men coming up behind me. There is no way out of this for you, with or without the girl. What can you want with her? She is nothing but a singing girl.'

'She has something I want,' he said.

'Do you mean that letter?' I said innocently. 'Oh, that is long gone. When we met in the lane, I had already despatched it. By now it will be with the king. You waste your time and imperil your immortal soul if you do any harm to the girl.'

I could see him hesitate, not knowing whether to believe me.

I took a cautious step forward, and as I did so I carefully loosened my dagger in its sheath, but did not dare to draw it. His attention had shifted from me to Azalais. He shook her roughly.

'Where is the letter, you harlot? Did you give it to this man?'

Azalais must have been exhausted and terrified, despite her defiance, and was momentarily confused by my ruse.

'I . . . I,' she gasped, then gathered her wits about her. 'Aye, it is true. I gave the letter to Master Elyot to send on to King Edward.'

But her hesitation had aroused his suspicion. He clutched her more tightly and shook her, till I could hear her teeth clatter together. Then a look of enlightenment

250

came over his face.

'You have it still. We knew neither of the men had it, or we should have found it when first we caught up with you. I was sure it was you. And now, see, you are betrayed by the rustle of the paper itself!'

He tried to reach into her gown, where he must have heard or felt the hidden letter, and she sank her teeth into his hand. He struck her on the side of the head, and I took my chance while his attention was on her, leaping forward with my dagger in my hand. Almost too late, he saw his danger and threw the girl aside, so that she fell, sprawling into the snow.

He stood, legs braced apart, his dagger poised, and laughed at me.

I could have laughed at myself, facing a man who clearly knew the use of arms, and I a sometime Oxford scholar, whose chief knowledge of armed combat came from the tales in the books I sold.

There was one compensation. He was not wearing armour today. He must have come in and mingled with the crowds unnoticed – and even in half armour he would have been noticed – thinking that he could somehow reach Azalais. By going outside to cool herself after her long labours of the day, she had played into his hands.

Like a pair of wary dogs, we circled. He feinted with his dagger, but I could tell from his eyes that it was not a real thrust, and did not make the mistake of parrying it and so laying myself open to his true intentions. We were more evenly matched than in the lane, for he did not have either his sword or his companions, but his dagger was longer than mine, and his skill clearly immeasurably greater.

Then he thrust at me in earnest. I ducked, avoiding the blade, and struck back, but he was too quick for me. Another thrust, swift as a striking snake. It caught my shoulder, but not deeply. Again I missed.

I had one advantage. He had donned a thick cloak to mingle with Peter's guests, while I had not stopped to fetch mine before I came in search of Azalais. I had been growing cold, but I was cold no longer, and it meant that I could move more easily. It evened the odds between us a little. Then I had another small piece of luck. He stumbled slightly over some hidden tree root, and I managed to slice into his left arm. It was no disabling injury, but it cheered me. Perhaps I was not so hopeless after all.

Azalais had been lying as if stunned, but now, out of the corner of my eye, I saw her stir. At least he had not killed her. Not yet.

Then my small gleam of hope died.

I had pretended that an armed band was following me into the orchard in the hope of persuading him to release the girl. Now, to my dismay, I could hear the jingle of harness approaching from the manor. The Frenchman, after all, had not come alone. He must have made his way here first, to try to find Azalais, while his companions waited in hiding to join him, once the guests of the manor had departed. They must have been lurking somewhere off the manor lane until they saw that the way was clear.

'Au secours!' the man shouted. 'À moi!'

Before they could reach us, and while his attention was briefly distracted, Azalais reached out and grabbed him around the ankle. Her intention must have been to bring him down, which she failed to do, but he lost his balance and staggered forward toward me. I brought my dagger down on his right wrist and his own dagger tumbled down and disappeared into the snow. By now Azalais had gripped both his ankles and pulled, while I thrust my fist against his chest and pushed.

He fell backwards into the snow and I threw myself on top of him, kneeling on his chest and holding my knife to his throat. Behind me I heard the horsemen come to a stop in a whirl of snow and a ringing of harness.

'Come one step nearer,' I said, in unconscious imitation, 'and I slit his throat.'

'You have my full permission, Master Elyot,' said a familiar voice.

I twisted to peer over my shoulder, where a tall figure

252

looked down from his horse.

Edward, the Black Prince, was laughing.

Chapter Twelve

The following morning found us once again in Peter's small parlour. A larger table had been brought in, and at its head sat Edward, Prince of Wales. He looked remarkably fresh and cheerful for a man who had been up most of the night, his only rest in a bed chamber of a modest country manor. A man, moreover, who had ridden the distance from London to Leighton through severe winter conditions, with but one overnight stop. However, although some of his life was spent amongst the magnificent trappings of the royal palaces, which I could only begin to imagine, he was often in the field with his armies, where he was rumoured to sleep in a tent no better than those of his men. He sat now with his right hand resting lightly on a folded paper, which I took to be the famous (or infamous) letter. It remained sealed.

Around the table, besides myself, were seated Peter Winchingham, Sir Henry Talbot, my cousin Edmond, and the three troubadours – Gaston de Sarlat, Azalais de Bézieres, and her twin Falquet. Azalais looked tired, with dark shadows under her eyes, but otherwise free of the strain which her face had worn since we had first met her. Apart from a sprained wrist, she seemed none the worse for her encounter with the leader of the Frenchmen.

'How did you manage to wrest his sword away from him?' I found time to ask her in a brief moment of quiet the previous night.

She curled a contemptuous lip.

'Men think they are invincible, with a sword in their hands,' she said. 'He was flourishing it about like a child with a wooden foil. I am strong. I grew up with two other brothers besides Falquet. I twisted it away from him and threw it into the snow, but I had no time to seize his dagger before you came.'

'No doubt you would have seized that also,' I said politely.

'Indeed,' she replied, ignoring the fact that when I reached them she had been held quite helpless, with the dagger at her throat. 'However,' she added gracefully, 'I thank you for your intervention.'

The prince looked around the table now, gathering our attention, and tapped the letter with his finger.

'I have yet to open this,' he said, 'although I have some thoughts about what it may contain. Last night we were all a little too occupied.'

That, I thought, was to understate the case. It had turned out that my guess was correct. The rest of the Frenchmen were lying in wait just off the manor lane, intending to join their leader, and might have done Edmond some harm as he rode down it, searching for Azalais, had not the prince's party ridden up from the village at that moment. It seemed the Frenchmen had made the mistake of breaking cover and were at once surrounded by the prince's men, when Edmond shouted out a warning. In the ensuing skirmish, two of the Frenchmen had been killed. The remaining three were now imprisoned in Burford pound. Their leader was here, locked up in the cellar which had once held the wrongfully accused Alan Wodville.

'The man you overpowered last night, Master Elyot,' the prince said, bowing, 'is not unknown to me. His name is Pierre de Dinan, although I am surprised he can claim any birthplace, and I believe his allegiance to Dinan was acquired in recent years. For most of his adult life he has led a band of mercenary soldiers, or rather freebooters, the like of which have inflicted damage throughout France under a weak king. Something I cannot regret, were it not that they have also, from time to time, turned their attention to our lands of Aquitaine.'

He flashed a smile at Sir Henry.

'Sir Henry will know of them, from his time at our wars in France.'

'Indeed, Highness, and long campaigns have made them skilled and dangerous.'

'Exactly. That has also made them a powerful weapon, when they can be made use of. And there is one man in France who has mastered the art of using them as his weapons. His name is Bertrand du Guesclin.'

The name meant nothing to me, but I saw all three troubadours stiffen.

'Du Guesclin is scarcely more than a mercenary himself, but a clever one, a skilled tactician. Whichever king can command him possesses a formidable leader of armies. The man I found last night lying under the point of Master Elyot's dagger is one of du Guesclin's right hand men, this Pierre de Dinan. Du Guesclin is himself of Dinan, or was born somewhere nearby, and I believe Pierre the-probably-nameless has taken the name from him.'

'So,' Peter said slowly, 'Dinan. These men are concerned in the war over the succession to the dukedom of Brittany?'

'Amongst other things. Du Guesclin is employed by the king of France both there and in his campaigns against Aquitaine, and it is my belief that this letter relates in some way to one or the other.' He turned to Gaston. 'Is that so?'

'Highness,' Gaston said, 'we were not told the contents of the letter.'

The prince nodded. 'Probably safer not to know.'

He took out a small knife from its sheath on his belt. It must be the knife he used for eating. The handle was beautifully enamelled with the arms of England and France, quartered, but the enamel was chipped, and the blade was sharpened so thin that it would serve as a small dagger itself. The prince slid it under the wax which sealed the letter, and lifted it.

He read the contents swiftly, and I judged from the look of shock on his face that they bore an import beyond what he had suspected. He laid the paper down, and looked again at Gaston.

'Who gave you this letter, Monsieur de Sarlat, and ordered you to bring it to England?'

Gaston glanced at his wife, and clenched his hands together.

'My name, I confess,' he said. 'is not Gaston de Sarlat.'

Peter gave me a quick look, and I nodded.

'My right name is Gracias de Gyvill, and I used to be court musician to King Pedro of Castile.'

Someone gave a gasp, and Falquet reached out and took his sister's hand.

'Oh, my wife and her brother know my true identity,' Gaston said, 'but it has seemed wiser to adopt a new name and a new country.'

Prince Edward was staring at him. Clearly the name meant more to him than to me.

'My sister,' he said faintly. 'My young sister Joan.'

That was the princess who had died at Bordeaux, I remembered, on her way to wed Pedro of Castile.

'Aye, that is so,' Gaston said. I could not think of him by this other unfamiliar name. 'My prince – for he was a prince then, his father still living – my prince sent me to entertain the lady on her way to Castile, having heard of her love of music, a love which he shares.'

'But it was thought that you also died of the plague,' Prince Edward said.

'There was a great deal of confusion, you understand,' Gaston said. 'It was the early days of the Pestilence. Terror and panic stalked the streets of Bordeaux. People were dying in unprecedented numbers. No one knew from whence the plague came, and there was no cure. The remnant of the English party eventually sailed for home, the few of us from Castile who survived also made our way back to our prince's court. Since then I have served him as an occasional messenger and intelligencer. France is hostile to Castile, as it is to England, and supports Aragon in its attacks on us. It was thought . . . expedient . . . for me to remain outside Castile, moving about, as troubadours must do nowadays. I could keep my eyes and ears open, and send reports back to my king, from time to time.'

'But on this occasion,' the prince said, 'the intelligence travelled in the opposite direction.'

Gaston bowed. 'That is so. A man we used as a go-between came to me in Bruges, with the order to bring this letter to England. I would have come here by some means in any case, but as it happened, Master Winchingham's daughter had just engaged us, so we could come quite openly, without arousing any suspicions.'

'Forgive me for interrupting,' I said, 'but you told us that you had been instructed to pass the letter to Reginald Le Soten at Leighton Manor. How could that be?'

'It was a fortunate accident,' Gaston said, 'that we were to come to Leighton. When the messenger from King Pedro heard that was where we were bound, he recommended Le Soten. Castile had had dealings with him before, as an intelligencer for King Edward.'

Prince Edward nodded. 'Aye, that is true. But of course word could not yet have reached Castile that Le Soten was dead.'

'We knew only that he had last been heard of here. When we learned he was dead, we were thrown into a quandary.'

'So now we know who you are,' Sir Henry said, 'and that your letter comes from King Pedro of Castile, and how it was meant to reach our King Edward. Are we to be permitted to learn what information it contains, that these men were so desperate to seize it?'

'Certainly,' said the prince. 'Especially since all those here have done much to secure its safety.'

He picked up the letter again, and ran his eye down it.

'There are three principal matters with which it deals,

and I will summarise them for you. The first two concern the plans of du Guesclin. He purposes a double-headed attack on English lands and strongholds. First, his army of mercenaries and French will attack the castles and towns in Brittany which stand for young Duke John of Brittany, who is our ally. Many of them are held by English garrisons. You may not know that ever since the death of their parents, Duke John and his sister have been wards of my father, and have been reared up with my brothers and sisters and me. They are, in a sense, our family. We stand for John's rights in Brittany. However, France, under the command of du Guesclin, stands for the rival claimant, Charles of Blois.'

He grimaced. 'Charles the Pious, some call him, for he constantly mortifies his flesh. So pious that he ordered the massacre of hundreds of innocent civilians at the siege of Quimper.'

'But we have him now,' Sir Henry said with satisfaction. 'He has been a prisoner in England these six years and more.'

'Aye,' the prince said, 'captured by Sir Thomas Dagworth, who was later murdered by the Blois party.'

'So, that is the first part of the plan,' Sir Henry said, 'a concerted attack on our garrisons in Brittany. What is the second?'

'While one army under an officer of du Guesclin moves on Brittany and diverts our attention, du Guesclin himself, with his main army, will march against Aquitaine, to make the most serious attempt at it yet.'

'When?' Sir Henry asked bluntly.

'At the earliest opportunity when the weather turns favourable.'

'And King Pedro of Castile learned of this plan?' Peter asked. 'How?'

'Aye, he is a man much set about by enemies, and Gracias here is not his only intelligencer. One who had managed to infiltrate the du Guesclin party learned this and took it hot-foot to Pedro.'

'Somehow du Guesclin must have discovered that word was being brought here to the king,' Sir Henry said, 'and so he despatched this Pierre and a body of men to intercept it?'

'So it seems. How it was discovered by du Guesclin, we do not know as yet.'

'You said, Highness,' I ventured, 'that there was a third matter?'

'Aye.' The prince smiled grimly. 'And that the most devilish of all. Troop movements in France we might have detected in time, but the rest of du Guesclin's plans carried the war on to English soil, and in a time of truce. These men who have been haunting your woods were not here only to get possession of this letter before it could reach my father. They had another task. Two tasks.'

We all looked at him with a kind of dread, but I reminded myself firmly that all the Frenchmen were now either dead or in hold. They could not hurt us.

'Sir Henry has reminded us that Charles of Blois is held prisoner here. Like any nobleman, he is held in comfortable surroundings, not in a dungeon, on his parole while he awaits his ransom. These men were charged with discovering where he is held and releasing him, to take up again his fight to seize Brittany.'

Edmond, who had kept silence until now, gave a soft exclamation. 'Could it be done?'

'By a determined group of men?' the prince said. 'Probably. As I said, Charles is held until his ransom can be paid. His piety did not prevent him condoning murder. I doubt it would prevent him breaking his given promise to await his ransom.'

I had been following all the items the prince had laid out before us. 'And there is one thing more?' I said. 'These men had yet one further task?'

'Aye, the most vile of all, for it concerns a child.'

The prince ran his hand over his face, and for a moment his eyes were bleak.

'God be thanked we have forestalled this!'

260

He flattened out the letter on the table, glanced down at it, then up again.

'I have said that young John, Duke of Brittany, and his sister Joan have been brought up in my own family. John is fifteen now. My little sister Mary is nine, and they have been dear companions all through their childhood. It is not always possible for us, children of the blood royal, to make our own choice in marriage. When my sister Joan was sent to Bordeaux, she was to marry a man she had never seen, Pedro of Castile.'

Gaston looked as though he might speak, but refrained.

'With John of Brittany and Mary, no alliance could have been happier. They love each other, perhaps more as brother and sister now, but it is a good foundation for a marriage. They are betrothed. Indeed, they were betrothed from the time of Mary's birth. They have been most happy together during this Christmastide at Eltham Palace.'

'There is harm intended against Duke John?' I asked.

'Against my sister, rather,' he said. 'A little girl of nine. One of her ladies has been corrupted. The plan discovered by King Pedro's intelligencer was to be the kidnapping of Mary with the aid of this traitorous dame. You may therefore understand why these Frenchmen were so determined to seize the letter before word of all these schemes, which appear to originate from du Guesclin, could be uncovered. In especial, with the last two, before their attempts to free Charles of Blois and kidnap Mary could be frustrated. You have told me that they were anxious not to be identified. I expect they feared that men like Sir Henry, who have served in France, might recognise one of them.'

'What would be their purpose in seizing the princess?' Edmond asked.

The prince smiled bitterly. 'Demand we exchange Duke John for her? Threaten to kill her unless we abandon our support of his claim to Brittany? Any number of devices which might occur to a cruel mind. Du Guesclin is no more inclined to be merciful than his Breton patron.'

'Then you must get word to the Court at once!' I said, half rising from my seat. 'There may be others tasked with this kidnapping – the woman in attendance on the princess must be removed!'

I sat down again. 'Forgive me, Highness. I spoke out of turn.'

The prince smiled at me. 'You do not speak out of turn, Nicholas Elyot, but very much to the point. Now that I have seen this,' he tapped the letter, 'I shall send a swift messenger at once to my father. He will take steps to protect my sister and to put a guard on Charles of Blois. I shall remain here perhaps two more days, if Master Winchingham is agreeable, to attend to these Frenchmen. Pierre de Dinan must be questioned closely. And Lady Fanshawe.'

He turned to Sir Henry. 'You might care to assist me in the questioning, knowing France and the ways of their armies.'

Sir Henry inclined his head with dignity, but I could see he was pleased.

'My father and I, and my little sister, owe a great debt of gratitude to those who carried this letter,' he bowed to the troubadours, 'and to those who kept it safe.' He smiled at the rest of us. 'For now, I must write to my father and despatch my rider.'

It was dismissal. We rose, still feeling somewhat stunned at the great matters of state which had been laid out before us, all from one simple letter, and drifted out into the hallway, while Peter brought paper, ink, and wax to the prince.

Sir Henry and Edmond went ahead toward the great hall, but before I could follow them, Gaston caught me by the arm.

'Master Elyot,' he said, 'it is not only the Black Prince who owes a debt of gratitude. You have twice been in danger of your life for our sake, and had you not gone to Azalais's aid last night, I think she would have been killed, for she would not have given up the letter while she remained alive. There is little I can do in return, but if there is aught, name it.'

I smiled at him. 'Your wife is a woman of great courage as well as great gifts of music.' I paused. 'Yet, as it happens, there *is* something you could do for me.'

Like Edward of Woodstock, we remained two more days at Leighton. We could not tarry much longer. Jordain must take up his duties as Warden of Hart Hall before his students returned to the university after their Christmas break. Margaret and Maud felt that they could not impose on Mary Coomber much longer to care for their hens, particularly if the weather conditions had been as bad in Oxford as in the countryside.

Walter had the keys of my shop, and he could reopen before I returned, but I preferred to be there at the beginning of the university term, for it was always a busy time, and I could not expect my scriveners to manage all the business as well as their scribing. I should be sorry to leave my family and friends here in Leighton, but Oxford called to me.

Emma spent the two days, from dawn until late in the evening, at the manor. She sat with Azalais, and sometimes with the other two troubadours, patiently making paper copies of the songs, both words and music, which seemed most suited to our book. For weeks I had believed it could never be made. Now it seemed that it would be one of our finest. I would be very reluctant to hand it over to Lady Amilia, who could not possibly value it as it should be valued. I began to think we might make a smaller version for her, and keep this exceptional collection for ourselves.

Several hours each day, I joined Emma and the troubadours, doing some of the copying myself, and writing down, on separate paper, the English translations of those lyrics which were in Occitan. They were rough translations, all that Gaston or Falquet could come up with at short notice. Later I would work at improving them, trying to catch the beauty I could sense in the original words, and ensuring that they could be fitted to the music.

Emma and Azalais talked eagerly of the illuminated borders and capitals which would enhance the finished work, once Emma had transcribed her hasty notes into elegant lettering.

'How I wish I might see it!' Azalais said wistfully.

'Then you must come to Oxford in a few months' time,' I said, 'after you have been in London. It is not far, nor a difficult journey, once the snow is gone.'

I was not sure whether they would indeed come, but I knew that Emma and I would want to show them the completed book.

When I was not working as a copyist, I spent some time with the prince. At his invitation, I attended the questioning of Pierre de Dinan, which was not gentle, but not brutal either. He was stubborn, and would give little away. I suspect we already knew enough of the business from the letter sent by Pedro of Castile, though I could not quite lay aside my suspicions that there could be more of du Guesclin's men in the country, who might make an attempt on the little princess.

Lady Fanshawe had disappeared, as had her husband.

'Never fear,' the prince said grimly. 'They will be found.'

The prince had sent one of his own men, carrying his letter to the king, immediately after our discussion that first morning. He would change horses at royal estates on the way, and was expected to reach London sometime on the following day. It would be a hard ride, but not much harder than the prince himself had, coming to Leighton.

After we had left Pierre de Dinan, stubborn in his silence, I walked with the prince toward the orchard, where Hans and the other boys were digging in the snow, hoping to find the Frenchman's sword and dagger as trophies.

'That boy Hans is the same age as Duke John,' the prince said. 'And see how carefree he is? Better far to be born thus, in the middle rank of life, than burdened for ever with the heavy duties of state.'

I hardly knew how to answer. The Black Prince had been famed – since he was of an age with Hans – throughout both England and France for his skill and courage on the battlefield. Like his father he was a man of great presence, a man whose fame could only grow, year by year. And yet, when I was alone with him, I felt him but a young man like myself.

'When I wrote to you,' I said, 'I never expected you to come to Leighton yourself. I asked – as I asked Mistress Walsea – for a reliable messenger, with an armed escort, not Edward of Woodstock.'

He smiled at me thoughtfully. 'I have not known you long, Nicholas, nor well, but I think I can judge a man. When I received that cautious letter, written on such execrable paper, I knew that something was seriously amiss. And do you not find, when something is seriously amiss, that it is better to attend to it yourself?'

I returned his smile. 'Of course, you have the right of it.' And I noted that he called me Nicholas.

At that there was a whoop of excitement from Thomas, who was flourishing a sword above his head.

'I believe that they have found their trophy,' the prince said.

It was decided that all of us would travel together. The troubadours had fulfilled their engagement with the Winchinghams, and could now travel on to London. The prince had business at Woodstock Palace, so we could all keep company until the turn off the high road took us south to Oxford and the royal party north to Woodstock. My former worries about our return journey, without the escort we had enjoyed on the way here from Oxford, were now swept aside. Surrounded by armed soldiers wearing the royal livery, we would be safe from the kind of scoundrels we had encountered near Witney.

'We are to go to Woodstock Palace with the prince,' Azalais told Emma, her eyes shining. 'We shall stay there and entertain the household until he is ready to travel on to London, then we shall have an engagement at the Court.'

'I told her,' Emma said, 'that all their distress and trials had been worth it, if they were to be thus rewarded.'

'As they are,' I said. 'I am glad for them. They have exceptional talent, and the girl's voice in particular is a gift from God.'

'What a fortunate thing it is, then,' Emma said, 'that she is already married. Else I should find myself quite set aside.'

I laughed but would not let her bait me.

Before we left Leighton, I paid a final visit to Sire Raymond in his small cottage beside the church. I found him reading, holding his book, the *Confessions* of St Augustine, at arms' length.

'Do you find difficulty in reading now?' I asked, taking the stool he indicated. There were no cushioned chairs here. He would not have felt them appropriate for a man of the cloth.

'Ah, it is age, Nicholas,' he said, with a sigh. 'We must all come to it.'

'You need not suffer for it,' I said, and I explained how the spectacles purchased at St Frideswide's Fair had helped Walter to read.

He shook his head. 'God has sent me this trial, and I must accept it.'

I would not argue with him, but thought when next the merchant of Venetian spectacles returned to Oxford, I would buy a pair for Sire Raymond. God, I was sure, would be pleased that his faithful servant could continue to read works of piety.

'It has been good to see you and Margaret back in Leighton,' Sire Raymond said, laying his book aside, 'and your children. I swear they have grown even since harvest time.'

'I came in some trepidation this Christmastide,' I said, 'for I feared to find my mother very frail, yet she is in better health than I dared hope.'

'She was seriously ill early in the summer, as you well know, and she was a long while recovering. You must have noticed, when you were here last, that she had grown thinner.'

'I did,' I said, 'but she seems to have regained some of her old strength. She is better living there at the farm house, where Susanna and Edmond can keep a watchful eye.'

'Her own old home for many years. Perhaps she can find more contentment there than in that small cottage.'

When I bade him farewell, I knelt for his blessing, then he embraced me.

'I am glad that you have come safe out of this latest scrape,' he said. 'As a boy you had your misadventures, but of late you seem constantly to be falling into trouble.'

'Emma says that I attract it, draw it like lightning to a tall tree.'

He smiled. 'Perhaps she has the right of it, but nevertheless, have a care.'

Later, when I spoke to my mother, saying how glad I was to see her back at the farm house, she shook her head.

'I shall stay here for the winter, Nicholas, for 'tis warmer and safer in these great snows, but when spring comes, I shall go back to my cottage. Two women cannot rule in one kitchen, and I do not want to usurp Susanna's place. When I am here, she must always be thinking that this was my home and my kitchen.'

'I am sure that is not so!' I protested, but she simply shook her head and smiled.

And then it was time to leave. Peter Winchingham and his children came to the farm to speed us on our way. Our cart groaned under the weight of food for the journey and provisions to take back to Oxford – oatmeal, honey, a large sack of flour, another of apples. The troubadours' cart was similarly loaded. Peter had brought us a huge ham.

'And where we shall put that,' Margaret said, 'I

cannot think,' though she smiled at him. 'I believe I must use it as a cushion on the journey.'

'It will be honoured,' Peter said.

I had consulted with the prince about how we should break our journey. There had been no fresh snow for a week, and the weather, although very cold, did not threaten any more as yet. I told him of our poor reception at Minster Lovell Priory.

He nodded. 'I should not care to spend the night there,' he said, 'even without this tale of your bad experience. The alien monks at the priory have no love for my family. What think you of pressing on as far as Eynsham on our first day? Could your party manage it?'

Despite wishing to agree, I was somewhat doubtful. 'The cart horses are slow,' I said. ''Tis a heavy load for them. And what of the troubadours? They have but a pony to their cart.'

'I have spoken with Gaston – or should we say Gracias? I can lend him a horse to ride, which will make their cart the lighter. I think if we make an early start . . .'

'Let us attempt it,' I said. 'In the summer we made the whole journey in a day. With no blizzards to contend with, surely we can manage it now in two.'

When I discussed it with the others, Jordain and Margaret were both reluctant, although they agreed it were better to avoid Minster Lovell. None of us, I think, wished to appear weak in the eyes of the prince.

So it was that we set off briskly, soon after dawn, a great company, with our two carts, and our royal escort. Most of the village turned out to see us on our way, still awed by the fact that for a few days the Prince of Wales had lived among them.

When we reached the high road, it was a relief to see that the surface was firmly beaten down, but not too slippery, so that the carts could move at a better pace than we had achieved on the way here from Oxford. Progress was helped by the fact that the two cart horses had been well rested and well fed during their stay at Leighton.

'Aye,' the prince said, when I commented on the road surface. 'When my men returned from Woodstock, they reported that it was sound.'

He had sent his prisoners ahead of us to Woodstock, so that we should not be troubled with them, and the men who had escorted them had returned that morning, having ridden during the night. In our turn, we made good time and passed Minster Lovell before stopping to eat our midday meal. Soon afterwards, we passed the beech spinney where the outlaws had lain in ambush.

'Your man from Oxford castle did well here,' the prince said, when I pointed it out to him. 'There are too many of these lawless bands preying on travellers. We have trouble enough in France, without these human wolves at home.'

To my relief, it was only just growing dusk as we reached the turn down to Eynsham Abbey. A rider had been sent ahead, to warn Brother Elias what to expect. I feared he might be overwhelmed, not only by our numbers but by the royal personage in charge, but he seemed all the more delighted. The prince himself was carried off to dine and sleep in the abbot's lodging, but the rest of us fared very well, as we had done before.

The next day would be our last all in company. Emma rode for a time with Azalais in the troubadours' cart, and for much of the way I found myself near the prince at the head of our party. He talked easily of the countryside, and his own estates, which he did not see as often as he wished, being so often needed abroad for diplomacy or war.

'This truce,' I ventured, 'how long, think you, that it will last?'

He looked grave. 'Not much longer. Certainly not when treachery is at work in France. My father will take steps at once to warn our garrisons in Brittany and Aquitaine of these plans of Bertrand du Guesclin. They may be forestalled, but I fear open warfare will break out again before long. I shall find myself in the blood-soaked fields of France once more.'

'You are famed for your greatness in battle, Highness.'

He gave me a sad smile. 'When I was younger, I thought no man could aspire to more than a warrior's glory. Now, I ask myself, did God put me on this earth for naught but to slay my fellow man? Is there not something more worthy a man might do with his life?'

'I cannot speak for God,' I said, 'but England feels safer under the shield of your strong arm.'

And then we had reached the crossroads and the parting of the ways.

Our farewells were brief. The royal party and the troubadours turned left, heading toward Woodstock and the palace where the Prince of Wales was born. Our cart and myself on Rufus turned right, to follow the road which led past the Godstow turn and on down to St Giles and Oxford.

Alysoun demanded, as she had done before, to ride into Oxford sitting before me on Rufus, and so I took her up. I feared there might be an argument from Rafe, but he was fast asleep in the cart, with his head in Juliana's lap. The cart horses seemed to recognise their road home, for they lifted their heads and quickened their pace. Rufus, in the lead, had to be held back from breaking into a canter.

We came out from the trees near St Giles church and looked down the wide stretch of road which led to the North Gate. The sun, which had been somewhat reluctant all day, lurking behind a veil of cloud, suddenly broke through, spreading a misty golden light over the scene before us.

'Oh!' said Alysoun. 'Oh, look!'

All the spires and crenellations of Oxford gleamed and sparkled, frosted over with glittering snow, so that the whole town seemed dreamlike, a jewelled casket, an unimaginable paradise. I feared that if I were to close my eyes and open them again, it would have vanished away.

'Oxford!' Alysoun breathed.

'Aye,' I said. 'Oxford.'

Historical Note

The so-called Little Ice Age, when the climate of Europe became markedly more severe, has been variously dated by climate historians, but some studies place it from around 1300 to the mid nineteenth century, although the worst period seems to have been in the seventeenth century.

Winters were very severe, and lasted longer, with bitter cold, heavy snow, and frozen rivers and lakes. By the seventeenth century, even the Thames, despite being tidal in its lower reaches, was freezing from time to time, making it possible to hold ice fairs on the frozen river. The paintings of Pieter Brueghel the Elder frequently depict the weather of the Little Ice Age in the Low Countries.

These severe winters meant a shortening of the agricultural year, so that fear of dearth and famine haunted the populace of Britain and continental Europe. Shortage of wheat for bread – the staple diet of the common people – led to frequent bread riots. At times, a kind of coarse bread had to be made from barley and oats, even mixed with acorns and ground nut shells. Shortage of fodder meant that fewer animals could be overwintered, resulting in a decline in flocks and herds, and so a decrease in the food supply. One historian has linked the growing persecution of alleged witches, which reached its peak in the hard-hit seventeenth century, to accusations of their responsibility for the increasing disasters in agriculture, due to the short growing season and the wet, cold summers.

Although in Nicholas Elyot's time the full impact of the Little Ice Age was yet to be felt, people were already suffering from the effects of longer, colder winters. Books of Hours produced at the time make much, in their illuminated illustrations for the winter months, of the bitter weather. Therefore the blizzards in *The Troubadour's Tale* were a familiar hazard, and simply keeping warm was a major concern. Travel was, of course, affected, and the sending of letters a chancy business.

As Nicholas recalls in the course of the story, a marriage alliance had been planned, between Edward III's young daughter Joan and Pedro of Castile, only to be defeated by the Black Death (or Great Pestilence, as it was known at the time). However, England and Castile remained allies for many years, both opposing the growing acquisitiveness of France since the Albigensian Crusade against the lords of Provence. England's great territories in Aquitaine, brought to the crown with the marriage of Eleanor of Aquitaine to Henry II, were always a tempting prize for the kings of France, while Aragon, aided by France, was a constant threat to Castile. It would be the Black Prince, some years later, who would lead the combined English and Castilian forces to defeat Aragon in a major battle at Nájera, although the circumstances also led to a falling out between the two countries. But that is another story.

The earliest surviving written evidence of the medieval lyric *Lullay, myn lykyng, my dere sone, myn swetyng* is dated to the first part of the fifteenth century, but it could well have been written down before that, without coming down to us. There is every likelihood that it was known and sung before that.

And as for the troubadours? Happily, a great many of their lyrics and musical settings have survived, and their spectacular if brief flowering created a lasting legacy for music and poetry throughout Europe.

The Author

Ann Swinfen spent her childhood partly in England and partly on the east coast of America. She was educated at Somerville College, Oxford, where she read Classics and Mathematics and married a fellow undergraduate, the historian David Swinfen. While bringing up their five children and studying for a postgraduate MSc in Mathematics and a BA and PhD in English Literature, she had a variety of jobs, including university lecturer, translator, freelance journalist and software designer. She served for nine years on the governing council of the Open University and for five years worked as a manager and editor in the technical author division of an international computer company, but gave up her full-time job to concentrate on her writing, while continuing part-time university teaching in English Literature. In 1995 she founded Dundee Book Events, a voluntary organisation promoting books and authors to the general public, which ran for fifteen years.

She is the author of the highly acclaimed series, *The Chronicles of Christoval Alvarez*. Set in the late sixteenth century, it features a young Marrano physician recruited as a code-breaker and spy in Walsingham's secret service. In order, the books are: ***The Secret World of Christoval Alvarez, The Enterprise of England, The Portuguese Affair, Bartholomew Fair, Suffer the Little Children, Voyage to Muscovy, The Play's the Thing, That Time May Cease*** and ***The Lopez Affair***.

Her *Fenland Series* takes place in East Anglia during the seventeenth century. In the first book, ***Flood***, both men and women fight desperately to save their land from greedy and unscrupulous speculators. The second, ***Betrayal***, continues the story of the dangerous search for legal redress and security for the embattled villagers, at a time when few could be trusted.

Her latest series, the bestselling *Oxford Medieval Mysteries*, is set in the fourteenth century and features bookseller Nicholas Elyot, a young widower with two small children, and his university friend Jordain Brinkylsworth, who are faced with crime in the troubled world following the Black Death. In order, the books are: ***The Bookseller's Tale, The Novice's Tale, The***

Huntsman's Tale, The Merchant's Tale, and *The Troubadour's Tale.* Both this series and the Christoval Alvarez series are being recorded as unabridged audiobooks.

She has also written two standalone historical novels. *The Testament of Mariam,* set in the first century, recounts, from an unusual perspective, one of the most famous and yet ambiguous stories in human history, while exploring life under a foreign occupying force, in lands still torn by conflict to this day. *This Rough Ocean* is based on the real-life experiences of the Swinfen family during the 1640s, at the time of the English Civil War, when John Swynfen was imprisoned for opposing the killing of the king, and his wife Anne had to fight for the survival of her children and dependents. Both are also available as unabridged audiobooks

Ann Swinfen now lives on the northeast coast of Scotland, with her husband, formerly vice-principal of the University of Dundee, a rescue cat called Maxi, and a cocker spaniel called Suki.

You can receive notifications of new books and audios by signing up to the mailing list at www.annswinfen.com/sign-up/ and follow her monthly blog by subscribing at
www.annswinfen.com/blog/

Learn more on her website
www.annswinfen.com